THUNDER FALLS

THE DARKTHORN SERIES

MICHAEL LILLY

Published by Vulpine Press in the United Kingdom in 2019

ISBN 978-1-83919-285-2

Cover by Claire Wood

www.vulpine-press.com

For my siblings: Felice, Joe, Tony, Stephen, David, and Olivia.
Lord knows Remy got his sense of humor from you lot.

Also in *The Darkthorn Series*:

Pond Scum

Roadrunner

PROLOGUE

TODD

"That guy? Came through here a few days ago. Maybe. I think? Can't be too sure, with all the faces I've seen lately. Whaddya need him for? He short you a bill or two on some blow? Ha! Just kidding. But really, I'm not too sure. Looks a bit generic, doesn't he? Maybe if he were a bit weird-looking, or had a good pair o' tits. But a guy like that, you can't really expect me to commit that mug to memory, can you? Ha! Anyway, good luck, pal."

"Hun, ya's lookin' in the wrong place. Me? I see probly two hundred faces a night, but only half that on Christmas and Easter. Double that on the days *after* Christmas and Easter, though, ya get me?"

"Who the fuck do you think you are, coming in here asking questions? I don't know anything about anybody, 'kay? Get outta here. And you learn your fuckin' place while you're at it."

"I'm not a snitch, man. Except perhaps to the right buyer. Couple of Benjamins never fail to loosen these lips, if you get me. Hey hey hey, take it easy, man! I haven't seen your boy, okay? Sheesh."

"Wha? Oh, sorry. Didn't realize you were talkin' to me. Sure

1

haven't been payin' much attention lately, but I'll take a look. Nah, sorry, don't recognize him. Might wanna try that guy in the corner. Swear to Christ, the guy fuckin' lives here, just sittin' and watchin'. Bit of an odd one, though. I wouldn't make any sudden movements. And maybe try to use small words. Yeah, no problem, guy. Hope you find your fella."

"Is he in trouble? I don't want to get anybody in trouble. Oh, yeah, I recognize him. Seemed like kind of a loner. Came in by himself, just had a coffee, very quiet. Equally polite, though. Said 'please' and 'thank you' just like we were all taught growing up. Seems he's the only one hasn't forgotten it though. Y'ever notice that? Oh, right, sorry. He came through a couple of days ago. Friday, maybe? Couldn't tell ya anything else, though—like I said, he was super quiet, liked to keep to himself. Yeah, sure, I'll give you a call if I see him again."

You won't see him again, Todd thinks. Remy disappeared almost a month ago, and Todd hit the pavement in search of him the minute he was released from the hospital. Todd had told him to flee, in a cryptic, Todd-esque way that wouldn't appear suspicious. A lesson he learned about Remy (slowly at first, then rapidly after he left) is that when he wants to be hidden, he will remain hidden.

One lucky break near the beginning of Todd's search, in Albuquerque, had spotted Remy as he, a passenger, zoomed up the on-ramp onto the interstate, heading west, toward Arizona. The last time either Todd or Remy took that road, they were together. On the way back, Todd pretended to be asleep; he always liked watching how Remy got at night.

For a moment, Todd allows himself to pause to reflect on that memory: Remy melting into a mix of rushed awe and nervousness about taking his eyes off the road for half a second to look at the stars.

So far as he can tell now, however, his lover is an anomaly, a phantom, a master of the art of active elusiveness. The paparazzi would be harder tasked to obtain a hi-res photograph of Remy than of Big Foot these days. The man is good at getting what he wants, and right now what he wants is to be unfindable.

He wonders whether Remy's note was sincere. On the night of the events that led to this search, the night Todd was admitted to the hospital, Remy sent their dog, Odin, in to find him. Odin had a note tucked into his collar. It was brief and concise: 'Message received. Love you.' Even so, Todd has clung to it ever since, as though enough exposure to it will eventually allow him to divine Remy's location, complete with active GPS navigation.

But alas, the now-crumpled piece of paper has yet revealed no such hidden power. Indeed, the only power it has thus far displayed is that of pouring salt in abundance over Todd's gaping, wounded heart. Even so, as he stands outside of a crowded bar on a warm, mid-September night, he thumbs the note inside his front pocket, his own little worry stone. The smooth wind against his face and the crumpled piece of paper against his thumb give him a small measure of comfort, but it's fleeting and inflated.

Remy has been here within the past few days, and that concept steels Todd just a little further.

He lost Remy's trail shortly after finding it. Without access to video cameras, he's had to rely almost exclusively on potential witnesses, and in most cases, he doubts those, anyway; it's a widely acknowledged phenomenon in law enforcement that witnesses will sometimes (often) invent bits of the story in order to be helpful.

But a few days later, Todd is floundering, and decides, almost as much on instinct as on logic, to check at a small gas station in Idaho—one they had visited in the middle of their move to Wometzia. He stops mostly to reminisce, but performs his interrogative routine anyway, and as it turns out, the woman at the register, a charming, elderly lady, remembers Remy from just the day before. As usual, Todd is prepared for the recollection to be false, but she mentions that he bought a liter-sized bottle of generic brand water and a bag of Bunch-a-Crunch. Remy's favorite road-trip snack. Todd buys the same thing, thanks the woman, and sets off with a renewed vigor. He's getting closer. He could feel it before, but feelings are painfully insubstantial without evidence—and now he has a small piece of evidence.

Really, it's fortunate for Todd that he has such an intimate connection to Remy; he knows that any other pursuer wouldn't be having a shred of the success that he himself is. Even so, 'close' is only so encouraging; in the dichotomous dynamic of 'found him' vs. 'not found him,' Todd still has a losing record.

"Where the fuck are you, babe?" Todd whispers into the clear, starry sky. He yearns in desperation for the stars to connect, forming letters or arrows or something capable of helping him find Remy. But instead, they sit and shine with the committed innocence of a sleeping newborn.

ONE

I can't sleep. Something about the day seems off, like I forgot to lock the door—even though I did that eight times. The door is definitely locked. Or is it?

It is.

My room's only light, for the moment, stretches in through the doorway; bright, luminous claws distorted by the handful of furniture through which it passes on its way in. I keep meaning to cover the light more fully, but it's one of those things I don't think about when it's convenient to do it. Oh well.

I roll to my other side and face the window, which is entirely blacked out by way of blackout curtains, the night owl's gift from the divine. Or from Target.

In any case, I often have difficulty discerning the time of day; my one-bedroom apartment is part of a complex that lights its hallways for improved security at night. A thoughtful, well-implemented feature, sure, but as I don't have any clocks that are visible in the dark, and my phone spends most of its time without a charge, I'm usually unaware of the time without the sun's approximate but consistent guidance.

Given that most of my time these days is spent hiding, it only makes sense to leave my dwelling as seldom as possible. I go out for groceries now and then, but mostly I order online. Frankly, it's incredible what one can manage over the Internet these days. Even so, I can't hide forever. Well, I could, but I would prefer not to.

I try not to allow my mind to wander much in this place, but with so much time to myself, it's quite difficult to manage my thoughts with the necessary vigilance to prevent it, and I thus fantasize, at least once a day, about existing in some timeline that parallels this one only in the areas that foster healthy, growing relationships with Todd and Beth. Perhaps a different upbringing would be nice, but my imagination can't contort to the appropriate dimensions to create a universe in which my father isn't an abusive piece of shit.

Besides, he's far from the star of such daydreams. I much prefer the ones in which I'm spending a morning with Todd, watching a movie with Beth, and finishing up the evening just being together, without the obligation of active interaction. The fantasies which most grip my mind are the quiet, intimate ones, so easy on the senses that my heart steps up to fill the gap with its own deep ballad. In short, I ache for this to be over, and to be able to reconnect with Todd and resume our lives as good little gay hipsters from the Pacific Northwest.

Tea and brunch and mediocre music playing in above-mediocre coffee houses. Rain as our anthem and the stars as our backup dancers. Before I met Todd, my life was a log, freshly deposited onto a lake, doomed to become saturated in murky, stinky pond water and sink eventually, entirely without direction or purpose.

Enter Todd, the gentle, deliberate craftsman who could

handle the fragile hunk of wood I didn't know I was, and build me into a canoe, then with buoyancy, direction, and purpose. Instead of succumbing to the waters around me, he turned me into a vessel that thrived on the water. Suddenly, the possibilities of life unfolded before me, like discovering the secret menu at In-N-Out Burger. The need to explore and experience the world through my new, appreciative eyes was akin to a blind person regaining their sight and indulging an itch to book an immediate flight to Europe to see Le Louvre and the Sistine Chapel.

I booked that flight, packed my bags, and boarded. I explored Paris and set off toward the mighty iconic museum, but the second I crossed the threshold, my vision went blurry, then faded completely. So to speak.

Todd as my sight and life as my Louvre, I can certainly remain in the building—loitering, listening to excited footsteps and tours getting started, testing my French against what I overhear from enthusiastic honeymooners. But the true experience, the beauty, the spectacle, will elude me without his influence—his empowering, liberating clarity.

I get out of bed, trying to coax into existence a will to do anything at all. I shower, shave, and eat a grilled cheese sandwich with a generous amount of Pepper Jack cheese on it. My apartment, though small, seems to host a vast emptiness, as though in an adjacent universe, this same area is occupied by a void, and the barrier between this universe and that one is thinning over time. The table and chairs seem hollow to me, and the counter and cheap appliances seem superficial, like props to be used in the show I'm putting on to try to convince myself that I'm living something of a normal life.

The thing about such a show, however, is that it lacks in plot, character development (and in my case, characters), and any kind of discernable substance. Mine is a one-man show, written by a depressed monk.

With reluctance and a sigh, I turn on my phone. I don't bother with it most of the time, as the only one who contacts me is a mysterious stranger, anonymous and ominous, who seems to be watching *(and manipulating?)* my every move, despite my recent and extensive efforts to disappear over the past month. Somehow, he's managed to stay on my trail the whole time. My attempts to lose him have had a similar rate of success to a man trying to shed his own shadow.

On the bright side, he seems to be on my team. At least, he hasn't given my location to my predators, constituents in an underground filth-peddling organization that seems to run as wide as it is deep, a concept that unsettles, even—I'll admit it—frightens me. So far, I've managed to elude their gaze, but with so many of their seemingly bloodthirsty minions involved, how long can I actually maintain my invisibility? Every time I step outside, I risk being found. I learned that the hard way—I tried Los Angeles first, in hopes that immersing myself in a dense, diverse population would offer some cover, but when some of that population is hostile, it turns from a refuge to a death trap. My friend, the nameless texter, alerted me to their approach in time for me to make an escape, and a narrow one at that.

Since then, I've been staying at various motels dotting the American Northwest, finally settling into an apartment upon realizing that this hunt may be a long-term thing.

Of course, I had to find one that would allow me to pay in cash and not have access to a real background check—I have fake documents, but I still would rather people not look into the history of someone who doesn't exist, and who I'm claiming to be.

Fortunately, my needs were met as a package. All I had to find was a town small enough that no big realty tycoons would touch it, but big enough to have an apartment building or two and allow me to exist in it without raising eyebrows. In essence, I needed a Riverdell, but with my history there, it would have been quite foolish to go back there, what with people looking to kill me and all.

However, I found another town (thanks to some not-so-subtle hints delivered by my mystery friend) nestled in the green mountains of Wyoming, a charming thing of a city with a population of 3,327 as of the 2015 census. Its foothills overlook the valley, a sea of green and, in mid-September, some of the greens are already being replaced by yellows—autumn is nearly upon us.

The thunderstorms here, while infrequent (especially when compared to those of New Mexico), are brilliant, rainy spectacles of light and shadow, and the thunder echoes around the valley as a heart-shaking tremor. Of the small measures of reprieve available to me, none has been more powerful, thus far, than a good, mountainous thunderstorm.

As I watch the animation for the phone's boot screen, I feel a tinge of anxious anticipation, but it dissolves when I try to inspect the sentiment further. The animation stops and displays my home screen, a photo of Todd sent to me by my secret inquirer to prove to me that he's okay. That he is (or was, at least) close to Todd is the only solid information I have about him, and my attempts to grill him for any more information ceased three weeks ago when I finally conceded that his will won't be broken. Of course, I have my suspicions of who it may be, but every time I try to wheedle at a theory, it closes up when I get to the finer details.

Since then, he has texted me once in a while, but oddly, it's always small talk, asking about the weather. I almost expect it to be some kind of ruse to trick me into revealing my location with some kind of program designed to pull weather forecasts and use that data to reveal what locations have had matching weather patterns over the designated amount of time. Whether such software actually exists is beyond my knowledge, but the possibility still grips me. My time alone has allowed for quite a lot of speculation about how I may be found.

Eliciting no surprise, my phone buzzes an incoming text as soon as it connects to the network. Then another.

The first text was from the same unknown person as before: "Mostly cloudy my ass, I'm getting sunburned, am I right?"

But the second number is one I don't recognize, one from a 208 area code. Huh. Idaho.

I open the text.

"You're being played. Get out of there, or they'll find you before you know it."

I received a similar message a month ago: *They found you. Run.* In that case, I heard thundering footsteps on my apartment building's stairs within seconds. However, this message was sent almost a week ago (Jesus, has my phone really been turned off for that long?) and I'm currently very much not dead, nor do I recall anybody suspicious or out of the ordinary over the past week. I've only been out once this week, and that, like most of my trips, was in the middle of the night, so as to garner attention from as few people as possible.

Not that being seen will immediately damn my chances of surviving here long-term, but it adds a measure of risk to the equation, one which I can't afford, even in this small of a town. After all, Todd's and my most recent dwelling, Wometzia, New Mexico, was even less populous than Ghost Fork, and we were sniffed out even there. To be fair, I hadn't taken any additional measures to preserve my anonymity there, and I even joined up with the tiny law enforcement force in Wometzia shortly after Todd and I moved in.

My decision to lay roots (however shallow) in Ghost Fork was a rushed one, but so far, it seems to have been the correct choice. Before I took off from Albuquerque, I withdrew quite a large sum of money from an account my mother had set up for me. When Todd and I lived in Riverdell, I refused to use the money with an almost childish defiance; the money, or at least a gross majority of it, came from a child porn ring, one to which my father contributed enthusiastically. He left all of his money to my mother, who reappeared in my life just a few months after I killed him. I kept that detail to myself. He left the house to me, and I listed it as soon as I could get over the idea of any innocent human living in the space where my father molested countless kids—including me. So far, no bites. I'm not mad.

Even thinking about it now makes my blood boil. On Maylynn Brotcher's behalf, and on that of Ellen Dodge. On Todd's behalf. On mine. May was actually Jeremy Keroth's victim, but he and my father were close friends and partners in their vile business. As I understood it, my father was most commonly the supplier of content, while Keroth used his contacts from his days in Undercover for Portland Metro to distribute it, which yielded quite the handsome profit, apparently.

So I rounded upon a solution I hadn't thought about in years, after the remains of Ellen Dodge turned up. She had been young, full of life, with promising talent in music. But those promises were left unfulfilled, the monstrous beast having ripped his way into the tiny, fragile life before she had time to become a woman. It was that moment that I decided, with a hollow certainty, that my hand would be the one to remove my father from this planet. No reasonable force could have been employed to halt my father's rampant perversion, and I was filled with an intense passion so deep that all other emotions were put on hold, right up until I pulled the blade across his throat and spilled his blood into the pond at Riverdell's favorite park.

I didn't feel it at first—drowning in that kind of adrenaline does that to a person—but at that moment, my father's body in my arms, a crack appeared in my emotional dam, one which deepened and widened until, at his funeral, the dam broke and I became something close to human—an encompassing metamorphosis facilitated by Beth and Todd.

In order to overcome my new adversary, Jeremy Keroth, I had to open up to them about my past—both the molesty part and the killy part. It took little convincing to get either of them to see that I did what was necessary. To my surprise, they took to the news rather well. Of course, any revelation like that warrants worse than any reaction they've given me over time, and my gratitude for that (and for them) runs deeper than they know, with an equally substantial abundance.

In my hurried search for a place to lie low, I stumbled into Ghost Fork and read up on it. According to its website, it was one of the most common rendezvous points during the nineteenth century trapping rush. It was centric to the northern states' trade routes, often dipping just below the Canadian border, and for a few years, it showed quite a lot of promise and growth. That was up until the late 1800s, when the Industrial Revolution blazed a trail through the nation on tracks of iron and steel and copper. These tracks were ill-suited for the twisting and careening paths through Wyoming, and any venture to Ghost Fork thus became a detour, an accident, demoted from its former role as a destination.

In that era, it was called Thunder Fork, not for the less-than-copious thunderstorms but for the roar of the waterfalls to the north and south. They aren't audible from town, but the article asserted that they once were. My thought, at first, was that 'Ghost' was to symbolize the town's economic death, but as the piece later reveals, it's an allusion to a legend that was popularized in 1905, that the downfall of the town was an act of penance, that the natives that were slaughtered en masse as a means to realize the American Dream had given birth to a collective vendetta so powerful that it was able to influence the fate of the town.

13

Why Thunder Fork, though? Why not San Francisco or a more alluring frontier from the gold rush? If the legend is to be believed, as most of the city's population seem to, it's because the 'spiritual magnitude' of Thunder Falls, the roaring waterfall west of town, was the only one strong enough for the natives' spirits to influence enough to make a difference through the barriers between worlds.

Although I consider myself quite a skeptic, I find myself intrigued by the myth. In addition to the blurry photos, the city website has a link to a paranormal forum and, more specifically, to a thread dedicated exclusively to Ghost Fork's legend. I clicked the link out of curiosity when I first settled in and, to my surprise, the thread had been active and rife with conversation since its creation eight years ago. So now, in my near limitless time to kill, I spend more time browsing the thread than I care to acknowledge. Many of the posts are speculative pieces by people who have never been to Ghost Fork. They often claim to be planning a trip here, but further investigation, apparently, leads them to canceling those trips. There are a few people who comment and post the most, but aside from undead_chaplain and xXDeathHunterXx, there's a healthy, diverse group breathing life into the page.

My natural, habitual impulse now, is to open my phone's web browser to read the new comments, but my mind is trying to kick into gear after a month of blatant neglect and operation in survival mode. If brains can atrophy, I'm certain I pulled it off. I can almost smell the rusty cogs of my mind trying to lock into patterns and mesh together, like turning on the heat for the first time of the winter.

Before, I had one person texting me, one force of influence outside my own mind. But now, another, only slightly less credible force jumps in to disrupt everything, to toss a layer of complex ambiguity onto the life I've worked so hard to make simple, easy, accessible to myself and no one else. A force trying to discredit the other.

I feel sick. I need Todd.

I have no clue how much time I spend with those received text messages displayed on my screen, occasionally tapping the text entry field to compose a message, only to delete the whole thing and back out. My first question of import isn't even how to play it, but rather, *whether* to play it. If I engage, become an active piece of the game, a moving part, another piece to keep track of, and though my movements will be, to me, far easier to keep track of, I also have to bear in mind how those movements will affect the other pieces. In those terms, the fewer moving parts the better.

So I close out of my text messages and resume my routine of scrolling through page after page of logically skewed recaps of definitely-for-real ghost encounters, a map of Ghost Fork that updates in real time to display the locations of the numerous paranormal visits in the area, color coded to indicate the type of encounter—red for a sighting with interaction, yellow for a sighting with no interaction, green for disturbances without manifestation such as rattling plates, knocking picture frames down, or whispered threats of scalping or dismemberment.

Interestingly, the town rests on a fault, and every influx of green dots, chronologically, coincides with an influx of seismic activity, as is revealed by another Internet search. I don't bring this point up, though. I am only an observer, and their enthusiasm for the lore and history is harmless; no need to burst that bubble. It's amusing to watch, too, and I keep being tempted to go and explore these places myself. I'm confident that I won't have a ghost encounter of my own, but abandoned buildings are a guilty pleasure of mine. The outskirts of the town are abandoned entirely, their former occupants having fled to greener pastures during the upswing of the Industrial Revolution: the town's center. The former tenants couldn't actually afford to leave town, but when their wealthier neighbors left their houses empty and unsold in favor of a profitable, accessible endeavor on the West Coast, they were able to move into the nicer homes at no cost. What a time it must have been.

I do my best to ignore the insistent goings-on of my life and my text messages, but they ache and wrap and strangle like a weed, and the garden of my mind is no longer of the zen variety.

For just a moment, I become almost angry about the fact, like it's a personal and intentional attack on the tiny, quiet life I've created. But alas, at least one of these messengers is not, unless the two are colluding, which seems unlikely. In the end, I circle back to my first plan: to ignore and observe until one or the other makes a decisive move. Though my will is strong, it will take quite a lot of effort to ignore them as I must, with so much time and energy unclaimed in my system these days. Perhaps I can find an outlet for it all.

I pull the map back up on my phone and study it. The most prominent cluster of dots is in the woods to the northwest, where some cabins' remains sit on a hill overlooking Ghost Falls.

Two

Ghost Falls is the only substantial economic asset of Ghost Fork. It's a behavioral treatment center that serves high-risk teen boys with various histories and diagnoses: abuse, substance abuse, alcoholism, suicide and self-harm, aggression, etc. It became a boarding school in 1972, but as the demand for higher security schooling grew in the '80s, the owner, Randy Thunderhorn, saw the opportunity and took it. Hiring and retaining therapists and administrators proved difficult, but in time, the facility found itself with a handful of dedicated, competent therapists, as well as some recreational therapists, administrators, and several dozen staff from within the town. The teachers, culinary staff, and maintenance crew also live in town. In fact, the only Ghost Falls worker who did not live within a five minutes' drive was Mr. Thunderhorn himself.

When the town was still a booming, prolific beacon, Randy's grandfather, Timothy, built an extra cabin near his house to take in a couple of homeless kids. Over time, he found that he loved it so much, he kept adding and adding. Sometime later, the kids he initially took in had grown, gone off to college, and returned full of ideas about how to make the facility more suitable both to Timothy and to a larger number of kids. At that point, the school was named Thunder Falls Academy; Timothy had liked Thunder

Falls better than Thunder Fork, and besides, why should he name it after the town, anyway?

So Thunder Falls Academy grew and, mostly by word of mouth, came to be known as one of the best, most accommodating schools in the country. Thunderhorn's students, according to reports, had a ninety-two percent graduation rate, and of those graduates, nearly all of them had gone on to college, and aside from a tiny percentage, the others were successful in their own trades. After some time, a sister school came to be, damn near identical to the first one but for girls instead of boys, and many of those went on to graduate as well.

However, the sister school got shut down when one of the staff was caught making sexual advances toward one of the girls, who then hung herself in the bathroom with a length of bedsheet. The schools both came under heat, but mostly they were only scrutinized. In the end, the girls' facility closed (despite the facility itself not receiving any punishment) due to nobody wanting to send their daughter to a school where a girl killed herself in response to the sexual advances of people who were supposed to keep them safe.

The boys' campus suffered in business for a while, closed for a week, then reopened and donned its current name: Ghost Falls. Randy Thunderhorn was reluctant to change the name, but the title of Thunder Falls had become associated with too much notoriety to retain.

Ironically, the town had been one of the few places untouched by the economic roller coaster that was the 1900s, as it was fairly small and independent. In its immunity, it was able to laugh in the faces of the throngs who left to pursue riches in California, only to be met with the impoverished nightmare versions of their dreams.

The growth of Ghost Falls as a treatment facility was much more gradual than when it was a boarding school, but business was steady—a nation in crisis produces a lot of troubled youth.

So now, the former girls' campus sits abandoned and, as I study the map, I find that none of the dots are actually *in* the school. They're all around it, on the lawn, in the woods, but none inside. Perhaps I can put one there. It'll be a nice way for me to get out and get my mind off of things without being seen, at least.

Beyond that, I have my curiosity about the case that ended up closing the school. A desperate part of my mind tells me not to get involved, reminding me of the horrors that occurred in Wometzia as soon as I started getting involved in their local law enforcement. But I'm not going to be associating with the actual police force in this town. Neither my name nor my address will go into their records (or any other, for that matter), so with a little extra caution, my investigation into this case will go unnoticed.

The debate in my mind about whether or not I should go lasts only a minute or so, then I'm packing a backpack with an extra pair of clothes, a water bottle, a flashlight, some spare batteries, a couple of snacks, a paperback, and a pocket knife. As I pack, I can't help but reflect on a couple of instances of my childhood, in which I was so stoically determined to run away, to leave that spectacular mess of a household in my figurative rearview mirror and let it sink beyond the horizon. Each time, I fled to the same spot, set on making it my new home. It was a nice little cave, cut into the rock behind one of the many small waterfalls that punctuate the streams and creeks of Riverdell. As a child, the area was quite spacious, but having used the same cave as a hiding place ten months ago, I could more accurately assess that that waterfall would, as a living space, accommodate no one.

I consider packing my gun, but the idea of being approached by a random cop on patrol and having to explain why I have a firearm on me while I trespass in an abandoned section of town douses that notion. It would be fairly easy to explain it away as having gotten lost in new, unfamiliar territory on an attempted camping trip, but in the interest of invisibility, having a weapon is a detriment; eyebrows raised means that I'll be recognized, remembered. I stow my weapon in the old nightstand by my bed and double-check my pack one more time. I screenshot the map so as to retain access to it even if I lose my mobile Internet reception, as well as to expedite its accessibility.

And with that, I'm off into the night.

My affinity for the hours of darkness is one that was born and nourished of a mind perpetually trying to tame the chaos around it. At night, much of the sensory stimulation dies down. The noise of the day—both visual and auditory—boils down to a much more stomachable whisper, allowing room for conscious thought of a caliber that daylight simply doesn't permit.

As such, my moonlit walk to the new city boundaries (implemented after the mass exodus and the school's shutdown), is easy and enjoyable. The crisp wind carries with it the RSVP of the coming autumn, cool and sweet with just the smallest hint of a bite.

After some time that feels like none, I stand at the town's edge, an abrupt collision between two worlds: behind me, the world of man, architecture, evolution, and civilization. In front of me, a remnant, a memory, an imprint of the world behind me, the Salvador Dalí version, dilapidated and a visible victim of the passage of time. The greenery, once neatly trimmed to man's liking, grows thick, unchecked, and unrestrained, now with a furious vigor known only by those who've been oppressed then freed. Whether in my imagination or in reality, an owl hoots. I continue walking.

A dirt road lies ahead of me, glowing in a pale blue light, a slave unto the night. I suppose that even the rejuvenated fervor of the plant life hasn't yet permeated the packed dirt of the past's traffic.

The moon is almost full, but not quite. I'm not terribly familiar with the lunar calendar, but it seems that another day or two of waxing will yield a full moon. Another few cycles and my good friend Orion will return to the sky to shepherd me through the winter.

It dawns on me that I never told Todd about my affection for Orion. The part of my heart that belongs to him throbs in ache before I can will my mind away from that intrusive, painful thought.

A minute longer of walking lands me closer to one of the famous waterfalls, evident by the low, steady roar I hear in the distance, growing just a bit louder with every step.

The ground beneath my feet is dirt and rock, in a ratio that might make footfalls loud under normal circumstances, but whether because of the recent rain or from the humidity of being within the proximity of the waterfall, the soil is damp and thus accommodating to one who wishes to be silent, like me. In fact, in a matter of time, I can't even hear my own steps over the waterfall's growing *whrrr*.

The earth has a tendency to release the most intoxicating aromas when it's damp, and tonight is no exception. I breathe in for a moment, and bask in the natural odors: the moist dirt, the rocks, and the plants smelling of a sweetness that reminds me of camping in Oregon.

I have only been camping once, officially. I was nine, and fear set in when we were told to pack our bags. My imagination went to all sorts of wild places—was my father really just…taking us camping? Like a Normal Family? Surely he had some kind of ulterior motive. My incredulity didn't waver until we reached the campsite. There was nobody we knew around, so it couldn't have been for show, but there were strangers in nearby sites, so he also wasn't planning to murder us, probably.

Then he actually taught my sister, Trina, and me how to fish. He didn't yell or threaten or by any other means attempt to intimidate us. Trina and I were allowed to run around and explore the forest on our own, and when we returned, Mom and Dad were waiting with hot food. Mom seemed to be in good spirits, and didn't have any new bruises—at least, any visible ones.

We ate fish for dinner every night on that trip, as they were abundant. As it turned out, Trina was better at fishing than Dad, and caught even more than him.

For a glorious few days, it seemed like maybe that was the

end, like the demon possessing my father had gotten bored and retired. Was my father changing? Turning over a new leaf, as they say? Was he even capable of such a change?

As it turned out, no. To this day, I have no clue what inspired that trip, nor do I know what got him to behave like a human for an entire week, but from then on, that was a memory I could escape to whenever I needed an out.

Hell, maybe *that* was the motive: to try to convince us that he had remnants of humanity in him, just buried under the steaming mounds of manure with which he normally manifested. Or so that when teachers asked what our favorite summer memory was, we could answer honestly with something other than, "My dad was out of town for a weekend and I didn't get hit once."

Whatever the case was, it didn't last long; when we got home, my mom forgot to put the remaining beers into the fridge. He beat the hell out of her that night. There were times I used to think of trust as malleable, flexing, expanding and shrinking over time. Since then, I've reflected on that memory and acquired a certainty that trust is not only rigid beyond belief, but just about impossible to repair, like a pane of glass.

However, when imbued with the beauty of a trusting relationship, it takes on a magnificence, and becomes the most lovingly crafted stained glass you'll ever see.

These childhood and adolescent memories and speculations shrink away, replaced by the blue-black of the night. If my direction has remained at least *mostly* true, I should be reaching the abandoned school before long. Already the buildings around me, sparse and almost camouflaged in the abundant green encroaching on them, are of the abandoned sort, derelict and time-whipped. The vegetation works tirelessly, if slowly, to reclaim the land that has always belonged to it, pressing in through floors, eating away at poorly treated wood, crumbling chimneys, and caving-in rooftops.

In one building nearby, an enormous tree has fallen right into a house and now occupies half of it. Wooden porches host tangles of weeds and shrubs, and here and there, a door is missing completely. I wonder whether nature confiscated these doors or humans have repurposed them. Some doors cling to their formal jambs by just one hinge, causing the brass to warp and bend.

Windows are covered in thick layers of dirt and grime, and even if they weren't, I'd imagine I wouldn't be able to see anything anyway, as little to no light could flourish in such dense forest. I speculate that the landscape was quite a lot clearer twenty, thirty, sixty years ago. Now, aside from the main road which led me out of the town, I can't even discern any paths for walking, not even blazed trails where bored teenagers might have come through on nights of empowered rebellion. This comes at my dismay; I do my best to leave as few traces of my passage as possible, and stomping over this dense greenery will be a direct hindrance to that goal. I'll probably have left some visible footprints on the main path too, but those are quite a lot subtler, nearly impossible to notice from a distance and more difficult still to discern from the other unevenness of the terrain. In contrast, a swath of trodden-on grass and weeds in the middle of an overgrown forest is noticeable from quite a distance away.

Still, my curiosity has a stronger grip on me than prudence, a dynamic that is a rarity indeed. Also a result of that is that I'm fully prepared to make some audible noises as collateral risk of my investigation. My normally methodical, silent movement is replaced by a clumsier counterpart, as though someone turned my volume up using a remote control that has been lost for a decade.

My feet *fush fush fush* through the grass, my feet and shins quickly becoming wet with dew and sending remaining droplets cascading to the ground. The first structure I approach, a cottage that looks like it was yanked from a fairy tale and planted in the pages of a much darker story, is missing its two front windows entirely; whatever force removed them left not so much as a jagged sliver of glass in the frame. I elect to use this as my entrance rather than the door, which is intact and almost certain to squeak loudly on its cold, rusty hinges.

Exploring places that have been abandoned, such as this, inspires in me an interesting cocktail of emotions. At the forefront, I feel a thrill—the same juvenile brand of it that accompanied me when I used to run away. Just beyond that sentiment lies a sense of curious wonder, and it seems that the only function of this feeling is to urge me to explore further and farther, to satisfy curiosity and to plunge myself deeper into the surreal. Underneath that, I taste the less-than-subtle undertones of melancholy; an empathy for the losses incurred here and a compassionate longing that echoes with phrases like *what if* or *could have been*.

Oddly, it's a sensation I quite enjoy. Perhaps it appeals to the morbid curiosity of the soul, one rarely acknowledged and just as seldom satisfied. Even more than that, however, we outlived them. We survived to see the answers to questions that these people didn't know they should have been asking. We get a rare, privileged glimpse into our past and their future simultaneously.

Plus, creepy shit is cool.

My feet descend upon a thick layer of dust and, from what I can see, no trespassers have intruded upon this cottage in recent years. When my shoes touch the ground, the familiar emotional clusterfuck runs through me like a current.

The living room looks as though it was inspired by *Little House on the Prairie*, but I suppose that when functionality takes up so much in the way of resources and materials, home décor and interior design take a back seat to livability and sole comfort. A wood-burning fireplace sits in the far wall, wide and sturdy, made of stones and built to accommodate huge pots of water for cooking or bathing. The structure still bears the chars from the last fire stoked in it.

A wooden bookshelf spans the entire length of the west wall, fitted with small nooks and shelves meant to display trinkets and photographs, though neither are present. I put on gloves and open the low cabinets, searching for nothing in particular, and finding just that. Cabinet after cabinet reveals nothing more than more thick dust, as undisturbed as the rest of the house, except for the very last one, which contains a picture frame that's cracked and completely without a photograph to frame.

My footsteps within the cottage are muffled by the excessive dust, but still collide audibly with the floor, popping through the silence. They sound of a firm but hollow sturdiness. The other half of the main floor is dedicated to the kitchen. It has the same rustic, musty smell as the living room, but the melancholy is thicker somehow, as if the ghosts of those who cooked meals here reach through time to cast their longing onto me.

Whether taken by the former occupants when they vacated or by looters later on, the cabinets, cupboards, and pantry are barren of cooking instruments of any kind. The dust on the shelves is substantially thinner than that on the floor and counters, but it is still a thick layer indeed. The nickel in the metal knobs and handles of drawers and cabinets has come forth in a green filter, and rust plagues the iron alloys.

As I snoop through the cabinets, a small, white triangle catches my eye, pinned against the back of one such unit. I pull the shelf out slightly and it slips below, where I am able to retrieve it by opening the cabinet beneath it. I pull a small plastic bag out of my pack and deposit the paper. This isn't a crime scene, certainly, but if I do decide, later on, that I want to find out more about this object, it's only prudent to be as careful as possible, and prudence is one strategy I virtually always try to implement.

The item is the corner of a sheet of paper, mostly white but mildly yellowed over the years. It looks to have been torn from some sort of handwritten letter. In an elegant, cursive script, the portion displayed on my trinket reads "Dear Dean," before cutting off so abruptly that the name could be Deanna or any number of things that begin with 'Dean.' Or even 'Deam.' But that strikes me as less likely. A gust of wind rattles the house. Or, what's left of it.

I tuck the paper into the pages of the book in my pack (*The Trespasser* by Tana French) and continue looking around for any

27

more forgotten relics, trinkets, documents, ghosts. But I find none. After one final visual sweep of the main area, I walk to the base of the stairs, set directly between the kitchen and living room, enclosed by a full wall rather than railings alone. Like the floor, the staircase is exposed wood, and I push outward, against the walls, stepping on the very edges to minimize the weight I put into the middles of the stairs. They seem sturdy enough, but you never know with these older buildings, and I'd much rather risk being overly cautious than risk falling through the stairs and getting impaled by a broken plank. Every step creaks loudly, calling out in pain after decades of disuse.

The upper floor is also wood, but a frayed runner covers the bulk of the surface in the hallway, an ugly crochet piece made out of the remains of old clothes, it seems. It sits perfectly centered in the hallway, which contains one door on the right and one at the end of the hall to the left, both facing me. As I step into the hallway, I notice yet another, on the south wall. I shiver even though the night isn't excessively cold.

The door on the south wall, now on my right, opens to a full bathroom—or the bones of one. There is plumbing installed (though it's quite outdated), but there is no tub, no sink. An old vanity decays in one corner. I imagine a beautiful claw-foot tub where the drain is, and a small, weak rectangle of moonlight illuminates a spot on the floor, giving its all to push through the decades of grime on the skylight.

The wind has died down and the few sounds remaining are my own. They don't permeate much of the darkness, being absorbed and muffled by the wealth of dust caked upon every available surface.

I listen to my heartbeat and my breathing, both cool, steady, calm. I used to have a fascination with ghosts, back when I was eight, maybe nine years old. Even then, I felt that their existence was unlikely, but it was nonetheless exhilarating to pretend, and once in a while, either Trina or I would dare the other to sneak out to the graveyard at night. Now, the skepticism of my youth has evolved and matured, but a faint echo of that thrill threatens to manifest if I keep this up. I welcome it.

I leave the bathroom and enter a bedroom, once more to the right. This room feels, if possible, even emptier than the living room. Really, there's nothing to suggest that much living had occurred here at all. The walls and floor are bare, sure, but there are no worn-down grooves or dents in the grain of the wooden floor, no tan lines on the walls indicating where a painting or a portrait may have hung. There's no wallpaper and, as I inspect it, no paint, either. These walls are simply exposed plaster. Interesting. Perhaps not so much in itself, but it does encourage me to keep exploring, sending me on another quest, and I am not one to leave such a task incomplete. My curiosity mounting, I inspect the rest of the room with a lesser degree of scrutiny than I've had up to this point. The closet is equally bare, equally boring, and only contains a couple of built-in shelves. There isn't even a rack for hanging clothing. The upper shelves contain only the uniform coating of dust.

I turn and head back the other way, toward what is most likely the master bedroom. As I reach the ugly rug's midpoint, I hear a low but distinct *thud*. I freeze and hold my breath to listen as closely as possible, but the only thing I can hear is my heartbeat. Damn thing won't shut up.

I wait for a minute or so, then continue, taking extra caution to minimize my decibel output. The rug and abundant dust assist me in that endeavor. There's a crack of moonlight underneath the door. My heart arrests for just a moment when I see shadows break that luminous stripe and eddy about, until I determine that the sole caster of those shadows is a dense tree outside, but I suppose I'll have to open the door to be sure. Just to lend to my certainty, I wait in a pregnant silence just outside the door, my gloved hand still hovering over the door handle, a plastic and brass atrocity. I half-expect it to stick or catch, but it slides open, and I'm met with more than just moonlight on the other side.

THREE

Rather than the easy, crude nakedness of the rest of the house, this room has been...*overtaken*. More confusing yet, there's almost no dust on the floor, and that which remains is only in small, accumulated piles in the room's corners. My mind kicks into overdrive to assess everything around me, if only, at first, to determine that no threats lurk in the shadows. The bedroom is clear, and I check the attached washroom before returning my attention to that which demands it: the mess of the master bedroom.

The walls are the same exposed plaster of the other bedroom, but they've been covered over much of their area by pinned-up newspaper clippings. The dates on them are missing, but their time frame quickly becomes apparent based on the subject matter: the suicide that closed down the school in the end. Her name was Willa Frye, and the photos of her, though worn, show a young girl who had a subtle, unique brand of beauty to her, the same way that the most arid stretches of desert can themselves be beautiful in an unidentifiable, desolate way. On the surface, she had been fairly plain, but her smile concealed a charm that only served to enhance her physical beauty. Such was confirmed to be the case by her peers, according to the articles.

I hone in on one article. "You'd never think it of her, she was always laughin' and makin' jokes," reported Nina Hesterly, a classmate of Willa.

"…doted upon from birth to become the loved and loving young lady we knew until the pain she hid became too much to bear. God rest her soul, and may she find peace in the afterlife," says what remains of her obituary.

Other articles are posted too, but I can't mentally connect them to this trend. I read on, in hopes that their relevance becomes clear. Closer to the window, I find a batch of articles about Thad Eboncore, the man convicted of raping Willa and ultimately initiating the emotional chain reaction leading to her suicide. These articles are complete, and seem to focus more on the investigation and trial process than the preceding events. I wonder where *those* articles are.

Thad Eboncore, only twenty-eight at the time of his conviction, was a typical entry-level staff at the school. The accusation of the rape was made just after Willa died. Willa was sixteen years old at the time, and would have turned seventeen had she lived two more months. She hung herself on the night of Halloween, and upon being found, her classmates first thought it was an elaborately executed prank on her part.

At Thad's arraignment, to everybody's surprise, he pleaded not guilty. Most were certain of his guilt, and those with any doubt only had shreds of it remaining, the last stand of the benefit of the doubt. A photograph accompanies this article, depicting what seems to have been the entirety of the town's population, bearing signs reading 'Thad is Bad!' or pointing out that 'Eboncore' means 'Blackheart,' and the biblical implications that that has regarding his soul. A couple of the signs, from what I can see, proclaim that an innocent verdict would mark the beginning of the apocalypse.

I feel my eyes growing tired, straining to read the faded print by the weak light of the moon, but I'm too wary of being seen from the window to use my flashlight, and the stuff is too intriguing not to continue reading.

The trial was short but brutal, according to reports. The evidence, while not much in quality, was tantamount in quantity, including witness testimonies ranging from classmates swearing they caught him trying to get an upskirt peek as she climbed the stairs ahead of him, to administration relaying their growing suspicion that Thad had made a habit of sneaking off to masturbate during work hours. Rumors flew that Thad had built, and possessed sole access to, a series of tunnels and secret passages within the walls and underneath the building, from which he could spy on the students without detection. The story goes that, eventually, he became dissatisfied with the fantasy and moved to bring his perverted daydreams to reality.

That's the extent of detail offered by the pieces here, but as a detective, I'm not satisfied. Certainly, a large part of my job is detecting the subtle connections that elude most people's gazes, but at the same time, my job is one that, aside from biologists and engineers, values completeness and accuracy of information over any other career.

The story seems pretty straightforward, and much as I'd like to believe in the infallibility of our justice system, I have seen, firsthand, overwhelming evidence of the contrary. Thus, I'm seldom satisfied with the accuracy of a verdict unless I work the case myself or am otherwise convinced—which takes a lot. But where can I find the rest? There has to be more information somewhere, accessible and waiting for me. But how? I can't exactly use my badge to gain all of the access I would normally have as a detective.

An old voice bubbles to life within me—the one that started this whole thing. Before I've even committed to this project, it has chained me to it and thrown out the key, because it knows that this is more than a project. This is what my life has become. My identity. And if I can't reasonably join up with the local police force, I can at least try to right the wrongs of the past with what few tools I have.

I'm called to this—commanded by it.

For now, I content myself with taking photographs of these articles on my phone. I'd prefer to avoid using the flash, but it's a necessary risk and it will allow me to revisit the information on my own time without having to revisit the abandoned house with the not-so-abandoned room. One thing that piques my interest, though, is the dust. On virtually every surface in the house, a heavy layer of dust rests, and has for some time. But in this room alone, the dust has been wiped nearly clean, in all but a couple of spots. Maybe I missed something, but as I mentally retrace my steps, I'm certain that the dust in other parts of the house was consistent and undisturbed. The window is shut, but not locked, on a simple metal joint. The dust on it is splotchy, but it seems that the activity has been exclusively on the frame. Careful not to touch the remaining, still intact film of dust, I push outward and the window submits, admitting a cool breeze that flutters the papers on the wall. I cringe in anticipation of the window's creak, but it doesn't come.

Feeling exposed, I pull the window shut. With the information here on my phone, I'm overcome with a sense of urgency, mandating evacuation. I do one more visual sweep of the room to ensure that I've gotten everything, then head back out the way I came. On my way out, I confirm that my own footprints are indeed the only ones to have blemished the otherwise serenely complete dust. How, then, has this mysterious other visitor managed to enter and exit without leaving a trace? My mind goes in two directions: either he goes through the second-story window (*not impossible, but not likely either,* I think) or there's some other way in and out. My imagination goes to the eccentric Victorian mansions with webs of secret tunnels, trap doors, one-way mirrors, inner passages, panic rooms, and doorways leading to nowhere. Certainly, the size of the cottage doesn't allow for most of that, but my curiosity is engaged anyway, and I spend a moment imagining an Indiana Jones-esque journey through the centuries-lost catacombs beneath Ghost Fork.

Perhaps there's a door or something in the closet of that main room. I'll have to check it out later.

To the best of my ability (and as much as is reasonable), I step within the footprints I have already made, so as to minimize the amount of disturbance I leave behind. It has the added benefit of disturbing each footprint, making it harder to identify. I exit through the same low windows through which I entered, careful not to kick the old rotting frame as I swing one foot over, then the other. The wooden porch isn't creaky like I expect it to be, but this is probably because the excessive moisture in the air cushions the cracks and softens the wood, muffling out any would-be creaks.

The contrast between the deadened silence of the house's interior and the perpetual, active life outside is a small shock; as I look around, flitting shadows and mischievous shapes assail my tense mind. I almost retreat back into the house and wait there until morning, but that panic ceases, its termination allowing for a fuller, more present lucidity. The moonlight hits the leaves in an ethereal way that seems to transcend the barrier between this dimension and the next, like mere holograms, massless and untouchable.

Down in town, the song of the crickets permeates the late summer like a dye disperses into clear water, but up here, they are either silent or absent. While a more survival-focused portion of me wants to call it a night, the rest of me, without such tedious inhibitions, itches to explore the other cottages around here. Chances are high that a person would only have one base, but as that was the first house I explored, it's a low chance that, as the first one, it alone contained all of the information of interest to be uncovered.

Before parting from the property, I head to the west side to look at the side of the house containing the window of the strange hideout room. A small rock trim lines the house and reaches maybe four and a half feet high. Above that, a wooden ledge wraps around the house. A window sits between these two. Unlike its south-facing counterparts, the glass is intact, with one thin crack, visible by the moonlight, bisecting the big glass pane vertically, a jagged line illuminated by the lunar light that makes it look like a bolt of lightning.

As far as I can see, this wall is quite accommodating to a climber, even one of average caliber. Protruding ledges are both abundant and sufficient, allowing for a swift, if a little labored, ascent.

One fact strikes into my mind like a blacksmith's hammer descending upon hot iron: the window is open. Adrenaline surges into my veins and courses through me with the purposeful charge of stampeding rhinos, their footprints a direct mimicry of my heartbeat.

Have I simply had excellent timing in my exit of the house, or have I been under observation this whole time? Surely, it must be the latter; any good karma I've earned in my lifetime has been spent, the last of my tokens being exchanged for finding this particular structure in the first place.

A morbid, heedless segment of me wants to call out to him, make my presence known, connect with him, but my inhibitions rematerialize, powered by my freshly charged sense of self-preservation. I have no idea what I could be getting myself into, after all; I have no insight into his mental status, access to weapons, or capability. I could be calling up to the window as if to Rapunzel, only to find that my princess is actually a sociopathic sharpshooter with a vendetta against intruders. That possibility is quite enough to deter me from intruding further.

Even so, my exploration itinerary isn't limited to the smattering of modest, decaying houses in the area. However, my discovery makes me think that my next destination, the school, may already have been picked clean by the squatter. Based on the nature of the material I found there, he has probably combed and sifted through every bit of accessible information in there, relevant or not. Regardless, the thrill of exploring abandoned places is quite enough allure for me, and my non-encounter with the mystery squatter isn't enough to keep me from it.

So I step away from the property with a half-fake confidence, trying to ignore the surveilling gaze I feel boring into my back. It buzzes behind my head like a persistent mosquito.

I do note the non-aggression in my observer's actions (or lack thereof); he knew where I was. He must have a familiarity with the layout of the house and the land. If he wants to harm me, he's had plenty of opportunity to do so already. He could have ambushed me at virtually any point during my exploration of the small house. So while I can't necessarily embroider a 'Team Remy' letterman jacket for him, I can infer that he's not necessarily aggressive in nature. Beyond that, the extent of my knowledge about him is only that he hides away in an abandoned house and that he harbors an unresolved obsession with the suicide that ultimately closed the school all those years ago.

I remain under my mask of nonchalance until I'm reliably out of sight from the cottage. Only then do I allow myself to look behind me, my sight able to join my hearing in my strained surveillance of my surroundings.

Adjusted to the dark and assisted by the moon's glow, I'm relieved to find that my visual assessment of the small ridge I just breasted to be satisfactory. No one is following me closely enough to worry me—not that I can tell, at least.

But of course, by law of the universe, where one sense is finally permitted a measure of freedom, another is limited, so although I'm glad to be free to look around with (presumably) no scrutiny, my hearing is impaired by the sudden increase in the waterfall's volume. Additionally, the spray and rumble of the crashing water are ever more palpable, further consuming my brain's sensory bandwidth.

From here, the trail wraps up and around the ravine, to a bridge that spans the river, which feeds the falls. The school is supposed to be on the other side of the roaring cascade, overlooking both it and a scenic, mountainous series of cliffs on its hind side. I find myself wondering, abruptly, whether they had stopped to consider the inherent potential risks of building a treatment facility so close to so many geographical dangers. I wonder if a student had ever had a bad day and attempted to hurl herself off the cliff into the churning waters below.

I shake myself loose from that morbidity and continue my trek, which has become something of a hike.

The other campus, for boys, is all the way on the other side of town, amid its own cluster of worn down houses. Again I visit the idea that other abandoned subsections contain interesting things, but I push the thought aside; it does me no good here and now. My consciousness is better spent assessing the area around me in case the squatter turns stalker. I don't see that as likely, but as already demonstrated tonight 'unlikely' does not mean 'impossible,' so I stay on my toes anyway.

I spend my hike breathing in the misty air from the waterfall and looking all around in case of followers. My left ear is pretty much useless for now, as nothing around creates enough noise to be heard over the falls to the left, and even my right ear has trouble picking anything up. I can't even hear my own footsteps over those formidable decibels.

When I reach the north side, the crashing roar of the water below is all but replaced by the innocent babble of the river, which is far quieter than I expected. This is a relief. Now, if there's anyone moving about in the surrounding trees and bushes, I'll be much more likely to detect it.

As I crest the hill, my right—the north—opens up just beyond the river to a gradual, sweeping slope which turns into a meadow full of wildflowers and long grass. I make a mental note to come back some day during daylight hours; the view must be absolutely breathtaking. But again, this thought can be categorized as 'irrelevant' and filed under 'entertain later.' So I turn away from the moonlit meadow, heading toward the school once again.

A chain-link fence surrounds the property, and a beaten, damaged gate sways and creaks gently in the breeze. Despite its state of ruin, the clinking gate sports a chain and padlock which gleam in the moonlight. Fortunately, I brought my lock picks with me.

Raking the pins is a lock-picking technique (though, in this case, I use that term generously) in which the lock picker holds his tension lever taut against the turning direction of the lock with one hand while the other uses the pick to pull outward while also applying pressure against the pins. The hope is that, with the pressure applied, the pins simply get locked into place as the pick pulls out. Obviously, such a crude technique is only likely to work ('likely' being another word used rather loosely) on cheap locks. Providently, that's what this lock is, and it clicks open with just a couple of rakes. The gate creaks an ominous song as it swings open. I stash the lock itself in my pack and walk toward the school, dark and tall and foreboding. Given the geographical setting, I half expect lightning to strike it, like Dr. Frankenstein's lab atop a hill all its own.

The locked doors attached to the school prove to be more challenging than the outer gate. I wonder whether the squatter also has lock picking in his arsenal. The lock clicks open (a heavy, industrial *click-thock*) and I hear it echo through the dark lobby even after the door swings open.

To my dismay, it seems that just about every door is locked. This makes travel through the facility slow and burdensome, but at least I'll get a hell of a lot of practice in lock picking. The lobby is dark; the only windows face to the east, and that's through two sets of glass doors facing the same, while the moon is currently at play in the western sky. A lingering sense of being watched keeps me from using my flashlight, but I'm sure that, after another door or two, I'll be unable to function in the darkness without it.

I've always had a fond affinity for darkness. I did not harbor a fear of it as a child (at least, no more than the fear which afflicted me during daylight hours), and in fact, it brought with it a restful sense of relief, as my abusive monster of a father would retire. Sometimes, during those starlit hours, I would perform a simple daily type of routine, like brushing my teeth or making breakfast, relishing in that I could do whatever I pleased without the otherwise constant fear that my father would see fit to interrupt me

41

with a belt, a dowel, a wet rag, or his bare hands. I would fantasize, not of my father undergoing an overnight transformation into a Nice Person—those fantastic hopes had long since been dashed—but that he was simply gone. Summoned permanently to some plumbing conference, abandoned us, turned up dead, I didn't care. Any way his foul being could no longer have power or influence over my life.

Perhaps it was the birthplace of my morbid indifference to death and my ever-deepening attraction to the macabre—wishing my father away, even if it meant decaying under six feet of earth. As long as his headstone was nothing worth looking at—the same amount of character as he had—I wouldn't have given the slightest of fucks.

Instead, it was my mother who left. I placed a lot of blame on her at first, but since she reappeared in my life I'm coming to believe more and more that she actually had no other choice. He was going to kill her. And if she took Trina and me with her, he would have looked for her, probably found her, killed her, and most likely turned and done the same to us. And while she knew that he would likely be enraged by her leaving, he would not pursue her, and he would not kill Trina or me. It was the only choice she had to keep all three of us alive. She could have gotten ahold of the police, but she's seen firsthand that it's not an immediate solution, and any solution *other* than immediate would have given Dad time to react—to retaliate.

Now, the standby hours of society, the ones in which most of the population sleeps in innocent naiveté, remain the ones during which I'm most at ease. In addition, it has always been a nice break from my anxiety. Walking the streets of Riverdell at night brought with it none of the compulsions to which I insisted the rest of my life adhered. The moon. The stars. Orion. And darkness. They are my oldest, most reliable friends.

The lobby opens to a small hallway of sorts, containing bathrooms and an office. Just across the hall is yet another set of doors, also locked. There are slim windows admitting a small amount of light into this area from the main entrance, but not enough to offer much insight as to the layout of the room. Immediately, my primary goal becomes to procure a key so that I don't have to keep picking these locks—they can be quite the time suck. I consider finding objects like chairs and small garbage cans to hold the doors ajar, but I disregard that idea; it would save me time on my return trip, but it would also lead any pursuer, should there be one after all, straight to me. I play, too, with the idea of opening and propping a couple of other doors to distract and mislead, but that will only work as far deep as layers I care to open by picking locks.

I have the sudden, panicked thought that should my lock picks fail me (or I them), I will end up trapped in here.

In modern treatment centers, the locks are engaged by electromagnets. Thus, the risk of anyone being locked in is drastically reduced. The locks disengage when a fire alarm is pulled (or when the building is entirely without power), so that the risk of both staff and students not getting to safety is minimal.

However, this school predates such uses for that technology, so every door has a traditional, mechanical lock instead.

I worry about how much time I'll spend in here if I don't

43

find a key and soon. I open the next set of doors and step into what seems to be the main hallway of the school building. One wall hosts several doors leading to what appear to be classrooms. They've been cleared of any desks or chairs, but the walls still bear signs with multiplication tables and sayings or poems designed to encourage kids to learn or to do their best. One such poster features a dog and a cat, smiling as they read a book together.

One room, a little farther down the hall, looks to have been a music room. It has musical staffs on the wall, charting the most basic of scales. In a far corner, several music stands are clustered together, contrasting against the white wall like a tiny, black forest in the deadened wintry cold.

Every noise I make echoes boldly through the dark, barren hallway, each footstep inciting a second and third and fourth and fifth, and for those moments, the ghosts of the past reappear here, filing to or from various classes, perhaps involved in chatter so easy that it could pass for jovial, of the immersive nature that, just for a minute, permits them to forget that they're in a treatment facility and allows them to remember that they're real, functioning humans.

Todd was in treatment for a time, years ago. In fact, the trauma that sent him there was inflicted by the same perpetrator as mine: my father. In the same fashion, even. Todd had been too terrified to tell anyone about it, and even if he weren't, he had no idea who my father was; he wouldn't be able to tell on him anyway. That being the case, the trauma festered and putrefied until he started to self-harm. Todd had no idea why he was being sent away. In his mind, he was being punished for being punished for being punished, which only piled on more angst and frustration to his already heaping plateful.

Todd never mentioned whether his experience there actually helped him, but I like to think that it did; that there are people, resources, organizations, willing to help struggling people through the hellish nightmares humans inflict upon each other. I'm not typically one for optimism, but even to consider the alternative—Todd, alone and confused and scared and wondering why everyone in his life wants to punish him even though he had no control over his life or his mind, all the while trying to fight through the tempestuous mental aftermath of physical and sexual abuse, akin to a dingy raft taking on a hurricane—is just too heartbreaking.

Even now I tear up a little, but the freshly stirred dust may also be a contributing factor to that.

Fuck I miss Todd.

FOUR

At the end of the hall, the doors rattle from the wind; apparently, a gale amasses outside. Most of the classrooms look the same, varying primarily in the degree and nature of decay and vandalism: a missing cabinet here, a hole in the wall there. Occasional graffiti adorns the walls, but it looks almost as old as the building itself. Most of it is unintelligible or misspelled, some of it both. Some looks like it was written by alumni, in pretty, loopy script with black or red paint; things one might expect: *Fuck TF* or *TF 4evr*. A penis here and there. The usual.

I head back east toward the main entrance. Along the way, I spot a door marked 'Jerome Batista, Program Director.' If I were a spare set of keys, I think that's where I would live.

I pick and turn the lock and swing the door inward to be met with a darkness like unto the devil's buttcrack. I stow my lock picks in my backpack's outermost pocket in exchange for a flashlight. I click it on. The room is cramped, but functional. A heavy wooden desk sits solemnly in the center of the room, and I suspect that the chamber has seen a great many staff fired here, hanging their heads, whimpering, some of them maybe ushering in a raging storm of defiance.

The walls are lined with empty, ceiling-high bookshelves that match the desk down to the wood and stain; perhaps even to the tree they came from. A worn metal filing cabinet at the back stands five feet tall and has an identical twin to its left. More matching. It seems that those behind the graffiti must have found a way into the school area without getting through any locked doors, as this room is seemingly untouched. Aside from the emptied shelves and the dust, it looks as though someone could have been going about his daily business here as recently as yesterday.

There are loose papers strewn across the handsome desk, and there's a bobblehead (a cactus with a sombrero and a maraca in each limb, all of which bobble) still upright. A fountain pen is lain across a couple of the papers, its inkwell sitting at the ready. Of course, the papers have yellowed a great deal, but they're still perfectly legible. The one on the desk, bearing the weight of the abandoned fountain pen, looks like an admission paper. A small, hypothetical movie plays in my head.

Batista, a hard-working hardass with a sweet tooth and a soft spot for human tenderness, sits behind his desk—and a mask of stoic vigilance. *Finally*, he thinks, ready to begin an economic upswing, after the Fucking Eboncore Fiasco. In relief, he dips his favorite pen—a gift from his late wife, Netty—and prepares to sign, to share one more triumph with his departed love, but then his door bursts inward, nearly coming off of its hinges. It's his assistant, Eric, a young aspiring social worker. His eyes are all panic, but gutted of the typically associated urgency. Panic may not be the right word, he decides. No; panic means action. This, bless Eric's soul, and Batista's, is despair.

"Sir," he pants, "it's over. They're pulling the plug. Our license is getting revoked. We're done." His face falls with the last word and a morose, defeated Batista calls upon every remaining bit of strength he has to prevent the situation from damning the demeanor of poor Eric, who is perhaps the only person who put more of himself into this place than he.

But alas, this facility has been hemorrhaging, faster and more profusely than Eric and Batista's combined efforts could prevent. And the end has come at last. *May my death rattle haunt Eboncore even into his next life,* thinks Batista. He stands, cups the nape of Eric's neck, and says, "Dear Eric, your talents are simply being summoned elsewhere. Heed that summon and help the world." He walks out, with Eric, pulling the door shut and locking it behind him.

With that, my mind snaps back to the present. My impromptu narrative doesn't cover that the shelves are empty now, but I'll just pretend he had already packed up those things as an act of preemptive acceptance, like making funeral arrangements for his company after receiving a dire prognosis. Perhaps Mr. Batista believed in his company and had hopes for a fighting revival, but the reality of the situation pressed in on him hard enough to permeate his optimistic barrier.

My need to explore is met with resistance in the form of a paralytic apprehension about disturbing this scene, this set and abandoned stage which has waited decades for its actors to return only to be drained of life by the strangling vines of disappointment. I have a reserved inhibition, as if the office's tether to the here and now are tenuous, strained, and any disturbance on my part might send it hurtling back in time to the moment Batista closed the door for the last time.

But that inhibition, eventually, is punctured by my pointed curiosity, and as the reality of the here and now continues to flush away my speculation of the past, the history (or what I imagine it to be) ebbs away, replaced by their less romantic counterparts; a frantic workspace becomes a desk, a pen, and some papers. Bookshelves starved for books and trinkets now seem nothing more than an aged assembly of handsome wood, dust-covered and forgotten.

However, the filing cabinets in the back of the office retain their allure: banks of information, names, dates, events, analyses—in the mind of a detective, evidence.

Not only could they contain information on past patients, but equally important, employment records. Disciplinary action, write-ups, suspensions, terminations, demeanor, performance reviews, workplace conflict. Short of a face-to-face conversation with the kid or a detailed report from his shrink, this is the most I could possibly ask for in regard to knowing the perpetrator.

That's when I sense it: my being drawn in to this case. This ancient, settled, ice-cold, long-forgotten case that should probably remain just that way: old and cold. My visit to the abandoned (or maybe not so much) cottage shed light on a possible case for the innocence of Thad Eboncore. Such is always a tricky situation: defending the accused. One typically wishes to believe the best in people, but over time there grows a distinct distance between that wish and reality. Still, the defendant tells you he's innocent and you want to believe him, save for those with a stomach for the scandalous or perhaps the family of the victim. Sometimes, you're particularly prone to this desire and you become a defense attorney, regularly going to bat for scumbags and shitstains.

But on the other hand, sometimes they really are innocent. In many cases, you find yourself asking the age-old question: is it worse for someone to be wrongfully convicted or wrongfully acquitted?

I've taken it upon myself a number of times to remedy the latter in my own, less legal way, but I only have so much influence on the former.

What must go on in the minds of the wrongfully accused and convicted? It probably happens more than we realize; modern forensics are good, but not infallible.

Fingerprints are usually partial, and even then, the final determination is made by a human, not a computer, and is thus prone to be victim to lack of sleep, distraction, or the rare but inevitable careless or incompetent tech. On top of that, the concept that no two fingerprints are alike is a myth. To be fair, chances of two people with matching fingerprints being suspected in the same case are incredibly slim, but it has happened, and a man who was not the perpetrator was sent to jail instead of the actual criminal. DNA is the most accurate, effective method of matching, but it's often much harder to come by. Still, fingerprinting can get us into the ballpark much of the time, and often, that starting point is all we need to get on the right track.

Thus, the question appears in my mind, more unearthed than fabricated: Did forensics fail Thad? Or was Thad set up? Of course, the simplest and most obvious answer is simply that he's guilty. It's widely accepted that, most often, the simplest explanation is the correct one. However, I always hesitate to count my own experiences among the 'most of the time.' Whether or not by my own hand, my life tends to be in a state of deep disarray.

Now, I itch to go back to the abandoned cottage and see if any more answers bubble to the surface. But for now, I have an entire school to explore.

As though the ghosts of the past are ushering me out of the office, a weak but sure chill settles over me. Goosebumps stand at attention in salute to the paranormal visitors from the past and I think I feel a breeze, even though the room has clearly been without one for decades. Although I'm aware that these phenomena are due to my adrenaline kicking my sensitivity up a notch, the intermittent creaks and gusty moans of the old facility seem to increase in both frequency and volume.

No wonder the alleged ghostly apparitions are more frequent in this area. If I were one to believe in such entities, I'd be preparing for an encounter any second now.

Trying to hold off a rush of dramatic urgency, I pull open the desk drawers one by one. In one, I find blank copies of various forms—releases for medical records, admissions forms, new hire forms, and training manuals mostly outlining restraint techniques and emergency protocol. I grab a copy of each and stuff the stack into my backpack. Despite the muffling quality of the thick dust, the noise I make with my movements seems to be exaggerated, like I'm listening to an audio playback at maximum volume.

I leave my bag unzipped on the floor, its mouth gaping and at the ready like a carnivorous plant waiting patiently for its next meal. Hopefully I can find more tasty treats for it.

The desk's shallow central drawer contains multiple sets of

identical keys, and jingles loudly as I open it. Each ring has two keys on it, along with a tag bearing a number. I pull one set out and slip it into my pocket. The weight of it feels empowering, freeing.

The filing cabinets are secured with built-in locks. Neither of my newly acquired keys fits. Sighing, I put them back in my pocket and revert to the old-fashioned method: picking the lock.

The upper drawer squeaks angrily on its tracks as I pull it out. I wonder whether it was this bad back when they were being used daily, hourly. The files inside do not disappoint; I find employee records, organized alphabetically. Judging by the number of names, I assume that the cabinet was updated with a measure of regularity, past employees being archived somewhere else.

Whether because of his ongoing relevance or simply because his name hadn't yet become a victim to the rotation process, Eboncore's file is still here. And boy is it thick. A wave of almost adolescent curiosity urges me to open and read the file now, but I prefer to do my reading at home, so I remove the file, probably better than an inch deep, and feed it to my backpack.

The middle drawer in the left cabinet is just as loud as the first, but contains no juicy spoils; just a handful of office supplies. A stack of legal pads, a small stapler, and little boxes of pens, pencils, paperclips, staples, and rolls of tape still unopened. They are organized so neatly as to rouse my suspicion that Mr. Batista had at least a small amount of OCD. Or perhaps he was just exhibiting some symptoms of it as a result of his world spiraling out of control, right up until the last bit of control he did have was wrested from his fingers even as he tried to tighten his grip. I muse for a moment at the depth of my speculation of this Mr. Batista.

Mercifully, the cabinet on the right is unlocked. The top drawer of this unit has stocks of various sweets. I only recognize a couple of them, and those I do recognize are only by name, as the packaging styles have changed so much over time, not to mention the ever-present dust and fading colors, unable to escape the damning wrath of time. The drawer smells stale and sickly sweet, with a touch of licorice on it, though I don't see any licorice. The middle drawer is empty, leaving not so much as a trace of what may have been contained here, if anything.

The final drawer is packed so tightly that it pushes outward the moment I release the latch. In my head, a flustered Batista teams up with an equally flustered Eric, shoulders to the drawer, trying to close it enough to engage the latch. That this drawer is bulging with material indicates that the second one did indeed contain something in the past, preventing these people from splitting the contents of this drawer between the two instead of stuffing it so full. I wonder what was in the other drawer.

There are almost three times as many names here as in the drawer containing employment records, and each one is at least as thick as Eboncore's. That these records even exist here would probably have been a serious breach of HIPAA, had it existed back then, but alas, that act wasn't put into effect until 1996. Still, there has to have been some unmet code of ethics, right?

As with the employment records, the students' names are listed alphabetically, from Ackler to Zoore. Reading each name, I check it against my memory, though a more effective method would probably be to seek out the most robust file. As it happens,

Willa Frye's file is twice as thick as nearly every other girls', filling one folder to bursting and nearing the same achievement with another. I pull both folders out and deposit them into my backpack, growing in equal parts intimidated and excited at my expanding collection of homework. With each item I put into my pack, a sense of melancholy presses more heavily upon me, but this is a familiar sensation, one which I can use as motivation.

Almost every one of my conscious functions tells me to leave this, to get out, to go home and watch old movies or read my book. The voice that silences these ones is one of wary justice, and amid the onslaught of opposition from sources like reason, apathy, and self-preservation, it speaks with a bold but quiet solemnity, and in that presence, the other voices cease.

Part of me wants to find out if Thad really did what he was convicted for. If not, perhaps I can clear his name. But that's only part of the drive; I also want to ensure that Willa Frye is properly respected. More than anything, though, I want to make sure that the correct man is in jail, for if he is not in jail (or dead, I reason), he is free to continue to commit atrocities. Sure, the case is old, but if there's a possibility that it was one young man at the time, then it could easily have been another. I've seen abominations active and repulsive well into their sixties and even seventies.

Without the police file from that time, I'll feel deeply underinformed, but armed with lock picks and a flagrant disregard for trespassing laws, I can make my own bastardized copy of a report, just without witness testimonies or updated photographs. Perhaps, before long, my bedroom will look like that creepy assembly of related articles and such from the cottage in the woods.

After I shove my new treasures into my bag, I zip it up, sling it over my shoulder, and exit the cramped office. The rest of the school awaits.

FIVE

The emptiness of the halls feels, oddly, full. There's a satisfying completeness to it, like someone built and designed it as the set of a thriller movie that takes place in such a place of neglect. It reminds me of when I traversed Wometzia's only school in pursuit of surveillance footage. That school had a similar emptiness, but it was temporary. In that building, the universe had pressed pause. In this one, the universe pressed stop. It's the implicit permanence that does it for me. With the school building in Wometzia, the imminent start of the school year on the horizon, I could almost feel the strain of the school simply holding its breath.

But this place…it's just *dead*. No office administrators 'just around the corner if you need anything,' no part-time janitors coming in once a week to empty trash cans and buff the floors, no promise of hundreds of feet shuffling and bumping into each other on their way to class in a matter of weeks.

The contrast seems so absolute now that it's curious that this place reminded me of it in the first place. Indeed, it's also odd to recall that that expedition occurred little more than a month ago. Even in pursuit of a solve much more complex and dangerous than I had had prior to it, it was also simpler times. No mysterious texter, no *other* mysterious texter. No hiding in absolution and isolation indefinitely, in attempt to elude the gaze and threat of past adversaries—at least, that we knew of.

Just good old police work, quiet evenings with Todd, and some fucking good thunderstorms.

I can't afford to dwell on that life long or often, however; it floods me with longing and melancholy so intense that it drains me of any useful shreds of motivation that have managed to survive the past month intact, and I'm overcome with the urge to surface again. To fashion a figurative neon sign, bright and colorful and gaudy, to bring Todd to me. To bring my home to me.

As a man with beyond respectable discipline and self-control, I'm not usually susceptible to the emotional draws in decision-making. Logic accommodates functionality, compromise, logistical obstacles, and overall cost, monetary or otherwise. But, alas, when Todd is involved, my impervious membrane melts away into nothing but a pitiful puddle at my feet as I'm assaulted by sentiments of longing that are almost more than I can handle. I wonder whether he, too, fights this battle.

The room adjacent to Mr. Batista's office is marked 'Medical Records.' I fish my shiny new keys out of my pants pocket and insert the bigger of the two. For a disheartening second, it catches on its way in, but it unsticks quickly and slides into place. I turn it and hear the springs inside the door, old, worn, and scratchy, and the latch clicks open.

This room is not much bigger than the last, but is floor-to-ceiling bookshelf around three of the four walls, allowing room only for a bare, modest desk. I wonder whether the contents of these files, thick binders filling the bookshelves all the way around, would offer more useful information (or if, indeed, any at all) than the ones in the office. I decide that it's probably worth it to have both, and hunt down Willa's file on the third shelf up on the wall directly opposite the entrance. It fits in my backpack, but only barely.

I sweep my flashlight's beam over the rest of the names, but none call to me. The desk is without drawers (qualifying it as much a table as a desk, I suppose), and I find nothing else intriguing about the room. I leave and lock it behind me, as I did with Batista's office. The latch clicks back into place, sending a reverberating echo down the hall and back, on the return trip carrying with it a small degree of the irrational paranoia of the supernatural that overcame me a few minutes ago.

Standing outside the Medical Records room, the hallway to my right leads to a cafeteria. Probably nothing of import there, but it may be worth checking out later. To my left lies a solemn-looking pair of doors, bisected by a metal piece of framework which supports both doors. I insert my key into its lock and it slides in smoothly this time. This door creaks open to reveal a second set of doors, these ones adorned with windows offering a limited view of outside. Rather than sit and look, I unlock it and walk into a courtyard.

The area is square, each corner overtaken by ambitious plant life. Creeping green fingers crawl their way up the sides of the enclosing walls, as though the plants themselves are attempting to escape, as students here may have done decades ago. Maybe in a few more years, they'll succeed. The far wall, the least entangled by plant life, features a fading mural, barely visible in the small amount of moonlight and starlight, in which a small girl pulls at the hand of her mother, all set to frolic through a field of wildflowers and grass which goes nearly up to her nose. The mother smiles wide in what must be a laugh—clearly, the boundless joy to be had in such an activity is a bit much for her to handle. I take a moment to revel in the irony that, just beyond a mural depicting a field of wildflowers, there's an *actual* meadow of wildflowers.

To the east, the wall, while mostly green from the insistent vegetation, still stands solid, foreboding, as if instead of wearing down over time, it ripened, solidified. All four walls stand at least twelve feet high to prevent being scaled—not that anyone who managed it would have anywhere to go, but I suspect that that wouldn't have deterred many of the clients here; lack of foresight and raw, reckless abandon blast through such inhibitions, I've noticed.

A giant building—the living quarters, I assume—spans the entire length of the western wall, the windows from the second floor up barred in like dusty glass prisoners in their cells waiting for the end of their sentences, marked by the eventual destruction and deterioration of the building as the tides of time pick it apart.

The building is four floors, a towering monstrosity of a thing, home, I'm sure, to abundant memories, healing, heartbreak, breakthroughs, and breakups. Friendships were born and cultivated here, and I like to think that some of those friendships persist today. The building, in its empty presence, calls to me somehow: *Come, discover my secrets, sift through the wealth of history here. Indulge your curiosity. Come.*

I walk toward it on the stone pathway, cutting through a

landscape that may have been grass once, listening to the rhythm of my footfalls, hoping that their steadiness extends to my mind and persists through whatever length of time it takes me to look through the building. Every foot I close between myself and the structure seems to pump into it a breath of life, like I'm slowly inflating its sentience, and soon it will take notice of my presence and decide to have some fun with me.

That thought is cast aside with a small amount of help from the mental image of the dorm bursting to life like the abode in the film *Monster House*. Confident that I won't have to tranquilize it first, I approach the building. The smell of damp, wild vegetation emanates from the excess of growth lining the base of the building. I can't see well enough to be certain, but it looks as though the plant life continues around the corner, possibly wrapping around the entire perimeter.

As I sweep my flashlight's broad, bright beam around, the light catches and twinkles on forming drops of dew stuck to the leaves and grass. A sharp wind rushes through and sends a small cascade of it to the ground from the exposed patches of overgrown grass. The bars on the windows of the upper floors whine here and there, and something man-made and wooden creaks in the distance, but I can't tell which direction it comes from.

The area around the courtyard, beyond the walls, is heavily wooded, in the darkness manifesting as a sinister tangle of branches and leaves. Some of the trees have shed their summer coats already, evident by thin, spindly fingers poking up through the otherwise solid mass of blackness surrounding the courtyard.

The heavy double doors are presumably locked, both by their

own mechanism and by a padlock and chain. The main lock wouldn't be much of a problem, but the padlock, with less outer protection, has succumbed to the prolonged exposure; it's rusted and corroded. My lock picks are useless here, as would be a key, as the keyhole is entirely inaccessible. My next thought is to break the lock; it's already been weakened by rust, and a good, solid hit should do it. However, I see nothing remotely heavy around, aside from the stones that make up the walkways, hopelessly embedded in the ground, beyond the possibility of removal.

I could try to jimmy it or look for something heavy in the school building, but before I try for that, I should circle the base of the building to see if there's another way in. To do so, I climb up a seam where the building meets the surrounding wall. It's sturdier than it looks, especially at the height of the stone that wraps around the wall of the courtyard.

I mount the wall and drop my weight, careful not to teeter over the edge. The opposite side has plenty of loose rock; I suppose that relying on these walls and locks to keep the students inside also frees up the mind from considering the anomalous surroundings as present dangers. Certainly, though, attempts would have been made to run. I wonder about the resolutions of those instances.

I lower myself down the other side as much as my arms' reach will allow, then drop the remaining few feet. On the outside of the wall, my comparison of the facility to Dr. Frankenstein's laboratory is plucked away and replaced by that of Dracula's castle. While not as immediate as described by Stoker, a steep and deadly drop-off chews hungrily at the landscape leading up to the north

61

and west sides of the building, offering maybe fifteen feet of safety between the building and the inky black below. It's enough of a berth to walk safely, but not without that bastard *what if I fall?* which is ingrained in human psyche.

The dorm building's northern wall has a degree of disrepair similar to the cottage I visited. Perhaps this side has just been exposed to much more weather. A handful of pipes and other various protrusions decorate the wall like a harshly pubescent teen's face. However, none of them looks sturdy and accommodating enough to climb. There's only one reachable window on this side, another grimy ground-floor pane so thick with dust that even with their face pressed up against it, one would have difficulty discerning any objects within.

Ultimately, nothing useful on this side. No doors. I pick up a sizable stone and toss it back over the wall, into the courtyard, to use to smash the lock if I can't find a less destructive strategy from this side. I proceed to the back side of the building.

This wall is another with windows, and at last, my luck takes a turn for the better; one of the panes is missing, similar to the cottage and, in fact, just as cleanly. No jagged edges remain to tear up would-be intruders, no teeth of razor-sharp glass on this maw.

I sweep into the black rectangle, a port to the unknown. Hopefully, some of that unknown can help me unravel this mysterious old case that my subconscious adopted without my permission. *I'm working this case now*, I think.

The voice that plants it in my mind is foreign, forceful, almost unrecognizable, but I am indeed able to identify it as my 'righteous vengeance' voice, the one better suited to an obscure superhero exclusive to Saturday morning cartoons (but the five o' clock ones, not quite worthy of the nine o' clock primetime). This voice, while noble, is the one that gets me into trouble with startling and increasing regularity. Even so, whether symptomatic of my remaining OCD or a genuine wish to see penance delivered, I find myself unfailingly unable to resist these urges. It's too bad these impulses don't come with complementary superpowers. The ability to fly, turn invisible, or walk through walls would come in quite handy on nights like tonight.

The main floor office, in direct contrast to the school building, looks like it has been meticulously, methodically picked through. The light from outside punches and kicks and slashes through the darkness on the walls and door, on its own sending the room into a disorienting, messy web of nuanced shadow. Distance and depth dance in an awkward foxtrot as my eyes adjust and, in time, manage to assign shapes and names to the various objects in the room. The dust on the shelves and desk is streaked and disturbed, waves and fingers and clumps of clean wood, in addition to the mostly geometric shapes where their objects originated.

Virtually everything in this room has been rifled through, which doesn't surprise me. What does confuse me are two things: First, that the streaks are fresh; barely any dust has settled in the tracks left behind by the stapler, the paperweight, the tiny stack of sticky notes. Second, that nothing of value seems to have been taken. There are only two reasons most people might break into an abandoned place like this: adventure or loot. But whoever came through here, or whatever number of people may have done so, left behind a couple of handsome bookends and their filling, a complete encyclopedia, standing together and presenting the alphabet on their outward-facing spines. The dust is thick throughout these artifacts, roiling off like tiny fireworks as I run my fingers along the volumes. Somewhere outside, a bird starts to chirp. I'm not familiar with the birds around here, but if their schedules match at all with those I am familiar with, I can't have more than a couple of hours of darkness remaining. After the sun rises, I'll run the risk of being spotted by hikers on my way back. I need to move fast and get back home. Surely, though, I have enough time to explore this building.

A brisk wind sweeps in, as if in response to the bird's call. It fills the room, dominant, like your classic high-school bully making his presence and superiority known, waiting for acknowledgment. The gust howls in the nooks and crevices, but this room has endured too many such gusts to take any more notice.

A door occupies the space between a heavy bookshelf and the wall, on the north side. I suspect that it locks and, upon moving closer, find that it indeed locks from this side, and that the lock is not engaged.

Six

This building feels somehow more immersive, like I'm a scuba diver or an astronaut, drifting through an alien world and looking out upon previously undiscovered planets through a tiny window in the front of my helmet. It seems that this building itself was, more or less, the nervous system for the school's operation in general. Sure, the other building had medical records, charts, and administrative offices, but this was where the students *lived*, where they could stop being students or patients or subjects or clients and just be *people*: Becky or Jennifer or Margaret or what have you.

Certainly, this structure would have filled to the brim with emotion several times over on any given day. I picture what it must have been like in the strained stretch of time after Willa's death: students wandering the corridors, not so much *refusing* to engage in their treatment as simply lacking the will or energy to make any sort of progress. Any kind of epiphany or breakthrough would carry with it the association of the oppressive melancholy permeating the very air. All but the strongest of friendships withered to the brink of death, due to the enigmatic answer to the question nobody could bring themselves to ask: "Is it okay to feel joy anymore?"

A difficult question indeed, a tricky, complex bitch of a

puzzle made only more confusing by the students' own personal, emotional, mental issues, especially in learning to deal with past traumatic experiences. How can one expect them to deal with past trauma, after all, when there's other trauma—present trauma—at the door, bearing a gift basket containing a slew of fun new emotional issues?

The office door opens to a foyer area that looks quite nice; if it weren't for the ever-present dust, one might look upon it and think it was used as recently as last week.

Of course, the décor is a little dated. I can't help but picture the decorator as someone who, try as they might, just couldn't quite escape the seventies. Brown carpet bears the clawed feet of squashy couches; it's hard to tell in this light, but it looks to be a dastardly mustard brown. A psychedelic-looking clock on the wall sits frozen at 10:47. I wonder how long after the school closed this clock continued to tick before the battery ran dry.

While cozy, that's the extent of what the room has to offer, aside from yet another door in the far corner. I make my way to it, stepping around the ugly couches. The door opens without creaking, which is relieving; though I'm confident that I'm the building's only current occupant, the chance that another person—a fellow adventurer, or maybe even a squatter—is within earshot is enough for me to make as little noise as possible. Worse yet, there's still a chance that my new acquaintance from the cottage in the woods was able to follow me here without detection. At this thought, my ears perk for any sort of movement they can pick up, but as far as I can hear, the building is silent save for the odd breeze whistling in the office where I entered. If another person is in an adjacent room, I'll be able to hear if he has a loud *thought*.

Although the door doesn't creak, the smooth clicking and metal-on-metal of the handle and lock ricochet off of the walls and up to the high ceiling in this grand hall. In striking contrast with the side foyer, this hallway is *extravagant*. Without my calling them, words like *fancy* and *exquisite* swim to mind. A couple of seconds pass before the noise of the door closing behind me is finally swallowed by the void, and after that, silence moves back in. I stashed my flashlight before scaling the wall outside, but now I pull it back out. The *click* of my turning it on, normally quiet and forgettable, now bursts, slices through the air like a samurai's blade cuts through a straw dummy.

In an instant, the atmosphere feels tense. For no reason I can find or observe, the ambience has become brittle, precarious, and tightly wound, like an old bear trap found still taut, well into the following spring. A hushed breeze whispers through the grand hall, licking my ankles and pushing bits of loose dust around, bullying little balls of dust into the corner and tossing them about.

The floor is sleek marble, and underneath the dust I can just see the remnants of its past, polished glory trying to push through, surely a gleaming sheen in its peak.

The marble extends to the staircase, a gaudy, wide thing that splays out at the bottom. Oddly, it reminds me of the Hogwarts entrance hall from *Harry Potter*, and as I look up, I can see Hermione stepping down the steps in her new dress and new confidence.

The stairs are to my right, my left bearing an expanse of wall with a pretty landscape portrait occupying much of the space. Long-withered potted plants sit in the corners and the small nooks to the sides of the stairs. One more door lies straight ahead, on the opposite wall, with a twin just a few feet to the right. The door on the right is marked as 'Supplies.' I almost dismiss it, but I remember the rumors of secret passages built by Eboncore and can't resist poking around in there to see what I can find.

I pull the door open and find a surplus of cleaning supplies, stacked neatly around the perimeter of the small room. I use my foot to shove pallets and boxes around, looking for a latch, lever, trap door, or seam of any kind, but I find nothing. I guess I didn't really expect to, anyway.

The other door is marked 'Study Area.' Using my key, I open this door and find several rows of desks, facing forward, organized in a near compulsively straight grid, four columns by three rows, facing the front with such an attentiveness that it almost suggests that their occupants are here, studying, entirely invisible to me.

A small bookshelf on the left wall contains maybe fifty or sixty books; ten to fifteen copies each of four different titles, all academic. Each of the volumes has a barcode and a label with a number on it ranging from one to ten or fifteen—whatever number of copies that title reaches. I begin pulling them off the shelf, one by one, and checking out the names on the inside covers.

Barbara Jensen was the last to possess this algebra textbook. Kelly Long's US History textbook came back riddled with angry notes, made to seem even angrier by its bold red ink. Upon more careful inspection, the user of that particular ballpoint pen had pressed hard enough to indent the notes into the hard interior.

Clearly, she was furious about the condition of the volume at the time of its return. "Ripped pages: 31, 39, 123-237, 341," one note said. "Bent lower right corner of cover. Defaced p. 137." Curiosity grips me. I turn to page 137. An imbalance of passion and creativity must have taken over here, heavily in favor of the former and equally lacking in the latter. Christopher Columbus, in comic contrast to his dignified portraits which are very much the norm, has a pair of penciled-in devil horns, an artificial goatee extending farther than his collar bone, and to wrap up the package and label it as the work of an adolescent, a gigantic, frighteningly detailed penis floats in front of his face without an attached body. A small, neat speech bubble next to Columbus's head contains the words, "I suck!"

While I recoil from the graffiti, I'm nonetheless impressed by the determined, focused dedication that this student had in her rage. Brava.

The other books have their own varying degrees of damage, but none quite so fully (or artistically) as Kelly's. As I continue my search, I find that one of each book is missing. Number eight, made easily evident by the books' neat alphabetical organization, is absent from each collection.

The teacher's desk is what one might expect: more sticky notes, staplers, a tape dispenser. Near the edge of the surface stands an empty black cup, partitioned through the center a couple of times, presumably used for writing tools at one point. Perhaps the pen used to scribble out the angry red notes once resided in this semicircle. In one drawer, dust blankets a thick plastic bag of rock-hard sweets. Whether or not they began this hard is beyond me. I'm tempted to unwrap one and smell it, but the waxy wrapper has hardened in such a way that I could just as easily unwrap a heavy duty safe while wearing oven mitts. It seems as though someone dipped these sweets in cement upon the school's closing, to give them a proper burial.

Another drawer contains folder files organized as neatly as the desks in the room. These files are thin and labeled according to the student to which their contents pertain. Each is accompanied by a number. Nicole Connell—9, sits just after Willa Frye—8. I guess that a numerical system must operate independently from the alphabet, as the frequency of their admitting and discharging students would have made filing and organization a colossal pain in the dick.

Willa's file is disappointingly empty. Just to find out what I'm missing out on, I open Nicole's file. Fortunately for me, it's nothing of much import.

One thing strikes me as interesting, though: Why keep an empty academic file of a deceased student around? Someone so meticulously organized must have seen it as excessive, unnecessary, inessential—as clutter. Maybe this teacher was simply trying to immortalize her. I slide the drawer shut and, perhaps it's a trick of the light or of my imagination, but I'm almost certain I see a shadow flit out of the glowing square of light admitted by the western window.

In reaction more than response, I whip my head around to look through the window, but see nothing in it save for an abundant peppering of Wyoming stars, all packed up in the four little squares of late summer sky I can see through the window. I listen

70

carefully, holding my breath, in case the shadow was not an illusion.

Nothing befalls my ears but the breathy mountain wind pressing in against the window. That, and my own heartbeat.

The building creaks abruptly and I nearly jump; my nerves are beginning to get the best of me.

I breathe in as much as this altitude will allow, hold it for a few seconds, exhale. Willing myself into a calmer state, I resume my perusal.

The third drawer is empty. The fourth opens with a clang and contains only one item: a nameplate. Mr. Arteno's name glints up at me in bronze lettering, through the dust catching only the most tenacious of moonlight breaching the classroom.

My work here is finished; this room has no more for me. I confirm this with one final visual sweep, then move on. The door shuts behind me with the same resounding, echoing clatter as when I entered through the foyer, but now some other sentiment hitches a ride on the acoustics, a coalescent fusion of longing and raw melancholy, like the ghosts and memories of this hall once again attempting to break through into this dimension. Having entered from this side, I spot a door on the same wall as the foyer, which evaded my notice before. It has a small square window about five feet up, and is without labels or signs. I open the door to find a small, empty room with painted cinderblock walls and a concrete floor. The probing beam of my flashlight tears away at the darkness, leaving naked and exposed a series of dents and obscenities drawn onto the wall with what seems to be crayon. These messages seem to echo the general sentiment of those spray painted onto the walls in the school area.

It takes me a moment, but I realize what this room is: seclusion. Isolation. Time out, to put it nicely. When a student behaved far enough out of line—violence or threatened violence—this is where they literally cage the rage. A creeping sensation of foreboding tickles at my brain, but not of the ominous haunting nature. Rather, this feels as though I'm overstepping boundaries, peering into some of the most vulnerable memories that many of the young students had ever experienced, flipping through the pages of their diaries without permission.

I look away, and the sensation of being watched rushes in to replace the out-of-bounds feeling. I look around, but the various corners of the hall remain empty and, save for the odd gust, silent.

My consciousness is not spared the awareness of the similarities between what I'm doing and an excursion through an asylum or an abandoned mental institution.

But! pipes up a defiant voice in my head, *they are not the same!* This is true, but I can't discount that the factors which make asylums creepy—mental illness, questionable ethics on the part of certain staff, and of course, death and the encapsulating feeling of almost-emptiness—may stretch into this place as well, if to lesser degrees.

The voice of ration speaks up again: *So what? So the* fuck *what?* A compelling argument, to be sure, and one I will keep in mind if occasion arises that I debate a believer about whether or not abandoned facilities like this are creepy.

But, to the voice's credit, well...so what? Sure, there are parallels between a treatment facility and a mental institution and the old insane asylums, but they only retained their power of fear as long as you subscribe to the belief that any of the past horrors have the ability to persist into the present. Without that belief, the daunting, haunted maze, ablaze with vengeful spirits and the unrealized fury of the damned, becomes a series of derelict walls and doors, stagnating and collecting dust until the next thrill-seeker comes along for a bit of ghost-hunting adventure. It goes from mystery to history, and from that perspective, I believe, we can appreciate it for its stories and healing, rather than for a place to send people on dares.

The darkness, always my ally, nevertheless poses a bit of an obstacle at the moment; I can't see into the darker pools of shadow as completely as I'd like to, but under my present feeling of being watched, I don't dare switch on my flashlight, lest some malicious stalker be alerted to my location. It's all I can do, I suppose, to rely on my ears and the hollow, echoing acoustics in this building. And, while my most rational thinking suggests that I'm alone, my instincts tell me otherwise.

I have a reputation for good instincts, but that's mostly because they have often led to a fake perpetrator I had already picked out for the case at hand. In this instance my withdrawn, half-exhausted, half-paranoid brain is doing its best to keep itself occupied without the stimulation of human connection. I'm not sure I trust my instincts any more than I'd trust a kiss from a hungry alligator.

Not to mention that, my mind being in its current state, I'm probably more prone to delusion and hallucination than I care to admit, and any creaks, shadows, or other occurrences adding to a sense of vulnerability are just as likely to be a product of my mind as they are to be products of a fellow intruder. Even keeping this in mind, however, my wariness heightens; better to be hyper-aware and wrong than to be unaware when a threat exists. I wonder for a moment at what point vigilant awareness becomes paranoia. I suppose it boils down to whether or not you're right.

The steps are only a dozen, ending at a landing. The painting opposite the stairs, in this darkness, is just a series of organic-looking shapes, blobs of inky blacks and grays swirling together but contrasting simultaneously, like ingredients pooled into a mixing bowl ready to be stirred. In either direction, the landing opens up to a hallway that looks like it wraps around toward the front, separating here and reuniting, it seems, on the opposite side of this wall with the painting. I circle around via the right hall and find myself at the base of another staircase. Rather than looking like the average staircase, however, it looks every bit as decadent and refined as the rest of this building has.

The staircase begins at my left as I enter and it hugs the outer wall as it goes up to the next floor. There, it remains level as it wraps around the other walls until it gets back to this one. Cast-iron railings extend from floor to ceiling like a column in a cave, stalactite meeting stalagmite in an overdue union. Welded to the inside of the bars is a handrail, coated in thick black paint.

On the main floor, I see the front entrance opposite me, its padlock and chain rattling weakly as though angry with me for bypassing them. A squashy armchair sits near the entrance, accompanied by a dusty side table with nothing on it but the inch-thick uniform of this time-worn place. Two couches each line the side walls, matching the armchair and each other in both style and their decay: not excessive, but certainly noticeable. A desk, heavy and handsome, sits just in front of me, centered perfectly in the room.

I walk to the middle of the room and look up to see that, although I can see straight up to the blackness of the roof several stories above, no floors are exposed; each level is caged in by the cast-iron bars. Presumably, this was a precaution to prevent suicidal clients from hurling themselves from the upper levels, similar in function to the bars enclosing all of the windows above the first floor.

As much as I would prefer to take my time exploring every last inch, I also acknowledge that if I don't pick up my pace, and soon, I will be in here well beyond sunrise, and thus risk exposing myself to people on my return trip, raising eyebrows and drawing stares, for sure; who knows how much of this rampant dust has nestled in my hair or on my clothes?

To that end, I exchange my typical prudent thoroughness for a rushed sense of purpose; I'm no longer perusing. I'm *seeking*. I'm not sure what my treasure is, but I have an idea of where I can find a map.

I kneel down and pull my backpack close, rifling through various snacks and tools and gear, and withdraw the file I took from the first office. I only want one piece of information, but the sentences and phrases jumping out at me from the page draw my attention and dilute my focus.

This stuff is mostly admissions information, office- and file-related documents, and (*aha!*) living arrangements and logistics.

I'll look through what I took from Medical Records when I have more time. All I need at the moment is some kind of indication as to where Willa stayed.

I flip through a number of old charts, lists, diagrams, and policy manuals; a comprehensive list of each client, her patient number, laundry number, and therapist, an obscurely labeled, hand-written chart documenting accrual of points of some kind; a handful of lined sheets of paper detailing their respective days' events in neat, black cursive; a shoddily folded love note (without a 'to' or 'from') in far less neat pencil, and riddled with spelling mistakes; and finally, a list of each client, sorted by which unit they lived on. I scan the list, hopeful that Willa's information hadn't yet been removed from this list's printing. But alas, I find her, one of the eight clients in a unit called Thunder Springs.

As quickly as I can without making a mess of things, I tuck the documents back into my bag and find myself surveying that massive hall once again.

A pregnant stillness hangs in the air, like a dam lined with explosives, waiting only for someone to detonate it; just that, just the press of a button to unleash havoc and chaos upon those once secured by that structure.

I stand and wait for a moment, as though some other entity will press the button, but this stillness is an old, patient one, and it seems none too bothered by the prospect of holding its breath for a few more minutes while I orient myself. That quality unnerves me just the slightest bit: the idea that this situation, this night, this *building*, seem to be reacting to me. Surely, it's a phenomenon all in my head. At least, that's what I keep telling myself. Whether or not it's true is a door at the end of a mental corridor I don't care to visit now—can't *afford* to visit now—while I have other matters to deal with, rendering each passing minute more and more precious.

From what I can tell, there are two sets of stairs on each floor, on opposite corners from each other. The closest one to me is to the north of where I entered, just to my left. Even in the crisp, mountainous September air, even in the scarce ether of the night, I feel a peculiar warmth, perhaps more within me than around me, as I begin my ascent up the stairs. Each footstep, despite my efforts to suppress them, echoes around the tall entryway with a clarity that surprises me; the relentless dust I've seen thus far would have led me to expect a more muffled sound. I suppose the amount of empty space coupled with the area of smooth, hard surfaces betrays me this time.

The sense of being watched threatens to encroach again, but I mentally bat it away, supposing (hoping) that these thoughts are baseless, formless, groundless. Still, sleeves of goosebumps envelop my arms, soon to be a complete jacket (a turtleneck, even). With the augmentation of adrenaline, I fail to keep the paranoia at bay and my senses go to town once more—the tired old building creaks and sways in the night, a lovely wind moans through the eaves, and shadows without casters dance and play in the moonlight's tricky, fickle gaze. That acute level of concentration is intriguing; an elephant could tap dance on the floor above me and it may escape my notice, but simultaneously, I would be privy to a fly sneezing three rooms away. It's as though all of my senses—and my mind itself—are operating through a microscope, magnified a hundred, a thousand, ten thousand times.

Aware of this, I attempt to calm myself, willing my nerves to drink in the tranquility, rather than speculate on the peculiarity and suspect, of this evening.

To an extent, it works—the rooms, temporarily transformed to a smattering of materials and dimensions and missing furniture, turn back into rooms. The shadows calm and settle, the easy creaks of the building lose their sinister presence, the face pressing in against the ground-floor window—

Holy Jesus—

scurries away, taking its shadow with it.

SEVEN

Ohgodohgodohgod.

What I've been dismissing as nerves and paranoia all night turned out to be true, solid, as though my very fearful apprehension coalesced and took shape. My heart's normally steady, rhythmic beat now hammers away without restraint. The shadow man having disappeared whips my mind into a hallucinogenic frenzy, my eyes flitting from corner to corner, window to window, watching the shadows dance and dance and churn and swell and heave and—

Knock knock knock.

My visitor is knocking at the door. There's the possibility that that, too, has been a product of my imagination, but I am able to yank my brain reins away from panic for long enough to dwell on it further. Yes, I believe that that was real. The fullness of it, the clarity, the resounding and echoing whispers of its vibrations—they're real. Is this person playing games with me? There have been times tonight throughout which I was vulnerable; if my stalker had intended to inflict harm upon me, surely he could have, just like at the cottage. Unless, of course, he just barely caught up with me. But then, even if he didn't intend to hurt (or kill) me now, maybe he's just waiting until after he finds out what I'm doing here. Frankly, if someone were to ask, I'm not sure I'd be able to answer, in a lie or otherwise.

Or maybe this is just one of the fabled ghosts of Ghost Fork, the volatile beings so saturated with rage or sorrow or longing or lust that it tethered them to this plane of existence, as though their emotional baggage was too much cargo for the flight to heaven, so rather than abandon it, the host stuck around to feed on it and nothing else for centuries.

Fortunately, I don't believe in any of that. That being the case, I must handle this inquirer, this stalker, as a human. That doesn't offer a whole lot of clarity, however, other than that circles of salt and crucifixes and holy water will be ineffective. No sir, no priest call necessary for this encounter, except maybe to perform last rites.

In my paralytic indecision, I end up doing nothing but standing, listening, and trying to suppress the volume of my breathing for a minute or so.

No further sounds fill this entryway. A human would normally try again, right? Not that there's anything 'normal' about these circumstances. And even if the knock were to come again, what would I do? He's already seen me through the window, I can't very well pretend I'm not here. And if I just elect to ignore him, what then? He has managed to tail me this far, who's to say he wouldn't maintain surveillance of me until the minute I walk out of here? It's probably best to face him now. I remind myself that there's a chain with a corroded padlock on the other side of that door, and take comfort in noting the drastic limitations imposed on how far the door will open. If he wants a fight, it won't be happening now. At least, not a fist fight.

I inhale deeply. Exhale. My heart rate is back under control. The door is thick and metal. If stalker turns assailant, it will provide a fairly reliable shield, even if fists aren't his weapon of choice.

I pull the door open and hold it close to my shoulder. A whooshing gust of wind gushes in, giving this hall its first breath of fresh air in many years. Swirls of dust skate just above the floor, kicking up small motes of it, which form whirling, curling shafts in the moonlight.

And then, nothing.

No flurry of gunfire, no grasping arm trying to claw its way in, no sudden explosion or thudding impact longing to ram through the precipice.

I look out the threshold and see a darkness only slightly more forgiving than that from which I view it. The shapes that are visible—the tree line, the mountainous silhouettes, the opposite wall, the school building—rush into place, like a liquid poured into a mold, ready to be baked into a solid by the sun's imminent rise.

Alongside that solidarity comes a stillness of light and sound, unbroken by crickets or birds, the whispering breeze or the subsequent chattering rustle of the leaves. Surely, the courtyard has its own muffling quality, but this is an ethereal atmosphere, more fabricated than natural, rendering it all the more unsettling. An abrupt, irrational (although recognizing its irrationality doesn't help to loosen its grip on me) fear seeps into my mind like a dye, that the world is balanced precariously on the edge of some great galactic cliff, and that any of my movements will upset that balance and send the world tumbling into the abyss.

However, as suddenly as it arrived, that fear is dismissed by the embrace of an unseasonably warm wind.

Perhaps my mind's tether to sanity is a bit more tenuous than I thought. I breathe deeply the night air, hoping that its refreshing fingers will help to augment the remaining functional faculties of my mind.

Deep breath.

An animal startles in the woods beyond the courtyard's outer wall.

Deep breath.

The birds return from their brief auditory absence to resume their singing (which will continue to seem premature until the sun rises).

Deep breath.

With a refreshed sobriety, I step back into the building, uncertain of whether that is a retreat to safety or from it.

As I step back, my flashlight's sweeping pool of light glints over something small and shiny. I crouch to see it better. I'm greeted by a tiny silver key, sparkling in its rounded edges, sitting perfectly centered atop a drying leaf, like a gift from Pan.

The key is old-fashioned, and brings to mind thoughts of music boxes and old piano covers. Despite its otherwise apparent age, however, the brilliant sheen is entirely without tarnish or blemish. Its long neck unites the simple-looking head with an ornate, loopy handle. I inspect it for a moment, then stuff it into my pocket. It feels heavier there than it did in my fingers.

My trinket stowed away, I scan the courtyard once more, but find nothing, no one. Had this key been here before? Did I overlook it completely when I came to find the corroded lock?

More than anything else, the casual ease with which this guy has been poking around makes me uneasy. When you see a stranger poking around in abandoned houses and schools, there are various assumptions you might make. Perhaps that man has an affinity for the old and derelict, or he is on some kind of dare or bet. In any case, the subsequent deduction would be that he's also pumped full of adrenaline, and that following him in too close proximity could result in a scare, or worse.

So, then, what kind of person is either unaware of or undeterred by such inhibitions? Is my stalker simply that fearless? Or does he have some insight into who I am?

Given that my mystery texter knows seemingly everything about me, maybe someone else found a way to access such information, as well, which makes me uncomfortable. The more likely situation, I deduce, is that if this person knows about me, there's a striking chance that he's connected to my texting buddy. That is a mystery, but I sense that the ball is beginning to roll on this. In any case, he hasn't shown any aggression or ill intent. At least, not yet.

I push the door shut with a resounding clang and head toward the stairs. In spite of the confusing and mysterious accompaniment I've (apparently) had tonight, I feel an odd sensation of comfort, as though having reunited with an old friend rather than a stranger shrouded in enigmatic shadow. I hope my intuition holds true in that sentiment; as much as I like to be alone, I could sure use an ally.

EIGHT

TODD

"Oh yeah, I've seen him once or twice. Quiet guy, but always polite. He in some kind of trouble?"

"Not at all. Just an old friend. Thanks for your help."

Finally, Todd thinks. He has always considered himself intuitive, and a logical, thoughtful detective, but Remy's vanishing act would make Houdini himself sweat.

Todd, saturated in hunter's elation, purchases an iced tea and a candy bar and heads out.

With this new information, he faces the crisp air with a renewed optimism. This intel was not so much that Remy has been here, but the one word that the store clerk used: *always*. He's *always* polite. That means that Remy not only *was* here somewhere, but *is*. The transition from the past tense to the present is an event he has been looking forward to for some time now.

The journey has been exhausting, tedious, and more guesswork and luck than Todd is ready to admit. But the drive to find Remy never wavered, and though he wouldn't confess to it, a part of him (the part more inclined to read cheesy romance novels rather than thrillers) believes that the raw strength of their relationship had more of a role in his success than his competence as a detective. After all, you can have the sharpest eye in the world, but if you're searching the wrong place, your hunt will prove endlessly futile. Indeed, on a not-quite-conscious level, Todd credits his intuiting the correct place to that magical bond (though, again, he would never mention this to anyone, even Remy or, indeed, himself).

Ghost Fork, then. It certainly has its appeal: small, quiet, isolated. He wonders whether Remy had picked this place before arriving or just hopped out of the car, nodded once in approval, and paid and dismissed the driver. Even beyond its small-town quietness, which brings its own appeal, he notes a certain charm about the place, though he allows for the possibility that this charm is a byproduct of the night, and that when the sun rises in a few hours, the darkness will take the charm with it, leaving behind a mess of buildings and vehicles and potholes rather than a sleepy, dreaming, calm little town. Daytime, Todd notes, has a way of stealing away the magic that always persists through the night. He doesn't care what time of day it is, though; Todd's singular goal for the past three weeks has been to find Remy, and now he is on the cusp of doing so.

The thought has occurred to him, of course, that a person interested in finding Remy would also be apt to follow Todd, as the two are romantically involved. The thought also occurred to him that Remy left in the interests of both his own protection and of Todd's. Todd would be in danger of adversaries if they suspected that he knew where Remy was, and indeed Remy would be in danger if a person tracking Todd followed him right to Remy.

It's for those reasons that Todd switched his phone into airplane mode before he set out. He has had to buy and use physical maps, but he prefers those, anyway. Yes, Remy can disappear with the best of them, but so can Todd. His main concern has been that if someone did manage to pick up their scent, it would smell doubly strong, so to speak. Asking around for either Todd or Remy would yield answers in more cases than if Remy alone had been through, without Todd following. Double the chances of being detected.

Naturally, if Todd had felt that the initial odds of that happening were even remotely significant, he wouldn't have chanced it, but as they weren't, he proceeded. The worry sometimes sneaks into his thoughts, a sticky burr he just can't shake with satisfactory permanence, but he spends most of his time unhindered by it.

Now he faces an awkward length of time, too short to spend sleeping in his car (though he feels that he's too excited to sleep anyway), but too long to sit and watch the night finish out. Remy has an ability to entertain himself for lengths of time with his thoughts alone which, to Todd, would be maddening. Todd has some patience for nothingness, but is more comfortable with a book or something else to do. Without some kind of anchor or hub, his mind operates on a treadmill, with lots of action but no actual movement.

He recalls that there was a rack of paperbacks in the 24-hour convenience store, but much of his cash has been spent and he decides now that prudence may yet prove beneficial. Besides, they're probably just shitty love stories anyway, mostly sex and without much actual substance.

Alas, he eventually decides to nap in his car despite the awkward length of time. After all, he doesn't have to turn off airplane mode in order to use the alarm functions on his phone. He sets an alarm for seven o'clock, turns the volume to max, tilts the driver seat all the way back, and submits to his exhaustion.

REMY

An elevator shaft gapes to my left after I reach the first landing. One of the sliding doors juts out from the right side of the threshold, the other missing completely. I poke my head into the shaft, aiming my flashlight's beam upward, and see the underside of the carriage a couple of floors up. I withdraw from the shaft quickly, as my mind floods with images of the carriage coming loose and falling down the shaft, decapitating me effortlessly, unceremoniously.

I do wonder what (or who) may have caused the damage to the doors, but dwelling on that now is a fruitless endeavor, the harvest of a dead orchard.

Another small set of stairs leads to what seems to be the entrance to one of the dormitory units. An odd feeling churns inside my chest—one of discomfort, foreboding, of being an *intruder*, made all the odder considering my hobby of chasing (killing) criminals, often going through their homes beforehand for various intelligence, or to purloin a comb or bloody tissue or something to add to my framework of falsehoods. My work is not honest work, but it is effective work.

The door to the dorm is solid and wooden and heavy-looking, but without the solemn quality that the metal ones have. The lettering on the door, reminiscent of a spa or a modern dermatologist's office—professional, bronze, stylish—reads 'Thunder Valley.' My stolen key opens the door without hesitation and in I go.

As I first enter, my mind is assailed by a barrage of thoughts of a thirteen-year-old version of Todd walking its halls. While it was a girls' facility, I imagine Todd in a facility identical to this one, but two states removed.

In this broad hallway, the darkness is almost complete, but it extends only about twenty feet ahead of me, at which point I see that some of the night's weak lunar shine spills into a common area. There's a doorway on either side of me, each shut by doors fulfilling their decades-long vigils. From what I can tell in the darkness, they're the same thick, heavy wood as most of the doors here. I suppose that if you're dealing with a demographic prone to aggressive violence, you can't skimp on the sturdiness of your building material. Most household doors these days will succumb to a single well-placed kick. Not these ones, though. These ones would hold up to a flurry of them, and I'm sure many of them probably have.

Signs above the doors label them as Bathroom 1 and Bathroom 2. Further down the hall, two more doors stare at each other in the dusty gloom, identical to the bathroom doors, save for the signs, which reveal that these are Bedroom 1 and Bedroom 2. I move to unlock Bedroom 4, but an intrusive thought gives me pause: that upon opening the door and stepping inside, the east window will be stamped by the inky black silhouette from before.

"He's friendly," I tell myself. I hadn't intended to say it out loud, but the breadth of my voice hugging the walls seems to shake away a layer or two of the fearsome mystery, filling the daunting void with the familiarity of my own words instead. A shroud of goosebumps envelops me, but this time as a result of empowering (if groundless) boldness rather than fear or the blooming paranoia that has accompanied me on my adventure tonight. Although, I remind myself, it's not quite paranoia if you're right, as I've turned out to be, at least in some part.

Having donned my new shield of bravery (or recklessness), I open the door. There is indeed a window on the east wall, but framed within it is nothing but a view of the courtyard, striped by the cast-iron bars on the outer side of the pane. The room is square, perhaps fifteen feet on a side, and contains two bunk beds, still made up with their sheets and comforters, albeit moth-eaten and tattered after all these years. Rather than a closet, the north wall is fitted with an open-faced shelving unit, separated into four columns and made of sturdy wood.

The silence in this room seems to apply a sort of pressure on its own, like the sheer weight of the atmosphere has doubled. My footfalls on the thin carpet sound crisp and clear, but somehow distant, like I'm listening to a high-definition recording being played back through mediocre speakers.

The beds are equipped with drawers in their bases—the only thing in the room not readily visible from the doorway. Unsure whether to expect anything, I open one of the drawers. It's empty, just like the shelves staring at me from the north wall. The other drawers (three more; four in total) offer the same. After a final scan of the room (and a quick glance down into the still-empty courtyard) I walk out, not bothering to close the door behind me.

Now I have a decision to make: Indulge my characteristic thoroughness or move on? Without a doubt, I would prefer to stick around and pick apart every small corner of every room and hallway, but already my time is wearing thin. The birds outside have been chirping for some time, and although global warming has fucked up their internal clocks, I sense that sunrise is fast approaching nonetheless. And for me, a person whose primary objective is to be invisible, the fullness of light brought on by daybreak turns into quite the obstacle indeed.

If I were somewhere like Riverdell, perhaps I might feel okay about chancing the sunlight, but in a town this small, to see an unfamiliar face is a rarity, and anyone who sees me will, thus, most likely remember me. My likeness isn't memorable—in my own opinion, I look perfectly average, so much so that it's almost a point of pride—but even so, an eye that catches mine is apt to remember the event, even if not my face. And if I *avoid* people's eyes, they'll remember me all the more clearly.

"Haven' seen you 'roun' these parts!"

"Well that's a new face!"

"Well hey, stranger, where ya from?"

All attention I neither need nor want.

That said, I don't know whether I'll get another opportunity to peruse this time capsule of a facility. I used to be able to rely on the cover of night, instinct, and a not-so-modest degree of prudence, but lately, my life has seemed to be intent (is 'hell-bent'

91

too strong a phrase?) on proving to me that, despite my efforts to salvage it, my situation, my circumstances are all as tenuous as a strand of spider silk clinging to a tree branch in a healthy breeze. If the past year of my life is any indication, the course of a day could have me on a plane to South Africa by tomorrow morning. So what, then, are my options for completing my search without making a return trip?

Not many.

I could finish my browse, and take the back roads (which, in this town, is a phrase nearly synonymous with bushwhacking) and pray that no one sees me, but that prospect doesn't inspire any confidence. The only other practical solution I can conjure is to wait for night to fall again. In that case, I'll easily eat through the supply of snacks I packed along. I amuse myself with a question as to whether there's enough exploration to be done to keep me busy for that long, but laugh it away; even without a vast, abandoned treatment facility to explore, my mind alone has quite enough twists and wrinkles in it to keep itself busy for a respectable amount of time. With this trove of entertainment to aid it, I could go without so much as a whiff of boredom for well over a week.

Of course, this place was built as living quarters, but can I content myself with spending a night here? The thought of sleeping in one of these beds makes me shudder, but maybe I could find a way to make them more accommodating. In terms of bodily functions, I'm sure I can find an acceptable place to relieve myself. The idea stews in my mind, occasionally branching into the logistical specifics and potential hazards, but most of the risk is that some other visitor may show up, and based on the thorough untouched-ness of this place beyond the immediately accessible, that risk is not a prevalent one.

I sift through the pros and cons, cripplingly torn between the two, until the curious, self-indulgent part of my psyche finds its voice. *What do you have to lose?*

So I explore with the mindset not only of dissecting the past, but of living in the present, scouting potential resting places, eating places. Not that I expect much, but finding the ideal place here could mean the difference between an acceptable night's sleep and a lung coated in dust, or between a quick bite and tetanus.

The other three bedrooms are, for all intents and purposes, identical to the first. No new surprises or nuances there. The common area features three couches that look like they would have been uncomfortable even in their prime. There's a series of cabinets and a sink on the northern end of the area, with a tiled floor and a window looking out at the cliffs and hills—through another set of rusty iron bars, of course. The cabinets yield nothing of particular interest, although they're also not empty. One has a scrunchie and a corner torn from a sheet of lined paper, now yellowed by time. I take mental note of the particular, jagged way the tear was done, but only in case I find the paper it came from and it thus becomes relevant.

There are two doors which lead neither to bathrooms nor to bedrooms. The first opens reluctantly, emitting a loud, pervasive squeak as its hinges flex for the first time in so long. It's only a supply closet, containing old spray bottles and a broom with a small fraction of its bristles remaining. A dozen rolls of paper towels and at least twice as many rolls of toilet paper sit on a shelf next to a neat stack of facial tissue. A mop bucket sits on the floor with its accompanying mop planted inside, their surfaces crusted together with dried dirt and grime.

I close the door and move to the other, the last unopened door on this unit. As I fish my key from my jacket pocket, I notice that the blue-black night sky has traded in much of its black for dull gray, and the stars have begun to fade, disappearing before man's eyes. The birds' songs continue.

The key I took from that first office has served me faithfully and fully until now, but this time it doesn't even fit inside the lock. Frustrated, I drop the key back into my pocket and pull out my lock picks, entertaining an odd sentimental attachment to them for a moment before putting them to use. From the assortment of picks, I select a sturdy, slightly curved pick and a tension lever. A half-second of ire sets in as my pick sticks fast. I'm about to switch and try another pick when the first pin slides into place. After that first pin, the other three follow suit without a fight, and I'm rewarded after a few seconds, with the satisfying grind of the tension lever turning the tumbler. The door pops open and swings, much more quietly than the last one, out toward me.

In some situations, the satisfaction of picking the lock successfully is more rewarding than what lies beyond the door, a concept exemplified by the rusty old water heater occupying this small closet. Deflated, I close the door and head toward the unit's entrance, back through the hall of doors.

After prolonged, meticulous thought, the entry hallway is

less frightening than it was before. It helps, too, that daylight continues to push its way into the sky, casting dim light into the corners of the room where busy shadows conspired just half an hour ago.

Continuing on toward the next unit, I open a door on my way there to find a sort of break room, with a small case of lockers, a board of hooks for hanging coats and jackets, two cheap tables in the center of the room, and counters and cabinets lining the walls. An old microwave still sits in the corner, plugged in to a powerless outlet. A coffee maker is not one of this room's amenities, but there is a hot water dispenser, complemented by various packets of tea, cider, and hot chocolate sitting tidily in a wire rack to its side. Flimsy plastic chairs with metal wire frames line the table in a disorderly way that suggests that the last time they were touched was when the break room's last loungers stood up to depart for what they didn't know was the final time.

A refrigerator bulks in one corner, to the left of the door upon entering. Out of fear alone, I don't open it; God only knows what sort of horror may have mutated from a forgotten bologna sandwich or tuna casserole after all this time. The stench would surely call forth what little I've eaten recently, as well. The same fear inhibits me from opening the freezer door up above. No sir, vomit is not on the agenda for today.

The cabinets mostly contain what one might expect: disposable dishes and plasticware, straws, napkins, and what is, in my opinion, quite an excessive amount of paper towels. I suppose paper products were never scarce around here. I grab a roll of them and shove it into my backpack, but there's little enough room remaining that the top of the roll sticks out like a standpipe. For a brief second, it almost looks like an extreme-looking bong, and I amuse myself with the image of the most dedicated stoner trying to use it as such.

I find nothing else in the break room and move on, back out into the towering entryway. By now, the sun's rays punch neat, glowing beams into the hall like great golden skewers. I continue along the pathway, which hugs the wall around toward the next staircase.

NINE

TODD

Finally, Todd locates the building—he's sure of it this time. He's still tired as hell, but more alert despite his exhaustion. They're finally going to be reunited. And Remy sure is good at vanishing. Never before has he had so much trouble tracking someone down—a significant feat, given his past as a detective. Anyone else would have been thrown off the scent several states ago. But he knows all of Remy's tricks, habits, and preferences. At every turn, Remy was able to host an imaginary conversation with Remy, and surely, had the conversations taken place in reality, they would have been damn near word-for-word identical to Todd's imaginary ones.

And as Remy was so careful not to be followed, Todd had to take similar precautions to preserve his anonymity and not leave a trace, lest he open a path leading to both him and Remy. No, Todd couldn't have that. Not after everything that transpired in Wometzia. All Todd wants now is to live in peace with his love. And if he has to choose between love and inner peace, well, peace be damned. He will wait here for as long as necessary. He will have his reunion. With eyes on Remy's front entrance, he makes himself comfortable. But as it turns out, he's too comfortable;

now, he drifts into a reluctant slumber. He only has time for a *What if I miss him?* to surface in panic before he's out entirely. His mind and heart disagree on the importance of this union, apparently. He sleeps soundly.

REMY

My heart beats intensely as I stare at the door. *Thunder Springs* is stamped across its surface. This is where Willa lived and died. The potent mystery of it all reminds me of one of those 'Escape the Haunted Opera' sorts of computer games, where you have to piece together clue after clue to advance, clicking every object at random and hoping that one of them turns out to be a piece of the puzzle.

However, the thing stopping me is not missing clues, but a festering uncertainty about whether or not I'm mentally and emotionally ready to process whatever I find, if anything at all. I've been dabbling, sure, but finding anything big would mean a full-blown commitment to this. I don't know how long that could take or how much energy, and one of the surviving symptoms of my OCD is that I cannot leave a project unfinished. Beyond that, if my mystery stalker is onto something, the result of my investigation may be that someone—Thad Eboncore—was unjustly locked up and I'd need to find a way to make that right without exposing myself to the public.

I insert the key into the lock and turn. The *click* echoes thickly in the entryway. The door swings open with much less noise, and I step inside. I'm pleased to find that my heartbeat and breathing, fickle little bastards lately, are under control.

If it hadn't been for the memory of standing outside the door to this unit, I could swear I was walking into Thunder Valley a second time. The same floor serves the same hallway which contains the same doors labeled in the same font.

Before going into any of the rooms, I walk through to the end of the hall, where it opens into the common area. I suppose the facility would have earned full marks for equality and standard issue; every bit of it, so far as I can remember, matches its counterpart in Thunder Valley, aside from that the hallway extends to the south instead of the north. I redo my familiar sweep—cabinets and cupboards, underneath and inside the couches, any nooks or crannies I can find—and find nothing but the usual abundant dust. I open the door to bedroom two first.

A chill sweeps into the room alongside me. The room looks the same as the other one, but still manages to feel different. I can't quite pinpoint the distinction, but it's undeniable. Todd would be able to find it. God I miss Todd. If he and Beth were here—if we had The Crew back together—I'm sure we'd have this cranked out in no time. With Beth's unparalleled reasoning, Todd's attention to detail, and my skills in execution, nothing could stop us.

However, as these nostalgic sentiments are a detriment to my focus, I must suppress them—for now, at least. Maybe I'll summon them back when I'm in the mood for a self-indulgent pity party. But now is not that time.

A few minutes of diligent searching later, I find why the room looks different: the bars in the window are missing. As I look more closely, I find that they weren't removed cleanly; the brick is torn up and a couple of screws didn't quite make it out along with the bars, and now dangle awkwardly from the holes that were drilled into the brick for them.

Like in the other room, the window overlooks the courtyard. Without the bars, it's actually a strikingly pretty view. So who removed them? And how? Also, when and why? It has to have been done from the outside—these windows don't even open from the inside, and the pane and its caulking are still intact—but that only brings me back to my one of my prior questions: How?

I move on from it. I search the beds in detail, pulling off pillows, pillow cases, comforters, blankets, and sheets one at a time for each of the beds in the room.

After I pull down the mattress of the second bed, I find a tiny lockbox in the corner of the frame, close to where the pillow was before I dissected it.

The box is wooden and painted over with a fading floral design. The hinges are tarnished and battered, and the wood chipped in several places. The lid slides just the slightest amount due to the poor condition of the hinges, but for the most part, the intact lock holds it steady.

As much as I want to believe otherwise, I'm certain that the tiny key, still weighing heavily yet snugly in my pocket, will unlock this box. Of course, much of that certainty comes from the similar ornate design between the two, but mostly, that confidence originates from my assumption about my follower: that he's looking into the same thing I am.

And, well, I suppose that's all well and good, but why now? Why is a stranger looking into a decades-old case now, of all times? Of course, it could be a coincidence, or maybe he's spent this *entire* time looking into it and I just happened to stumble upon him in the midst of his work. I don't place much stock in the latter possibility. Or the former, really.

No, I think that, as seems to have been the case of late, my arrival here has somehow triggered the onset of some series of events that I'll initially think are independent of me but are actually intricately woven into my life, in ways that cut deep into my past and shape my future. Or something.

That line of logic opens even more questions, however. I sit on the lower bunk to think, and the mattress issues a *sigh* that seems, strangely, equal parts muffled and amplified.

Who could that be, and how could he find me here? Why would someone follow me here and set to work on an old case? How long has he been here? What is his ultimate goal? Is he friendly? And if so, why doesn't he reveal himself? And if not, what is he waiting for? If he was able to find me here, he almost certainly knows where I live, and has thus had plenty of opportunity to strike or to call in the cavalry, if that is his goal. That he's friendly is the more likely conclusion, I decide. Even if he were just keeping tabs on me, something would have happened by now if he's been here long enough to have assembled all of those newspaper clippings and organize them in such a Beth-esque manner.

Indeed, I think that my new friend is just that. But that takes me back to the question of why he has stayed concealed for so long.

A couple of other feeble explanation possibilities surface in my mind, but under critical scrutiny, they shrivel and die rather quickly. I'll have to set that one on the back burner for now.

The lockbox feels oddly foreign in my hand, like picking up a controller to an unfamiliar game system for the first time. And certainly, I've never held it in my hands before, but it has a deeper level of enigma than simple novelty. The air in the room is still, but its chill does not relent.

I fish the tiny key from my pocket and admire how closely the loopy handle mimics the floral pattern on the box. I expect to meet a worn-down, tarnish-induced resistance, but the key slides in easily with a satisfying *click*. A similar one follows when I turn the key, and the lid opens up.

But there's nothing inside—at least, not at first. Upon more attentive inspection, however, I find that the bottom is false. I can't pry it up with my fingers, so I hold the box upside-down. The false bottom, a square of thin wood, falls into my waiting hand, and an off-white, folded slip of paper follows it down.

Someone went to great lengths to keep that a secret. How the staff never found the box itself is beyond me, but based on what Todd has told me, something like that, especially with its metal parts, would definitely be considered contraband. Perhaps this student had a way of hiding it elsewhere when time came to search the bunks. Or maybe they were just incompetent or lazy staff with no regard for thoroughness.

Becoming ever more aware of the cold (despite the sun's steady ascent), I lift the folded piece of paper and unfold it with the careful precision of a neurosurgeon. The creases are worn down almost to the point of breaking simply from being unfolded. When I've managed to unfold the note completely (intact, miraculously), I hold it in the brighter area by the window, but still have trouble reading the faded text—it was written in pencil, decades ago. To say that time has had an adverse effect on its legibility would be an understatement.

But alas, the light of my flashlight, in tandem with that shining in through the window, is enough to make out the short message: "I love you, Dubz. We'll be together soon."

Dubz? Must be referring to the 'W' at the beginning of 'Willa.' I must admit that I'm a bit deflated at my find. I'm not sure what I was expecting—maybe a telling, hard-hitting, undeniable piece of evidence that would blow the thing wide open.

I *am* inclined to think that the note belonged to Willa and, if not, is at least related to this case somehow. Why else would my mystery friend have come and dropped off the key?

That leads into a bigger question, one which has been skating around the outskirts of my mind like a spider caught in a tub, now circling the drain before plunging into it: Does this guy ever plan on contacting me? He ushered me into a piece evidence regarding Willa's death after I discovered his collection of relevant newspaper clippings, but if he ever plans on reaping the benefits from that endeavor, he either has to confront me or steal it from me. I remind myself that neither scenario is outside the realm of possibility.

Carefully, carefully, I fold the delicate paper back up, following its creases to ensure that I fold it the same way it was done before, tuck it into the lockbox, fit the wooden concealment piece back in, and close the lid, locking it with that same satisfying sound as with which it opened. I wrap the box in several layers of paper towel from my backpack and place it snugly inside.

An interesting, potentially juicy find, to be sure, but without a bit more context, it's not all that damning. Maybe it will be more substantial when pieced together with other, more established evidence. But I remind myself, too, that I'm in a uniquely advantageous position in that regard. Sure, people have come through here, but as far as I can tell, none of them were equipped with the necessary knowledge and tools to get into the locked areas. In this moment of reflection, I remember that the window at the back had been smashed in, but the door leading from it remained locked, and everything beyond that has seemed entirely undisturbed. This allows me a much more honest look around than, say, a rogue thrill-seeker looking through the front entrance area.

For now, though, I'm starting to get tired. It seems to be sometime in the late morning, and if I set aside eight hours for sleep (a sort of joke I play with myself, apparently), that leaves me with three or four hours of exploration time before night falls again. I could probably get away with leaving a bit earlier, but I'll make that call later on. As for how I'm going to split my time, I think the sooner I get some sleep, the better. That way, I'll be sharper in my calculations and, should the need for some action arise, I'll be better prepared for it. Besides, my misadventure in New Mexico last month taught me more than any human should know about sleep deprivation, and since then, I've seized any opportunity I've gotten to sleep—within healthy parameters, of course.

With that in mind, I head back out toward the common area. The couch doesn't seem too dusty, but that might just be a result of my total immersion in and subsequent desensitization to it.

So I lie down, and my nostrils fill with a concentrated version of that old mustiness, and before I have the time to recoil from it or perhaps adjust to a position in which I'm less prone to it, I find myself relaxing into that position. The room is chilly, emphasized now that I'm stationary, but the old, stiff couch holds my body heat well and I find that I'm actually quite comfortable.

I lie for quite some time, awake, in that tricky mental limbo between subconscious and conscious. I can feel thoughts, analyses, and speculations struggling against the partition from one direction, while the primal emotions and sensations hammer away at the other. The strange, elusive state I'm in allows me only the briefest view of both, and for a split second, I amuse myself with thoughts about how I so often consider those two planes to be so separate and distinct, a thought which is only amusing because of how entirely it contrasts with reality. Indeed, cognition and emotion are different, but with very few exceptions, the two do not exist independently of each other. Many decisions are solely calculated ones, and many are born exclusively of emotion, passion, the heat of the moment, as they say. But most decisions are rooted and executed in a measured combination of both.

And as this thought manages to champion the pensive side of this dichotomy, leading it through the barrier, my last act of cognition before drifting off to sleep is to wonder whether these thoughts and ideas will persist once I've woken up.

I fall asleep.

My life, up until about a year ago, was very measured. Figuratively in most cases, but still literally in many. And even as I plunged myself into the events that catalyzed this seemingly endless chain reaction, I took steps that were measured and calculated. My damning mistake was to underestimate Keroth. But all it takes is for one variable to be misvalued to fuck up entire equations.

That being the case, my life *since* then has been anything but measurable and calculated. It's been a dizzying flurry of hiding and evading, picking fights from the shadows, getting shot at, doing some shooting of my own, and various messages—cryptic, threatening, and endearing. But even so, never before have I been quite as disoriented as I am now, waking up with my nose (and mouth, it seems) full of dust. It takes longer than ever for me to blink my mind into focus. The room comes into view, but everything seems foreign and comes together at odd angles. It's still blurry from my slumber and a tricky evening hue lends its colors all over the spectrum. The ordeal seems to last several minutes, but in reality, it probably only takes a few seconds for me to float back into mental clarity.

On the last of those seconds, a flood of memories rushes in, one full of sneaking and lockpicking and perusing. Last night, this seemed like quite a thrill. Right now, however, the prospect of rising from my horizontal haven to do anything is less than attractive.

Eventually, a sense of urgency prods at me hard enough to

overcome my apathy, and I sit up in preparation to leave my little patch of warmth. The room has heated up considerably, but it still takes a colossal amount of willpower to push myself forward.

Onward. I have more to explore. Briefly, I go to the window to see if I can get a better idea of what time it is. The sun still has some time before it hits the western mountains, but I did sleep for longer than I anticipated. That itself is a relief, but it may bite me in the ass if I find much more interesting content during the second half of my excursion. And while the adventurous part of me hopes for just that, the rest of me longs for the quiet, safe, dark solitude of my apartment.

In that small moment, a more vocal part of me awakens— one that went to sleep not hours ago, but weeks ago. This is a part of me that got buried after I parted ways with Todd. And the function of this part, simply put, is to appreciate. To act as an audience to the natural spectacles of the world and the less natural spectacles of mankind. To indulge in the beauty of everywhere and to gawk at the marvels of life.

That part didn't see much use growing up, but as I got into college and began to explore who I really am, that section awoke with the mighty hunger of a grizzly coming out of hibernation. As such, I immersed myself in movies, music, video games, and books. Of course, we were allowed books growing up (they aren't in the least noisy), but with my newfound love for art, I was able to appreciate them in a new light, an enlightening luminescence that seemed to reveal to me previously unseen secrets as though translating them from some lost language written in the stars.

I was able to empathize with the characters, immerse myself

in the plots, and connect my senses to the settings laid out by the pages. Finally, the ideas and dynamics involved in the pages offered me something beautiful. Something beyond the intricate patterns of the words: *story*.

That understanding, vague and rogue and wondrous and fascinating all at once.

Then that part thrived, on and on until about a month ago. It was shut off as a side effect, a precautionary measure, like how one shuts off a water main in order to prevent leaking and flooding from broken pipes farther up the line.

It was dangerous, a detriment to my efficacy, an indirect hurdle between me and my goal of self-preservation. And now, that newly awoken chunk of me has a request to make: *Let's go outside, so we can watch night fall. Just like old times. Let me watch the sunset.*

This thought ushers me into action at last.

For now, I'm willing to oblige. My imprudence seems to be reprimanded almost immediately, however, as when I stand to go outside, I hear voices. They're distant, almost faint enough for me to miss them, but as I train my ears upon them, I become more and more aware of the risk I was about to take. The voices belong to a minimum of two males, as distinctly as I can hear.

Their tones are without passion; they could be discussing the weather, or the freshly begun school year. In any case, I'm too far removed to discern any specific words or phrases, and in reality, I'm not sure whether I want to close that distance. If they move close enough to me that I worry about being discovered, I will then occupy myself with the particulars of their intentions, but as it seems that nobody else has managed to explore this area before me (and as I have closed all of the relevant doors behind me), I have confidence that my identity and even my very presence here shall go undiscovered. Still, my sudden and thirsty impulse to go outside is, for the moment, quelled, and I thus resolve to continue my search of the school for the time being.

Party poopers.

When I approach the door, I wipe away a thin film of tears. Perhaps my water main has been opened back up. I must will it closed, though, lest I be caught in a vortex of emotion at a fatally inopportune time. Indeed, this flood is inevitable, but what I can control is *when* to indulge it, and now is not that time.

What I *can* see of the sunset is beautiful and brilliant, the birds chirp merrily and the wind is low, but something in the air buzzes with the sensation of imminent bad news, like a phone call or knock at the door at two in the morning.

I can't afford to dwell on that, however. I tack that in with the other exploding sentiments threatening to turn me into a blubbering mess and, with tremendous effort, summon my mental spotlight (thoughtlight?) to the present—not only the now, but the here. The gentle stillness of the room, my self-inflicted adventure, and the pregnant potential of breaking open a case widely assumed resolved decades ago. And while I am able to re-focus myself and steer my actions toward my end goal, my mind is still aflutter with the case, with building a present out of the past.

The note and the tiny lockbox stick out in my mind. Surely, these would have been discovered when the case was hot. Right?

Beyond that, my rogue companion had the key to it. Was he closely involved with the parties in the case, or had he come across it in another way?

Also, it doesn't escape my attention that he not only trusts me, but most likely wants to meet at some point. He probably left for home (or wherever he's sleeping) immediately after leaving the key for me, as the sun was apt to rise not long afterward. I wonder for a moment whether he spends his time at that creepy, newspaper-laden room in the abandoned cottage. Perhaps he stays in a different one and only uses that one for his obsession. Maybe he's even a resident of Ghost Fork.

My questions about the mysterious man's involvement with the case turn into questions about the man himself—his identity, his purpose and intentions, and—most pertinent of all—whether he knows of me and my identity. Not knowing makes me uncomfortable, but if I can't find relief in confidence of his benevolence, I can at least rest assured that he is not malevolent.

And again, he may not even be aware of who I am. Maybe he's just another passenger on this mystery ride and we just happened to occupy the same car at the same time (although my doubts from before still hold strong). In whichever of these cases (or others) may be true, one consistency compels me to forge an alliance with him: that he seems to be a key component in bringing about the entirety of the truth about Willa Frye and Thad Eboncore.

The note I found rings in my head at the thought of them: *I love you, Dubz. We'll be together soon.* My mind grasps for anyone else who could be called 'Dubz,' but I'm forced to admit to myself that my familiarity with the context is likely insufficient to make that assessment. Still, though, I resolve to be open about the possibility that it's not Willa.

My remaining search yields nothing much of import. A few pairs of socks were abandoned and left in the side table drawers in the common area for some reason, and some squirrels have found their way into the one of the bathrooms in a unit on the next floor up. On the next floor were the therapists' offices, and just in time; I've been growing bored and increasingly eager to finish here (and I don't bore easily). But if anything can offer insight to the mental states of the involved parties, therapists' notes and charts are the surest bet.

I reflect on my experience with a therapist, in a time that was scarcely more than a decade and a half ago but feels to me like eons ago. She was neat and polite. She wore a happy face and her office was cozy, inviting, and visually interesting.

Trinkets from all over the country—maybe even the world; my eleven-year-old brain couldn't tell the difference either way—lined shelves and tabletops, and each had its distinct spot, as though they reserved their places with nameplates before retiring each night.

The sun sinks ever more rapidly, soon to share the western horizon with the mountains, cutting a jagged shadow into the valley. As I dig through the therapists' files, I can only hope that I can find the correct files quickly; with dusk coming in soon, the last of my natural light will be banished to tomorrow. While I do have a flashlight (and spare batteries), such luxuries would render me nakedly visible from the outside. I didn't worry about that quite as much last night, but two major factors have changed since then: First, that I'm several stories high, and thus visible to greater distances. Second, I'm not certain of the whereabouts of those guys from earlier. Their voices ceased some time ago, but that's not hard confirmation that they left; only that they're no longer talking within earshot of me. That is mildly comforting, but still not enough for me to act rashly.

With these things in mind, I fish through stacks of reports and filing cabinets with greater speed (and less thoroughness) than for which I've always been reputed. Beth used to watch me process crime scenes with one eye on the clock, tapping her foot and sighing on the minute every minute just to drive home how long I was taking. It blanketed the beginnings of our camaraderie with some tumult, but as soon as I started finding things that she missed, it opened doors for growth, both in regard to my career and in terms of our friendship. The foundation of our relationship was built firmly on my failure to be a misogynistic asshole, but this dynamic sparked a competitive streak that rocketed the pair of us through case after case.

God I miss Beth.

I finally close the last of the drawers in Janey Tramish's office—the last being in her desk, containing only a handful of pens—and leave, preparing myself for the next office. But as soon as I step out onto the landing, I hear a strange grating noise on the west side of the building, followed by a loud, rhythmic series of bangs.

For a wild second, my imagination spins into overdrive, fashioning all sorts of scenarios in which vengeful specters of the past manifest and use some ancient power to close my throat and strangle me. However, my mental return to reality is rapid and I regain enough of my gall to follow the noise. It sounds like it's coming from that combination hallway and lobby area where I first entered the building, and I realize that they're probably those guys from earlier, trying in vain to explore the locked areas of the school. Like me, but without success.

Bang. Bang. Bang.

Nonthreatening as they are to me now, I would be much happier if they turned tail and left. The doors here are indeed strong and heavy out of necessity, but I don't know these guys or how far they're willing to go to get inside. So I make a fast decision.

I descend the stairs as fast as I can without making much noise and slip through the doorway back into the lobby where they're trying to enter.

Bang. Bang. Bang.

I can hear their voices more clearly now. There are indeed two guys, but whether because they were quiet before or because their voices simply didn't quite carry to me, I hadn't perceived the two women with them.

By the sounds of the conversation and the general way the guys sound (that is to say, like assholes), this strikes me as a cliché scenario: take the girls on a date out to the creepy abandoned place so that they get frightened into the big guys' arms.

I suppose I can help with that.

Three more crashes come. *Bang. Bang. Bang.*

My turn. In between sets, I raise my knee up to my chest and kick the door with mighty force. Two of them scream, and they aren't the women. Without a window through which to view me, they fall silent for a moment—to be sure they aren't just imagining it, I'm sure.

One voice says, "Did that just—" before I cock and launch another kick.

"Hello? Is someone there? How did you get over there?" asks one of the girls. While her bravery (or persistent skepticism) is impressive, I'm afraid that I may have to find another way to deter them, but then the guys speak up:

"Jesus, Melissa, are you fuckin' insane?"

"For real, let's go! Shit's creepy as hell." The girl laughs, but evidently submits; I hear some hastened shuffling, and duck into the shadows, relishing in their hasty retreat as I go.

I make a mental note to check the forums later for a post about this. I feel that this particular encounter will be deliciously embellished when it makes it to the Internet.

But for now, I need to rush back up to the fourth floor and make use of what little time I have remaining before this sudden twilight turns to inky black night. I don't necessarily need to read the pertinent information right away, but rather, I'll be most efficient in snatching anything with Willa's name on it and perusing it later. As I resolve to do so, I almost feel HIPAA glaring in my direction.

In Mary Crankle's office, I finally find what I'm looking for: a simple yellow folder marked 'Willa F.' Even in my resolve to collect my prize and get out, I'm yet tempted to open the folder and flip through its contents. But I will myself to get going. When I reach the bottom floor again, the sun's light has since faded entirely, and its relative warmth has dissolved quickly along with it.

A mountainous chill wraps me in its frigid fingers before long and I can see my breath against the twilit sky, even in the limited light offered by the entryway. My opportunity for escape is fast approaching.

I run through a mental checklist, assuring myself that I left nothing behind without proper scrutiny. I will have a wide window of time to leave, but I'm getting tired and I miss my bed.

Before making a beeline to the exit, I sit in silence for a time, listening for any other adventurous souls, sure, but also immersing myself in the quiet. Yeah, it's been this quiet the whole time, but only in terms of decibels. In regard to *mental* volume, this excursion rivals any concert you might imagine. Now, though, the writhing tentacles of perpetual thought finally grow weary and slow to a less daunting, more restful level, even going as far as to border on full-on repose.

And for a minute or two, I'm too lethargic to risk sending my mind into action again, and thus content myself with sitting on the bottom step until I'm ready to leave. Such a cognitive tranquility is a scarcity in my life, and I'll be sad to see it go, but the pregnancy of my newly purloined documents and their potential impacts on this old case are enough to shake me free of my complacency.

I slip through the dark hallways, this time without a turbocharged curiosity. Once again, I close all of the doors behind me.

They're spring-loaded so as to shut on their own, but many of the doors' springs seem to have expired, so instead of the authoritative *whoosh* with which those kinds of doors normally close, they shudder rather than swing closed, and lack the shutting power to latch properly.

Once more in the school hallway, I consider exploring the cafeteria, but disregard that urge when I think about my bedroom.

In the awkward buffer between the school hallway and the main lobby, where I first entered, I'm halted by the noise of a car's tires crunching on gravel outside. I can't see anything from where I am, and while it's tempting to look around through one of the windows, I also acknowledge that my own invisibility is dependent on these visual obstacles.

Such prudence turns out to reward me; after a minute, bright, sweeping headlights' beams surge in through the windows, temporarily brightening the room. A few glass frames glint briefly before going dark again. The car's crunching returns and the beams drift away, leaving me in a solid darkness once again. As my eyes readjust to the blackness, I listen to the car as it turns tail and heads back down the dirt and gravel outside. I wait for a few minutes longer, just in case my path is blocked by crunching footsteps or a searching flashlight beam. But no such threat arises, and at last I leave through the same door that admitted me earlier.

The air outside is familiar but oddly estranged, like returning to one's hometown after living abroad for a long time and finding things either more worn than you remember or replaced by new buildings. I breathe it deeply and feel a sense of relief I haven't felt for some time.

TEN

TODD

Todd parks outside of what he learned is the only apartment building in town. He first considered searching the abandoned houses he learned about, but knew Remy wouldn't have chosen a place without water and gas—in his time of deep grief or stress, his longest-standing and most reliable form of relief is a hot shower—so hot that Todd must let the bathroom air out for a while afterward before he can stand to be in it.

In the back seat, Odin whines—he must have caught Remy's scent.

The apartments consist of a single building, with only four apartments. Numbers one, two, and three have already had traffic since Todd parked. Guests and visitors, mostly, but number two's tenants left and returned with groceries.

With these factors in mind, Todd watches number four with an obsessive attentiveness. He of all people is aware of Remy's gift of subtlety. If Todd gets distracted for even a minute, he might miss him.

At first, he knocked on the door. Of course, he didn't expect it to be answered right away, but he also knows Remy would have liked to know who it was, and if he had seen Todd through the peephole, no doubt he would have thrown the door open and lunged into his arms.

But now, he is starting to worry that Remy might be out adventuring. He likes to consider himself careful, but in certain emotions' holds, he can be quite susceptible to impulsive decision-making, particularly when driven by justice or some kind of penance. This is a quality Todd holds dear most of the time, but in crucial moments of self-preservation, he sometimes wishes that Remy would keep that in check a little better.

At length, Todd determines that Remy must indeed be some kind of 'away' at the moment. So where to begin looking for him? If he's not here, he's either on some heroic adventure (Todd tenses at the thought) or he's familiarizing himself with the area. To that end, Todd pulls out his phone to search for any local crime lately, with which Remy may have gotten involved. To his relief, no recent crimes show up, but among the search results, virtually every single article is about a suicide from decades ago. Todd reads the article, and two words jump out at him: *"…now abandoned…"* Suddenly, he has an idea of where Remy is.

The path to the school hasn't been maintained ever since it closed, but Todd is still sure that he can navigate his car up there. It's too early for snow, at least, so he won't have to worry about that. In any case, it can't much hurt to try. So he sets off after committing to memory a rough map of the area. The road is indeed rough, but after a particularly bumpy patch, it smooths out.

Just as Todd picks up speed, however, movement in his headlights incites a small panic and he arrests his momentum up the steep hill. Four people, two men and two women, it looks like, are running down the hill at a dead sprint, seemingly either unaware of or unyielding to the rocky and uneven terrain on which they tread. Todd can't quite see well enough to be sure, but it sounds like one of them is in the middle of a hysterical fit of sobs.

If Todd were one to perceive such events as signs from the universe or a higher power, he might turn back, but as he is not that type, he continues up the hill. Sure, logic might indicate that that group was running from something, but it's most likely either an animal or a paranormal encounter, based on what Todd was able to find out about the town.

In the case of the former, he has the protection of his car, and in the case of the latter, it was most likely that they frightened themselves into terror by attributing natural phenomena to supernatural culprits. Todd is satisfied in his safety and presses onward.

Though he keeps a distinct barrier between his rational thoughts and those rooted in emotion, Todd notices that he can't help but let his imaginative speculation circle around the highly improbable what-ifs, even going so far as to consider ghostly apparitions, such as those that dominated any lore or history he tried to find regarding the town. He pauses briefly when he comes to an overlook, and rolls his window down to hear the mighty roar of the waterfall, previously inaudible over the hum of his engine and the crunching progression of his tires over the unpaved road.

The mist from the waterfall dampens things this high up, however, and as Todd curves up and around the drop-off, he enjoys the smooth quiet. He eases his way upward and comes to the bridge which, according to his recollection of the map of this route, lies immediately ahead of the school. He finds this to be the case as he finishes the curve, and his headlights' beams cut through a chain-link fence to illuminate the entrance to the school. There's a gate which, if opened, would easily admit his car, but it's locked with a shiny padlock, glinting and taunting Todd before his eyes.

Just like at the apartment, Odin perks up and whines.

He considers scaling the fence for a moment—without barbed or razor wire, it poses little challenge—but then where would that leave him? He's confident that Remy is inside, but Remy has the advantage of years of experience trespassing and picking locks. The two champions of Todd's mind, his love and his ration, battle for the reins of his being. On one hand, he's closer to Remy than he's been in over a month, but on the other hand, his subject is entirely inaccessible. Surely there are locks upon locks upon locks inside, especially if his own experience in treatment is anything to go by. Remy has probably figured something out, though; he always does.

He resolves to catch him at his apartment, like he originally intended. He swings his car around and heads back down the damp pathway, the last bits of his emotional draw to the school diminishing with less rapidity than Todd would like.

The drive back into town is devoid of panic-stricken twenty-somethings and feels just slightly bumpier than the uphill counterpart. He crosses the unofficial barrier back into the inhabited districts of town, aiming for Remy's place once again. He parks in the same space he occupied before, and sees a figure emerge from behind the building, beyond where Todd is able to discern any real shapes. The backdrop is just a line of trees, and the twisting, sinuous shadows and silhouettes make it more difficult to discern shapes or objects.

Todd's heart begins to race—the figure, a man, is the same height as Remy and has the same general build. He zips to Remy's apartment—with all of the grace and agility Todd has seen in Remy. But he doesn't pull out a key and unlock the door. He only lifts the mat and leaves something underneath.

Odin cocks his head out of curiosity. Todd's hand hovers above the door handle as he watches—he was fully committed to opening the door and initiating the reunion for which he's been longing for so long now. But his heart won't allow it now, as that isn't Remy. Just a similarly built, similarly moving imposter. But that *is* Remy's apartment, so who is this guy and what are his intentions?

Whoever it is, Todd is inclined to think that his presence here isn't one that Remy brought about. Remy, Todd thinks, is most likely still reeling from the resulting effects of his imprudence in Wometzia. He's not about to go making friends (or, hopefully, enemies) just after getting all settled and anonymous.

The man glances over each shoulder before flitting back out into the night, quick and quiet as an owl on the hunt, but only after pushing the mat just a small bit askew. Smart. He must be acquainted with Remy's compulsive tendencies.

And, Todd reasons, this mysterious man must trust that Remy will be home soon. Otherwise he wouldn't be so comfortable leaving anything of import just lying under the mat. For a moment, Todd is tempted to go and look at the contents, but he, like Remy, is averse to creating any sort of reputation for himself, including that of snooping trespasser.

This reasoning gives him the self-restraint necessary to sit and wait in his car.

REMY

My confidence is much bolder on the return trip than it was on the way here. The moonlight still dances in that mysterious way, but now, I feel like I have an ally. Even if the stalker isn't friendly, at least we have a common goal: to find out more about Willa Frye. Perhaps he already has an angle he's working. Certainly, it would be interesting to discuss this with him.

I think my newly bolstered confidence comes, in part, from a mantle of purpose, of *doing*. I had been sitting in my apartment, stagnating, for far too long. My sense of being and my identity were crippled, mangled. But now I'm Remy Thorn again. I don't know all of the implications that that holds, but I am glad to be *doing* things again.

And maybe the risk I took in being out and about will turn sour, but my current high has elevated me beyond the point of giving a damn. If my life is at risk, or is even forfeit, that's unfortunate, but is it any better to hole myself up and refuse to live for fear of dying?

The chill of the waterfall's spray sends me into a mild shiver, and coupled with the cold of the night, it persists for some time before my body heat is sufficient to pull me out of it.

I consider doing a bit more exploration as a detour on the return trip—maybe visit some of the other abandoned cottages around here—but my body and mind ache for the safety of my apartment. Of my bed. Perhaps tomorrow.

With the added weight in my bag, I have to adjust slightly in my weight distribution in order to keep my footsteps quiet, which is made more difficult by the varying decline. The moon lights up the path well, but even with its assistance, I find myself stumbling and tripping here and there. Logic would suggest using my flashlight, but even my newly emboldened confidence isn't enough to dilute my aversion to running into people right now.

Before, it would have seemed suspicious at worst, maybe a little weird at best. But if a cop stopped me now and happened to find me with a backpack full of stolen property, the vast bulk of which being privileged documentation on a teenage girl and her supposed suicide from decades ago... well, there's no perspective from which that looks good.

Add to that my newness to the town and that I keep to myself, and instantly my reputation bursts into being as some weirdo or a pervert or something. So while my general confidence has indeed seen an uprising, I must still take the necessary precautions to avoid drawing attention to myself. With that in mind, I observe all of the precaution I can think of, and with a surprisingly clear head.

Soon, I see the town's lights twinkling into view. The leaves even thin out enough for me to make out the moonlit sides of buildings, one of them with windows reflecting the moon's brilliance. The streets are quiet, like early Christmas morning before normal families are piling into minivans to go visit relatives or are outside playing in the snow. That mysterious inhaled breath that acts as an odd limbo between things gone and things to come.

It settles with ease on me and I on it.

The path levels out and I walk into the town's outer limits. It's just as quiet as I perceived from the trail. In fact, being this close to it makes it seem even more so, like being submerged in a settled snow globe.

On my way to the apartment, I walk casually, but still stick to the shadows as much as I can. I think I'm free of observers, but the chance that I'm not is enough to keep me careful. An amusing mélange of sentiments stir in my mind: amusement, purpose, indulgent melancholy. But above all, I appreciate the simple feeling of…*feeling*. Of sentiment in any form. Of having a connection to the world and its inhabitants that is more than just cognitive.

I won't pretend that the pains don't come floating back in, too, however. The pain of dragging Todd through this with me, the pain of having left him so quickly, and with such a brief good-bye. That vein is one through which hope and anguish flow in equal parts. The source of the pain is obvious enough. The source of the hope is the prospect of putting an end to the pain. Maybe one day soon I'll read a headline about how Todd Love single-handedly brought the entirety of a sex trafficking and child porn ring to its knees, and we'll be able to make a safe, happy return to Riverdell.

Maybe other conditions could occur to enable our reunion, but this is the one that fuels my fantasies. There are other varieties, of course, as one might expect of a man who spends more than ninety percent of his time alone. Maybe the whole of the issue bears down upon me, gun-wielding pedophiles in throngs being handled in some way or another, the bounty on my head going unclaimed. Perhaps he finds a way to send me the cryptic messages of our style. Sometimes I fantasize that he somehow manages to find me, knocks on my door, and is just…here. In each case, the desperate gravity of longing and the subsequent frustration are counteracted by the driving hope that one of these can come to fruition.

As much as I want to treat this new, unfamiliar town like the hornets' nests the last two were (or that I turned them into), I can't help but feel at ease, looking at the warm glows of the street lights tonight. Even if only by habit, I avoid these pools of warmth, but tonight, their connotation is not one of danger.

It brings to mind a trip to Portland I went on with my mom, when I was young. I always enjoyed shopping with her. Not that the activity itself was all that exciting—what child enjoys tagging along through department store after department store, really?—but to be out in the Real World without the remarkably short leash of my father's gaze was magical in itself, and I always felt like a dog whose owner left its gate open by accident.

This particular trip was for clothing. My dad was always content with buying Trina's and my clothes locally, but he held my mother to an insane standard of beauty, and she thus had to do her clothes shopping in the city. She enjoyed it, too. I liked to think that she, also, would imagine a different life for herself in those times, like maybe her husband sent her out shopping for a dress for their anniversary dinner, and when she got home, he would be waiting there with soft music playing and a bath drawn, after which she would put on her new dress and he would show her off to the world—not as his property, but as his beloved.

That day was unusually cold, for coastal weather. Our normally mild winter took a frigid turn and dipped into the single digits for the only time I could remember. Reflecting on it now, I think that my mother was more panicked than I thought about the change in temperature. If snow had come, the journey home would have been quite treacherous indeed, and that part of Oregon wasn't very well equipped to handle its removal with any degree of efficiency.

But my mom also treasured these abuse-less outings, and her spirits, though shaken, would not be broken. Instead, she laughed a shrill laugh each time the chilly wind picked up. Eventually, we ducked into a cozy little coffee shop and ordered hot chocolates with extra marshmallows.

I remember sitting with my mother, drinking my hot chocolate and looking out the window at all of the city lights, and wishing that every night could be so—strange though it was—warm and magical, no matter how cold the thermometer read.

Tonight isn't as cold as that night, and Ghost Fork is definitely no Portland, but the warm lights in the buildings and on the street, in contrasting harmony with the tranquil darkness, pull me deep into that memory. I welcome it.

My apartment building's parking lot is unpredictable; my neighbors have their cars, sure, but they also often have company or go to visit friends, so sometimes the small lot is empty, while other times it's full and a few cars line the street. Tonight, all but one space is full. I can't see any movement from my angle, but just in case, I circle around to the back of the building. My front door is visible to the parking lot, but by taking the back route, I'll appear in that visual space for only a moment before slipping into my apartment and out of sight again.

As I view my apartment, though, and increasingly as I approach it, something seems off. Ah. My door mat has been moved. Has someone been in my apartment? I look around for any more movement, but still detect none. As I bend over to fix the placement of the mat, I notice a slight rise. I pull the mat away to find a manila folder with no markings or labels on it.

I fix the mat and step into my apartment. The night seems less quiet now, as though my apartment itself is abuzz with anticipation from the moment I step inside. As I sit to open the envelope, a car door closes outside and a dog whines.

I read the headline of the topmost paper in the envelope, a newspaper. *"Thunder Falls Student Takes Own Life After Sexual Assault Allegations"*

Then there's a knock at the door. This is no time to be soliciting, and I don't know anyone in this town. Perhaps my stalker is dropping by to make sure I got his gift.

Quietly, as quietly as I can manage, I creep to the door. The moment is pregnant with potential. I could be only seconds from meeting this guy and finding out who he is.

ELEVEN

I look through the peephole and see…the only thing better.

I fling the door open and throw myself into Todd's arms, Odin jumping excitedly at our sides. Even now, I know that in years to come, this is a moment I'll remember with reverent fondness. His sturdy warmth seems to spill into me, filling the landscape of my soul with a light so full that it illuminates places I didn't know were dark. On the rare occasion in which I allowed myself to fantasize about Todd materializing in my life, it was always layered with a tenuous uncertainty, the surface knowledge that it must come at a price and that that price would be one (or both) of our lives. Instead, what befalls me is a peace I didn't think I was capable of feeling anymore. The pent-up confusion and anger and rage that I had been concealing beneath a steadily weakening barrier of apathetic indifference melted away and for the first time in what felt like decades, I experienced a sort of reliable peace—like crossing a rickety rope bridge and finally finding oneself on the sturdy earth on the other side.

"I missed you," Todd says.

"I missed you, too," I say.

In all of my fantasy versions of this reunion, Todd melted into a tearful monologue about the treacherous voyage and hordes of antagonists through which he had to fight in order to reach me.

But this is better. Our exchange of 'I miss you' was a formality—everything he wanted to communicate to me was visible in his eyes, his body language—the subtle ease with which his hand found my tricep and the thick glaze of tears over his eyes. It was all there, with the fullness in impact I had gone over in my head upwards of a thousand times since I left him in Albuquerque.

I don't know how he managed to find me. In the fantasy versions of this moment, he had also vanished and found some way to track me down, some way to which the opposition has no access, thus closing the door on my worries about the situation. In those versions of this moment, I was still plagued with the perpetual worry that has seemed to be the signature of my life. I guess I must have forgotten how calm Todd makes me feel, because this wordless embrace beats all of the fantasies, banishing my preoccupations with commanding authority.

It doesn't matter how he found me. I don't even care whether he was followed, or someone else found success in the same method as he did. It only matters that he's here now.

My hold on Todd only loosens when Odin's persistent, excited whines finally win me over. I kneel to pet and hug my German shepherd and he greets me with an abundant face full of his tongue.

I usher them inside, still half expecting to wake up any second, maybe having fallen asleep on those dusty, musty couches at the school again. But the dream doesn't end, and little by little I let myself trust that this is reality—that Todd and Odin are truly here.

Inside, more silent embracing precedes our first words to each other since last month.

Apparently, Todd has been searching for me since mere days after I left. Part of me—the romantic part, admittedly—expected that he might, but I never expected him to *find* me.

"How did you find me?" I ask. I'm still beaming.

"Honestly, I got in my car and drove. I figured I'd be able to find you if I put myself in your shoes. I did some asking around, and now I'm here." This detail also agrees with the more romantic side of me.

"And that's it? That worked?" I can't quite mask my incredulity.

"Well, it definitely took a while. You don't fuck around when you disappear."

I let out a low laugh. "Nah. Can't afford to." We're sitting on the couch in my apartment, Todd on my right and Odin on my left with his head in my lap, subdued but still breathing rapidly. Naturally, I'm in the process of fire hosing him with questions. Next up:

"Who was that who took your picture last month? The one who's been texting me?"

"Oh, yeah. You ready for this?" He raises his eyebrows in the *you won't fucking believe this* way that he's mastered.

I nod, although now I'm not sure.

"It's your mom."

"…What?"

"Yeah. It's this whole crazy story. Apparently, when she left your family and went off to New Zealand, she actually just went to Washington. The first thing she did was join a support group for abuse victims. She started asking questions about how to get you and Trina back, and it caught the attention of a shady-looking lady there.

"So, this lady started asking your mom about the lengths she'd be willing to go in order to get you guys back. Obviously, there's the legal route, with attorneys and Child Protective Services and DCFS and the likes, but there's only so much they can do without a *dickload* of evidence"—this is a word he picked up from me. I'm proud—"and she was afraid that if an investigation was initiated, your dad would kill you two before they were able to get you out of there.

"So more and more, she got involved with this lady, but she was almost ethereal, the way she would only *sometimes* be there. She would be gone for weeks or months, then come back just when your mom thought she had dropped off the face of the planet. She was always leaving vague hints about being underground or some kind of operation.

"This is where it gets interesting."

"*This* is the interesting part?" I say.

"Yeah. So your mom started getting even more deeply involved with this lady. As it turned out, she was part of this group called Deliverance."

"Deliverance," I say.

Todd nods and continues. "They're this group dedicated to

finding and rescuing people who have been abused, abducted, or otherwise caught in all that nasty shit. So your mom got all excited. She wanted to solicit their help, and try to get them to go and get you and Trina. But the leader didn't like it. Said it would be a bit of a lengthy process to figure out exactly how to do it, and she couldn't afford to have so many of their crew across state borders for so long.

"Your mom argued and argued, but still they said no. So you know what your mom did?"

I raise my eyebrows.

"She fucking joined them. She said, 'Either help me do it, or teach me so I can do it myself.' So they taught her. And man, they don't fuck around. They taught her, all right. From what it sounded like, your mother is well qualified to be in the FBI at this point. We're talking self-defense, weaponry, tech and digital forensics, the whole nine yards. She could star in an action film. So, after you disappeared, she hopped onto her computer and within *minutes*, had lists up of all the phones activated near Albuquerque within the prior hour. She had your phone number and fast. And she wouldn't fucking give it to me."

I chuckle at the teen-like angst dripping from that last part.

"So for a while, she convinced me to back off. That was okay for all of a minute, but I got sick of it. I plotted to sneak into her phone and laptop to find out where you were, but all of the relevant information was locked inside an encrypted folder. So I got fed up and decided to find you the old-fashioned way."

"By hopping into your car and hoping you're going in the right direction?"

"Exactly."

I laugh again, and this time he joins me.

I shake my head. "Damn. So my mom is a closet badass."

"Like you wouldn't believe."

"So, where is she now?" I ask.

"Probably at the house—our house, in Wometzia—stalking you on her laptop or something. She's been doing that a lot."

I pull out my phone to see if I have any missed texts, but my phone's screen is black. Dead. I put it on its charger in the kitchen and see the manila envelope. It's interesting to think that a case that consumed my whole being less than an hour ago can now seem so distant and irrelevant and unimportant. I'll admit that I forgot all about Willa Frye the second I saw Todd through the peephole.

Todd catches me thumbing the envelope.

"Oh yeah, some guy dropped that off while I was waiting for you," he says.

"You saw him?" Did you get a good look at him?"

"No. I tried, but he was fast and well covered. He was agile; at first, I thought it was you."

"Hmm. Well, I'm sure that he and I will meet at some point."

"Do you know him?"

"Nope." I tell Todd about the past couple of days. He follows along in appropriate Todd fashion. He nods, furrows his brow, gasps, and laughs all in the right places. He asks the right questions and skips the wrong ones. He's Todd, and even regaling him with my tale, I find it hard to form words under the thick haze of renewed infatuation.

At the end of the story, he sighs animatedly. The message is received and the feeling is mutual: *Let's not worry about anything tonight.* Hours ago, I couldn't have imagined a force great enough to pull my attention from Willa Frye. Now, the idea of wrapping it up only persists in my mind, by the shallowest of roots, due to my compulsive need to finish everything I ever start.

So we call it a night. We're both in desperate need of a shower, so we take one (at a normal temperature, for Todd's sake) and change into comfortable clothes for sleeping.

It almost feels like we're back in Wometzia, or even Riverdell, retiring after a busy day. Almost. That 'almost' turns in my mind, though, the sole inhibitor of my full appreciation for the night. The rogue pebble stuck in my shoe as I try to appreciate the Grand Canyon. The 'almost' is the essential difference between now and Wometzia.

Wometzia was, for a time, safe. But our safety was compromised by yours truly, in the name of having something to do. And now here I am, doing the same thing. Do I get bored like this? Bored enough to risk my life (and, by extension, those of my loved ones) for the cheap, temporary rush of the hunt?

Apparently.

No, this isn't like Wometzia. Wometzia was where were escaped to for safety—and we found it, at first. But here in Ghost Fork, we're in the middle of a hunt. I have a target on my back, and with Todd at this proximity, he's got a good chance of getting caught in the blast, should my adversary manage to fix their sight on me for long enough to pull the trigger.

The thought makes me wary of growing too attached to the situation, but at the same time, this is the singular thing, the sole desire, I've had ever since I settled back down. I've been dying for Todd to find me somehow and move in, and now here he is. But now that the fantasy is reality, I'm obligated to consider the potential consequences of it.

This stream of preoccupation comes as we fall into our old sleeping position. I want to revel in the movement, to invite the repose of the night, but I'm sure that neither of us will be able to sleep all night anyway.

My intense need to be the custodian of Todd's safety is at odds with my tenuous willingness to rock the boat now that I'm finally at a comfortable float. I don't want Todd to leave—unless he's not safe here. But there's a chance that that's the case.

But feeling Todd's steady breath against my neck, these worries float away as easily as if his exhalation carried them away. Maybe I can allow us this night of rest after all. We deserve it, for fuck's sake.

After I make that concession, I do in fact fall into a sleep more restful than I've had in…well, a little over a month.

In that descent into unconsciousness, the stage of my mind opens on a horribly familiar scene: a dream I had on my way out of New Mexico, in which I was ravenously consuming Todd's hand. Relief sweeps over me this time, though, as my plate has none of his limbs on it. Instead, it's a heaping pile of pretzel rolls, which we enjoyed on his birthday a couple of months ago. He's laughing at a joke or the general silliness of that night or something. I'm not concerned with what's funny. Only that he's laughing.

The curtains close on that stage and I emerge into the light of morning. Late morning, judging by the amount of sunlight marking the seams of my blackout curtains. Todd's breath is steady and smooth as ever, and his thumb gently moves back and forth in the center of my chest.

"Are you safe here?" I say. I fear the answer more than I care to admit, but for the sake of allowing myself to enjoy his presence, I must know.

"As safe as you are," he says. I believe him, but it doesn't make me feel any better; I'm not entirely confident in my own safety.

"I guess we need to talk about that, huh?"

I roll over to look at him. To my surprise, his look is not one of melancholy but one of joy.

"Your mom is a badass, remember?" he says.

I give him my *not following so far, but continue* look.

"She's tapped into the communication systems of the bad guys. She knows what they know. So, just like she warned you about those guys in Los Angeles, she can warn us about any impending fuckery. If they get so much as a whiff of where we are, she'll know, and she can let us know in turn. We're safe."

At that, my prior worries flutter away in a cloud of euphoric bliss; I'm entirely free to enjoy Todd's presence. And in this realization, I bury my face in his chest and pull him with force just shy of breaking my nose on him. He pulls on me, too, but with a merciful gentleness.

"So, what now?" I say.

"Whatever we want, m'dear," he says.

In an instant, my mind goes to the old days: eating our snacks and reading books, watching movies, and cooking together. However, my apartment is sparsely equipped in regard to entertainment or cooking equipment, so our options are quite limited.

"Let's do nothing," I say.

So we do.

Many people belong to the school of thought that *doing* something is a requisite to quality time, that the time in those transitions—driving to a restaurant, sitting through the previews of a movie—don't count. But Todd and I have our own lowkey versions of quality time. Sure, we do the regular things, but something as simple as sitting in each other's company while we read our separate books is quite enough for us. In this case, we simply hold each other and listen to each other's breaths and heartbeats, a luxury we've been without for too long. And that's enough.

While I enjoy our little bout of nothingness, I'm left to wonder where things are set to go from here. To remain in this state of hidden bliss together forever sounds wonderful, but the more realistic faculties of my brain respect that that won't be happening. This confusing yet satisfying limbo is a small, effective pocket of comfort, but as much as the passage of time brought Todd to me, the same threatens to whisk him away, and I'm left to guess at what the catalyst might be.

Even if the universe permits us to stay here with each other, will our natures allow us to sit tight and wait for things to right themselves? Already I've shown myself how easy it is to lure me out of hiding with the appropriate bait.

Todd is more patient than I am in the long-term, content to busy himself at home with cooking or reading or home improvement projects. Last month, he built a bookshelf. Who knows what endeavors he might undertake in my currently far less accommodating apartment? He might take up crochet or knitting, or writing, art, or film. Todd's capacity for appreciation of these things—both creating and observing—is one of my many draws to him. Try as I might, however, this is not a trait we share—at least not on the same level. It's true that I can become engrossed in a book or a television series, but the process of creating things was always more frustrating than gratifying to me. I'd commit to drawing a bird, but let myself get distracted after detailing only a couple of feathers. As a child, I tried to write stories now and then, but if my damsel was still in distress after two pages, the poor bitch would either have to save herself or stay in her distressed state forever, because I was not going to write out a proper ending for her.

As if Todd were just strolling in my mind, he says, "So, what of that Willa Frye case? You still haven't really looked through that envelope yet."

I know it will only keep us occupied for so long, but my excitement balloons at the prospect of working a case with Todd again, even if the case is technically closed and colder than week-old penguin shit. Given his peerless ability to enjoy obscure, irrelevant stuff, I figure he'll be just as into this case as I am.

I've told him a handful of details from my past couple of days, but I didn't get into the details of the case, so I do that now.

TWELVE

I always enjoy watching Todd puzzle over things. He gets this serious, concentrating look on his face, and you can almost see the image of his mental workings through his eyes. The pieces form, with their unique and specific edges, and he flicks them around in his head until they come together, all at once in a coalescent mesh.

So I lay the pieces out in front of him. But as soon as I'm finished, I can tell that he has reached the same conclusion as I did.

"We need more. Evidence, testimonies, whatever. It's incomplete."

"Well, shall we see if there's anything useful in the folder?" I say.

"We shall."

Once more, the headline slides out of the envelope, naturally followed by the article itself, which offers no new information. Todd and I agree that the article is included as a sort of cover page for the contents of the folder; our mystery helper is organized and thorough, as I've seen.

The next item in the folder is an interview with Ginger Garrity, who apparently shared a room with Willa at the time. Most of the interview, conducted by a reporter for Thunder Rumble Press, runs in labored circles around information we already know, but one small exchange is highlighted, a series of bright yellow bars on the otherwise black and white print.

"You said she was acting strange?" said the reporter.

"Oh, yes. She was all giddy the day it happened, but she wouldn't tell anyone why. She had this little box, too, she always had it with her, and that day especially she clutched it to her chest like her heart would stop if she let go."

Todd looks at me. "Didn't you—?"

"Yeah," I say. I pull the tiny box out of my backpack, carefully removing its protective layers of paper towels. The key, I recall, is still in my pants pocket. I retrieve that, too, and fit it into the lock.

The same satisfying *click* as before marks its opening, and I pull the note out and unfold it for Todd to see.

"Dubz," he says. "Like 'W?' Like for Willa?"

"That's what I assume," I say.

"What else is there?" he asks. I smile; he's like a child sorting the contents of his stocking on Christmas morning.

There's only one more piece, tucked behind that interview. It's yet another interview with Ginger Garrity. Again, most of the interview presents no new information, but a few yellow stripes tell a bit more of the story.

"Oh yeah, Thad was weird to her. I can't really put it into words, but he just treated her different. Not like he was *favoring* her. Just…different. But I guess we know why now. I wish I could tell you I'm surprised, but I'm just not. We kind of suspected maybe something was going on, but maybe a little more tame."

I look to Todd, but he seems just as stumped as me.

"We still need more," he says. I can tell he's getting just a touch agitated. This delights me, as it means he's been drawn into the old case with me.

"Well, you've come to the right place," I say in my best old-timey salesman voice. I fish the remaining contents from my backpack and slap them onto the counter with a heavy *thwap*.

"Done some homework, have we?" he says.

"Well, I picked it up. I haven't really looked into any of it yet."

"Can we dig in?" His child-on-Christmas-morning resemblance deepens.

"Well, I think it may be time to meet my secret admirer."

"The stalker guy who gave you the key?"

"And probably this folder, yes. I feel like he's the one with the most solid insight into the case. And if nothing else, I can show you the creepy room where he put a bunch of this together."

"All right," says Todd after a second's consideration.

I put the heap of papers back into my bag and sling it around onto my back.

It's still early in the day, but I'm not as worried about being seen in daylight with Todd at my side. One person walking around on his own may be conspicuous, but two people just look like a couple of friends out for a hike. I'll really only need to worry

143

about visibility when we arrive.

"So, where are we going to meet this guy?" Todd asks. "We don't have much of a way to contact him, do we?"

"No," I admit, "but I figure he'll probably be at the cottage, and if he's not, we can look through the stuff he has there until he shows up."

"Perfect. Ready to roll when you are."

The morning air has a nip in it just like last night, but to a lesser, more friendly degree.

If my freshly bolstered confidence last night made me feel good about tackling this, Todd's arrival has accomplished that tenfold. The pair of us stroll through the town, heads held high, straight on out toward the western boundary. The sun warms our backs and provides a pleasant contrast to the slight but noticeable chill in the air.

I suppress the mighty urge to grab Todd's hand—that *would* draw attention. Instead, I content myself with glancing at him every few seconds. The minute we're out of the general town's line of sight, he pulls my hand into his and squeezes tight.

Conversation flows freely and easily between us, and unless I'm actively thinking about the case, I accidentally convince myself that we really are just going on a hike, like we used to do back in Oregon.

The weather certainly accommodates it; as the sun rises, a warm breeze plays at our hair and faces as it whispers by, now with just the slightest dampness.

These woods are more charming than I would have believed

during my journey the other night. I was hopped up on adrenaline and the thrill of exploration, augmented by the adventurous rush of leaving my apartment for the first time in the while. The moon cutting through the darkness at night cast a sense of mystery and enigma over the vegetation, and every tree and bush was rife with the potential of critters or other people hiding behind them. But now, bathed in the fullness of the late morning sun, the intoxicating sense of obscurity is all but banished along with the darkness. It lacks the artistic melancholy of the night, to be sure, but it fills that gap with brilliance of the senses. Where before I appreciated the *nothing*ness of it, now I can appreciate the opposite.

The colors themselves seem to come alive, leaping and shouting and bouncing and singing. Various hues manifest on flowers and even weeds, all wild and in the final leg of their cycle before winter returns to claim them. The sky is a magnificent blue, a concept almost foreign to me as I grew up in rainy, cloudy Oregon, but which I now enjoy. Birds' songs fill the air with the same abundance as the colors—fast, timid chirps as well as contented little melodies. In the few intermittent gaps during which the birds are quiet, the wind—even the wind!—seems to take on life. The long grass sways and brushes in sweeping *whshhhh* noises. This sensation *is* familiar to me, as I heard it many times in Riverdell, but after the flat desert of New Mexico, I surprise myself at how excited I am to hear this again.

The higher we climb, the more of the waterfall's mist we get, and the dampness in the air takes on a chill as we approach our destination, but we still have a way to go yet.

Before I know it, we're outside the old, abandoned cottage. In an almost mocking contrast with the surrounding environment, the abundant light does nothing to lend the cottage beauty. The awkward angles at which the joints have worn and sagged look even more dilapidated, the broken boards and planks seem even more jagged, and the darkness inside is at a much opaquer contrast with the light outside. In that contrast, the shadows fold and stretch and bend.

"This is the place?" Todd says.

"Home sweet home," I say.

"To whom?"

"I guess we'll find out."

"Hello?" I call as I step through the empty window frame. My call is largely muffled by the dust and elicits no reply.

Todd climbs in after me with slightly less grace and looks around. I can almost hear his brain at work, committing everything he sees to memory.

Todd has the best memory of anyone I've ever met. Not that there are regularly held 'Memory and Retention' competitions, but his ability to recall and pinpoint is astounding and I'm confident that, were such a competition to exist, Todd would be second only to Kim Peek, the man who inspired the story for *Rain Man*. That man is simply superhuman.

In addition to his memory, Todd's company and assistance on cases is invaluable thanks to his fully efficient 'what-if' machine, useful in creating and dismissing scenarios rapidly. In most partnerships, to achieve the same result requires much back-and-forth.

Though I can feel Todd's curiosity pulling in every direction, I lead him away from the living room and toward the stairs.

"You came here alone at night?" Todd asks.

"Yes, sir."

"Jesus. It's creepy as hell."

"We've done worse. Remember that creepy-ass barn where we found Stan?"

"Well yeah, but we were together for that. No way I would have gone in alone."

"As I recall, you were the one to suggest splitting up in that house."

"I bluffed. Thought it would make me seem tough. Did it work?"

"Totally."

I take Todd upstairs and toward the bedroom dedicated to Willa Frye. For a wild second, I worry that I'll open the door upon an empty room, but as I enter, all of the stuff that was there before remains so, exactly as it was that night.

I step to the side to let Todd in. He reads each piece with enthralled and concentrated intensity. I could have shown him the photos on my phone, which is now freshly charged. However, this trip has a more prevalent, pressing purpose: to meet my mysterious companion. He's not here in this room, but according to the mental feelers beyond my immediate, conscious understanding, he'll be here soon. And, even if that sense is incorrect, Todd and I can busy ourselves with this small treasure trove of information.

As Todd becomes engaged in the articles on the wall, I cross to the open window and pull it closed. This, I think, will signal our presence to the man.

We're here. Come, new friend, and we can indulge our mutual interests.

"Most of these are all the same exact thing," says Todd, "and he doesn't even have anything highlighted like he did on the stuff in the envelope. Also, they used the wrong 'its' in this headline. Hopefully there's some good stuff in that backpack or this might come to a sputtering halt before it even gets going. And since you got me into this case, I'll hold you accountable for blue-balling me after such a dry spell."

I chuckle. "I'll make it up to you later," I say.

Todd smiles and opens his mouth to answer but stops when we hear a noise outside.

A series of whispering *fshh* sounds joins the organic ones, too rhythmic to be the wind and too infrequent to be a quadruped. Either our guy is here, or some lost gorilla is a long way from home.

Todd listens hard, his concentration on the articles and headlines paused for the moment. I look through the window—with difficulty, due to the grime—and see a figure walking toward the house with a steady casualness, like someone whose bus schedule allows a more leisurely walk thereafter to his place of work. Perhaps he'll stop for coffee on his way to us.

From what I can see, Todd was right: this guy could be my stunt man.

He approaches without looking up at the window, but I entertain no doubts that he knows I'm here. Todd might be a surprise, though.

The cottage creaks and sighs, punctuated by a couple of light *thud*s and the clopping sound of sturdy soles on sturdy wood. This, of course, muffled by the dust. We listen to him climb the stairs and walk the hallway toward us. A strange giddiness grips me, like an enamored fangirl waiting to meet her rock star crush, as he reaches the door and swings it open.

"Morning, gents," he says.

For a moment, I think my mind is playing tricks on me.

"Are you—"

"I am."

Todd observes this exchange and supplements it with a look of exasperation.

"So, who are you?" asks Todd.

"My name's Creed."

"He chased me through Los Angeles," I say. I feel naked, exposed suddenly, craving the cover of my gun, but it's in my bag, and if I reach for it, I will leave myself vulnerable. I mentally kick myself for not having had the foresight to equip it when I saw him approaching.

"Relax, man. I'm not with them. I'm a friend of your mom's." The urge to retrieve my weapon relents.

"Wait, he chased you through LA?" says Todd.

"Yes. He was with the group of guys who showed up there. I ran and most of them fell behind pretty much right away, but he kept up. I only got him off my back with the fear of making a scene in one of the busier streets."

Todd raises one eyebrow, his badge of skepticism. "How the hell did you keep up with him?" he asks.

Creed and I both laugh at this, and creed answers. "It wasn't easy, that's for sure. Your boy's fast. Frankly, if he'd run much farther, he woulda lost me. I spent a good few days recovering from that. But it was the most fun I've had in years."

"I'm sure it would have been fun for me, too, had it not been for the prospect of my imminent death."

Creed laughs a hollow little chuckle, like it was shaken out of him rather than coaxed. "Sorry about that. I was undercover. I was there only to keep you safe."

"Oh good," I say. "Too bad I didn't know then. We could have grabbed a beer or something." Dry jest seems to be my default.

"No way, they would have executed us both."

Both Todd and I cast him a prodding gaze, urging him to spill details. Such a person can't just surface like this and not tell the involved stories, and he's more or less painted himself into a dynamic corner. He knows he's said too much not to divulge the tale that led him here.

THIRTEEN

"Well, it's a pretty involved story. I guess, to begin, I was a foster kid."

Oh. It's going to be one of these stories. I adjust my sitting position and get comfortable—so do Todd and Creed.

"I was kicked around from home to home, rarely with the same family for more than a few months. Usually I was fairly neglected, though. I never knew where my next meal was coming from. Because of that, I learned to take care of myself pretty early on.

"I used to shoplift food wherever I could—a loaf of bread here, a can of tuna or chicken soup there. Sometimes adults would get suspicious, but then I would retreat to the nearest possible family and stand or walk just close enough that onlookers would think I belonged with them. As soon as they looked away, I would pocket whatever I had been looking at and book it out of the store." He says this last part with an almost nostalgic laugh.

"Anyway, fast forward ten years. I never went to high school, but I had made some friends in foster care and on the streets. So all I was really doing was surviving. I never had time to think about the long-term future because I was always so focused on the immediate future: where I would eat next, which friends' couches I could crash on this week, the likes.

151

"I had my typical answers, of course. People asked what I wanted to do with myself. I'd tell them whatever bullshit answer came to mind. Contractor, crime lord, whatever."

"Sure," says Todd.

"But at some point, I actually started to think about it. Maybe I just got good enough at stealing and hustling that I finally did it well enough to allow room for those thoughts, to begin thinking in time frames of weeks and months, rather than minutes and hours. Anyway, I had been slipping down that thought route for a week or two when I met Carol."

"Carol?" I say. Doesn't ring a bell.

Creed nods and continues: "She was in a situation not unlike my own: homeless, no education or work experience. Her eyes were always so full of hope, it just made ya want to go out and change people's lives. She had that effect on people.

"Well Carol and I, we hit it off, fast. She had the most amazing heart. Her daughter was just the sweetest girl, too. Called me Keed, because she couldn't quite pronounce my name yet. Her name was Taylor." His use of the past tense when speaking about them makes me nervous; I sense a southward turn coming up in this tale.

"Things were pretty rough at first, financially and logistically. Obviously, Taylor took priority. Only after we made sure she was fed, warm, and healthy would we start to seek those things for ourselves. That's how we operated for some time.

"At one point, Carol had an idea. She was always teasing me for getting distracted by interesting-looking trees or clouds. So she took the money she had been saving for a down payment on an apartment and bought me a camera.

"'Take it,' she told me, 'This is how we'll pay our bills.' It took hours of discussion after that to convince me to keep it, and even then, I told her that if Taylor went hungry for even one meal, I would sell the thing.

"It had quite a steep learning curve, but eventually, I got pretty good with that camera. Before long, I was able to afford some new lenses, which increased the potential for my photography just that much.

"Even so, it was a rocky start. Seattle isn't exactly a drought of talented photographers and artists, after all. But slowly, I built a clientele. I put my work in coffee shops and bookstores and little Mom and Pop diners, and sold some prints here and there.

"Things were on the upswing. I couldn't wait to get home to our new apartment every time I made a big sale or got commissioned for a big job. And each time, she was just as excited as I was. Taylor was excited about our excitement, too. She could even pronounce my name by then, but instead called me Daddy. She only called me Creed when I was in trouble.

"One day, I had been haggling with some cheapskate from Spokane. He wanted me to drop a hundred bucks on a three-hundred-dollar canvas print just because it wasn't 'of the season.' I told him, 'Bitch, we're in Seattle, we only have like one and a half seasons.' He got all mad and left without buying anything, but the shop owner blamed me for the whole thing and wouldn't let me sell my stuff there anymore. I sold my stuff all over the place, but this particular shop was a pretty major hipster hub, so

I had some great success there.

"So, I was pretty bummed. But then on my way home, I got a call from a modern-style interior decorator. Not only did he want a dozen of my most expensive prints, but he wanted to commission me for an entire series of city life shots. I was ecstatic! Money like that would keep us going for a good long while.

Creed places his hands on his lap and turns his gaze upward, indulging in the sweet euphoria of nostalgia.

"I nearly ran home after that phone call. My excitement was augmented by the thought of buying a ring for Carol at last. I leaped up the stairs at the apartment building and opened the door…and found Carol on the floor, face down in a puddle of blood. She was cold. And even worse, Taylor was nowhere to be found. The apartment was a mess. Carol clearly put up a fight, but they got the best of her.

"The cops started a search for Taylor, naturally. The effort was colossal. Dozens and dozens and dozens of cops and volunteers crawled the streets to look for her based on her photo and the last thing I saw her wearing: a pair of red sneakers, blue pants, and a red shirt with yellow flowers on it."

Tears stream from Creed's eyes and his voice trembles. "She was so excited to be picking out her own outfits. Anyway, the search went on and nobody found anything. I spent all of my time either on the street looking for her or on the Internet looking up any cases of children lost in the Pacific Northwest. That's when I came across Maylynn Brotcher's case. I saw that she had been found, and that gave me hope, so I looked into the reports and articles and stuff.

"Days later, your mother arrived at my apartment. She talked a little about you, and a little about me. Then she left. It was strange, but I was too preoccupied to think much on it. A few more days passed and she showed up again, asking all these questions about Taylor. I didn't really know what to think. She was so…powerful, your mother. I started to think I'd been sent a guardian angel. So, I talked to her and told her everything I could think of that might be relevant.

"They found Taylor in a couple of hours. Your mother and this group. I didn't know who they were at the time, but they led me to Taylor. Well…what remained of her."

Creed's silent tears become sobs for a minute or two, until Todd finally jumps in and manages to calm him down. I offer him a tissue and he cleans off his face, which has been bearing not only snot and tears, but a small amount of dirt. This, too, gets wiped away by the tissue.

After composing himself, Creed says, "Thanks. Anyway, that happened. So, I started asking her questions about who she is, but she revealed very little at first. She was polite, just vague. But at the same time, I figured if she was going to disappear off into the sunset, she would have done it already. Well, after she started to trust me, she told me a bit about her past, but still nothing about her present.

"Then it happened, all at once, like a thousand firecrackers going off in one synchronized blast. She picked me up at my place, took me to a random, obscure park, and told me that I'd have to trust her. I thought it was weird how serious she was getting about it all. I understand now, of course, but at the time, I just thought she was being dramatic.

"She filled me in. Apparently, they had set up a sort of bait article online and tracked its viewers. They found my IP address and looked into who I am. When they found out about Taylor, your mother mobilized them to help. At first, that was her only intention. Or, at least, so she says. But as we got talking more and more, I kept telling her about how I wished I could do something.

"That's when she decided to recruit me. I didn't fully understand what I was getting myself into, but the idea of *doing* something was so alluring. I thought it was maybe a volunteer group. To raise awareness and funds and provide resources.

"When I learned the truth, I think they expected me to run off with my tail between my legs. But be it because of my Scandinavian bullheadedness or my still unsatisfied need to do something impactful, I jumped in with no hesitation. I found out pretty quickly who you were after that."

He looks at me meaningfully, but I can't discern whether that meaning is 'May Brotcher's Rescuer' or 'Retributive Serial Killer.' Strangely, my feelings toward these two possibilities is the same.

As the day's heat rolls in, the room becomes musty. Creed opens the window. "Let's keep this open, shall we?" he says.

We chuckle.

"Had to flag you down somehow," I say.

"Of course, my visitor must announce his arrival."

"Cordially, at your service."

"My service? How's that?"

I pull my scavenged (purloined) documents out of my bag and sit cross-legged on the floor. Todd sits to my right and I pat the floor to my left, inviting Creed to sit.

"What have we here?" he asks. I sense that he already has a fair idea, but I indulge the mock curiosity.

"Well, I feel like we may have a mutual endeavor," I say, gesturing to the abundant news articles and interviews plastering the walls.

Creed smiles. "You get anything good?"

"That remains to be seen. I was waiting for our little pow-wow to break into it."

"Well, let's get to it!" He's quite chipper, which is a relieving contrast to the sinking twist to his story.

Creed helps himself to the uppermost document, a stapled packet marked 'Incident Report' in bold letters at the top. He reads ravenously, but as the rest of it is handwritten, his reading is laborious. He still finishes quickly, furrows his brow, and hands it to me. I hold it between Todd and me so that we can both read it.

Pt walked into a bedroom where she found a peer hanging by her neck. Pt screamed and staff moved all other students into the common area. Pt was escorted to another unit where she was secluded. In seclusion, Pt retreated to the corner of the room and bawled. Staff attempts to console Pt were not acknowledged, and Pt continued to cry.

The name at the bottom is Ginger Garrity.

"Isn't that the one from the interview you sent me?" I say.

Todd nods his affirmation before Creed can answer.

"Huh."

"Yeah, she didn't seem too torn up about it in the interview. That she even consented to the interview is a bit telling, in respect to her disposition to the whole thing, don't you think?" says Creed.

"I don't know about that," I say, "she may have buried that experience in her mind enough that she could talk about it. Notice that she didn't go into any detail regarding her own experiences. It was all about Willa and Thad. Of course, that's what the interview was about, but most people, especially teens, would like to bask in the attention at least a little bit."

"Hmm. Let's look for some more to go on. I like where you're going, but it doesn't feel like enough yet," says Creed.

"Yeah, I agree," I say. "Let's keep looking."

As if either of them needs the prod, I think. They both compose themselves in preparation to receive more information, like a hungry couple who finished their appetizer well before their entrées arrived.

"Oh, here's a statement from Ginger," I say, pulling the next sheet from the stack.

I read it aloud: "'I went into my room to get my journal and saw Willa hanging there. I screamed and staff came and took me to the time out room and put me in seclusion. Willa went into her room a few minutes before me. She told staff she was going to get something for her costume. She was dressed up as a ghost, and there was staff going to each unit doing makeup for the students. So I thought it was a really scary prank until I saw she wasn't standing on anything."

"Huh," says Todd. "It sounds like Ginger went in almost immediately after Willa did, if nobody was concerned that she was taking so long; if she had been in there for longer than a minute or so, and she was 'just getting something', they definitely would have wanted to check on her. And if she told staff she was going in to get something, shouldn't the staff have had just that concern?

"We'll see if there are more statements, though. When I was in treatment, sometimes some of the boys would distract staff while other stuff was going down, intentionally or otherwise. Maybe there will be something else in there to shed light on why no one noticed."

"Good point. Let's keep our eye out for that."

The next page is a statement from Iris Alcazar. Again, I read aloud: "'I was sitting in the common area and Willa told staff she needed to go to her room to get something for her costume and staff said ok. Ginger went in a minute after that and screamed real loud. One staff stayed in the common area with us and the other one went to see what was wrong. Our staff was Kelly and James that night and James stayed with us to make sure we were fine. Ellen got triggered and started crying in the kitchen area. Josalyn went to go talk to her and she calmed down. Staff removed Ginger and called more staff to keep us away from the hall but then the rest of the night went like normal.'"

"Huh," I say. *That may be the word of the day,* I think. "Here, at the bottom: 'Pt came to staff shortly after submitting this statement, recanting it. Pt refused to point out which parts weren't true and how. Pt would not write a new statement or speak any further about it.'"

"So she knew something she wished she didn't," says Creed.

"Sounds like it," I say. "Say, how long have you been working on this? Have you been able to speak with any of the interviewees about it? They would probably be pretty useful."

"Well, I haven't looked up Thad yet, but I did track down Ginger's number. She's actually just living about two hours away, in Cheyenne. I didn't get an answer when I called, though, and I haven't been out to Cheyenne since then. The rest of them, well, this is a bunch of new names for me. We'll have to look into them moving forward."

"Perfect. Shall we continue?"

Both Todd and Creed nod with enthusiasm. I draw yet another sheet from the stack. It's still another statement from that night, this time from Donna Stempson.

I'm confused for a few seconds—at first, I think that I've accidentally picked up Iris's statement again, but the name at the top is definitely Donna Stempson. It's just a word-for-word duplicate of Iris's.

I tell Todd and Creed such.

"What? Let me see," they both say. It's not that they don't trust or believe me, I sense. Just that they're incredulous at the degree of high-form fuckery presented here.

Todd holds the two statements side by side and says, "Damn. The only differences are in the handwriting and the names at the

160

top. And even the handwriting is similar." He passes the pages to Creed, who nonverbally agrees.

"Wait, look," I say, "This one wasn't recanted. Whatever Iris was too afraid to confess seems to have sat just fine with Donna."

"Well, you know the drill, then," says Todd.

I nod.

At Creed's questioning gaze, I say, "When someone recants a testimony that puts someone in an innocent light—such as this one—you interview the shit out of that person. Because not only do they know what happened, but at least a small part of them wants to tell the truth, to make things right. Plus, after all these years, she has had plenty of time to get over the holdups she was having back then. In my opinion, if we find Iris, we learn the truth."

Todd nods knowingly and Creed pulls his phone out. "Let's see if we can't find this Iris Alcazar, then," he says.

"Do you have some kind of massive database at the ready in there, Mr. Bond?" I say.

"Close," Creed replies, "Google."

Todd and I watch in anticipation as Creed's face goes from concentration to exasperation, then from that to shock, finally ending in disappointment.

He looks up from his phone and says, "Iris is dead. She died just a couple of months after leaving the treatment center, after it closed."

"Oh shit," we both say.

"How did she die?" asks Todd. "She must have been pretty young. Eighteen at the oldest."

"Right. She was only sixteen," says Creed, evidently reading form an article as he speaks.

He taps and scrolls for perhaps another minute before speaking again.

"I guess she was one of the last girls to discharge from Ghost Falls before it shut down and forced everyone there to go home or back to whatever care they were in beforehand."

"Did she finish her treatment or get discharged for some other reason?"

"It says she completed her program. Her parents were excited to have her home; they threw her a welcome home party and everything. A few weeks later, she turned up dead in the back of a stolen pickup. They had to thaw the body before the autopsy could be done. Jesus.

"The autopsy revealed that she had been strangled, and based on witness accounts, she had been perfectly happy and in good spirits—no more or less than usual—the days leading to her death. Suicide wasn't ruled out at first, but the bruising around her neck and wrists were indicative of an attacker. But the assailant left no prints and no DNA. No witnesses, no leads. By the time they found her, the trail was colder than the corpse."

"Ginger, Iris, and Donna. That's three roommates. How many did she have?" asks Todd.

"There were eight beds to a unit," I say.

"So let's see, seven total, excluding Willa, obviously. Four to go, then. I wonder if every one of them wrote a statement."

"Probably," I say. "Or at least they asked them to."

"Right. Oh, and the other testimonies mentioned an Ellen and a Josalyn, too." Clearly, Todd's mind is busy at work creating the scene. I wonder if, in his mind, the stage is built from what he remembers from his own days in treatment.

"Okay," I say, "So we have Willa, Ginger, Iris, Donna, Josalyn, and Ellen. That leaves two, if all of the beds were full."

"Well, let's keep reading, then."

The next paper is a statement from Josalyn. Her account matches those of Iris and Donna, but that's not to say that it *supports* it. Rather, it only provides a handful of details, leaving room for the others' statements to be either true or false.

The paper underneath Josalyn's statement is one from Rhonda Beus, and to my surprise, is well written.

"'I'm not sure exactly what happened. I was sitting on the couch, reading. I heard Willa telling staff that she was going to her room to get something. After that, Ginger got up and said the same thing. I didn't think much of it. Sure, Ginger hated Willa, but she wasn't usually one to start things, if she could avoid it. What was weird was how long they were in there. I couldn't help but think, oh god, are they secretly dating? Of course, we're not allowed to date, so it's always secret from staff, but then there are the *secret* secret relationships, which we even keep from our friends. So that was weird. But then the scream happened and I thought Ginger finally pissed Willa off enough that she hit her.

"'But it seemed really weird. Some of the girls in the common area with me kept looking at each other, like they were planning something for Ginger to distract staff from—I've seen it before—but they didn't do anything. I thought maybe they chickened out.

"'Anyway, then staff came and removed Ginger. The other staff wouldn't let us leave the common area. Ellen had a flashback and Josalyn helped talk her through it. To me, it seemed like any other staff assistance call, except for how Iris and Donna were acting. They seemed like they knew more than the rest of us did.' This one also makes it sound like Ginger practically followed Willa into their bedroom."

Todd and Creed nod in pensive agreement.

"Plus," adds Todd, "she herself got suspicious of how long they were in there. So again, we have to wonder why no one else thought anything about them having been in there for so long. That definitely wouldn't have been the case at the facility I went to."

I shrug and pull another sheet from the stack, which is becoming something of an indulgence.

"Up next on the roster, we have Ellen Norman. Ah, this one's boring. She couldn't remember anything other than having a flashback. Understandable. A note at the bottom says that her therapist doesn't want her being pressed for information. And that's all.

"And lucky number eight is Gina Tawney," I say. I turn the paper outward so that both Todd and Creed can see the entire body of text: "'No comment.'"

"God damn it, Gina, you ruin everything," says Todd. In

jest, of course, but I do detect a small amount of frustration in it.

"Just you wait, m'dear," I say. I gesture to the still intimidating stack of paperwork waiting to be perused.

"So what's next? That was seven statements. Well, six. Five and a half."

"Therapists' notes," I say. Todd perks up considerably at the idea of reading in intimate detail about the complex neurological and cognitive issues of teens past. I try to judge him for it, but I can't deny that I have a similar sentiment.

"Now, these are exclusively about Willa," I say. "If we want the others, we'll have to make a return trip." I mean for this to dismiss the idea, but the statement backfires.

"I'm in," says Todd.

"Me, too," says Creed, "I've been stuck on the outside of that place for too long."

"That reminds me," I say, "where'd you find that key?"

"Ah, yeah. I looked up Willa's mother."

"And what, she just gave it to you?"

"Nah. I stole it."

"You stole a woman's key, which she used to remember her dead daughter?"

"Well you can make anything bad wording it like that," Creed says, becoming visibly defensive. His guard drops when he sees that Todd and I are laughing, both with our eyebrows raised and shaking our heads.

"Well, then," I say, pulling a thick packet toward me, "time for some incredibly unethical readings."

"Arguably one of the best kinds of reading," says Todd, as though he's discussing wine.

FOURTEEN

There's a fair amount to sort through, as Willa had been a student at Ghost Falls for nearly a year before her death. I thumb through the bulk of it, really only keeping my eye out for anything that might be more than a page long, but nothing catches my eye before I reach October. I figure if something were to have been going on, it would mostly have taken place within the month leading up to it, and depending on Willa's ability to conceal it, I assume that much of her behavior and demeanor in these sessions will reflect that something was going on. I make a mental note, however, to be wary of falling victim to confirmation bias; seeing things that aren't there can be as damning as missing things that are.

"October fifth, 1987. Patient is of a much happier demeanor than usual, but either can't identify why or won't disclose why. Patient continues to participate in verbal altercations with peers, particularly patient GG."

"October seventh, 1987. Patient's good mood has finally been broken, but just like when it started, she either can't or won't tell me the cause. Both cases are unusual, as Patient has never had issues with being open before. Must speak with staff later and find out if they know anything."

"October twelfth, 1987. Patient back to her euphoric

demeanor, seems distracted, absent. Apparently had a great shift, but isn't quite present enough to tell me about it, which again, is unusual for her."

"October fourteenth, 1987. Patient is moody again. She blames her mood on being on her menstrual cycle, and refuses to acknowledge any other contributing factors."

"October sixteenth, 1987. Patient got into an argument with her peer, GG today. Spent the majority of the session actively and directly speaking badly about GG. Felt a little better afterward."

"October nineteenth, 1987. Patient continues to struggle with peer relations, and even lashed out at peer EN, who she last said was her only real friend here."

"October twenty-first, 1987. Patient verbally aggressive toward GG today. The fight almost became physical but staff put her in seclusion before it escalated that far. Patient was banging on walls and cursing about GG the whole time. She was perfectly happy when I spoke with her, though."

"October twenty-third, 1987. Patient is apparently getting along with peers again—even GG. No one knows what's gotten into her, but she's well behaved and respectful again."

"October twenty-sixth, 1987. Patient is calm, contented. She had a good morning and made a goal to have a family one day."

"October twenty-eighth, 1987. Patient continues to be positive, about staff, peers, and it seems even herself. Patient even recalled a pleasant interaction with GG."

"October thirtieth, 1987. Patient is on cloud nine. Even though her family call was stressful and her visit had to be postponed, Patient remains unbelievably positive. Is she perhaps in the middle of a manic episode?"

"And that's all she wrote," says Todd, who has evidently been paying attention to the dates of the entries.

"Interesting roller coaster of a month," I say. My mind lingers on the entry about Willa wanting a family. To be a mother. To raise children. As though reading this, Creed says, "You don't think she was pregnant, do you?"

"No, she mentioned being on her period, remember?"

"Oh, right. That's an interesting goal, then. Strange timing, too, don't you think?"

"Yeah, but find me a piece of this whole thing that isn't strange," I say.

Todd shoots me his *fair point* look.

"I think you'd be hard put to find any month of any student that wasn't a roller coaster, though. So many people and emotions pressed so tightly together. It's quite a volatile environment," says Todd.

He wasn't at this facility, sure, but he was at a treatment center. He doesn't much talk about it, and I don't try to get him to. Just like some wounds heal with rods or screws in them, I'm content to let that one heal however it's doing on its own, without being ripped open.

"So, what can we take away from the therapists' notes?" asks Creed.

"Well, the goal part gets me thinking," I say. "What's normally going on in the life of someone thinking about families and having children? A relationship. Or at least either the delusion of one or an intense desire for one. Maybe this is our indicator that she had some kind of infatuation, whether or not it was reciprocated."

"It could have been anyone, though," says Todd. "Peers, teachers, therapists, other staff—hell, even medical or culinary staff. Do we have any evidence that it was Eboncore?"

"Nothing solid," Creed says, "just a bunch of incoherent witnesses. And really, none of them actually *saw* anything happen. Just a whole heaping pile of speculation and judgment about his character."

The air takes on a slight chill, more characteristic of the coming autumn than of the current late summer. The elevation does that. Todd moves in closer to me.

"So on what grounds was the accusation even made?" I ask. "I know it was thirty years ago, but it's not the Salem Witch Trials. You couldn't just get someone burned at the stake without something pretty substantial, right?"

"Well, that's the thing. Eboncore didn't have a defense attorney. Some people thought that this was his way of conceding to the punishment he had incoming, but others thought that it was because he truly believed he would be let off without one. Obviously, this school of thought is the one that thinks he's probably innocent."

"Is that a popular position?" asks Todd.

"No, but still more so than you might think," says Creed. "There have been petitions and campaigns for a more competently conducted trial, but the judge has remained firm."

"So, the accusation was made, a bunch of people sat at the stand talking about what a gigantic piece of shit he was, and then they whisked him off to prison?" I ask.

"Yeah, sounds like it," says Creed.

"Damn. Our job would've been so much easier back then," says Todd. I nod. Creed laughs.

"Okay, so there's no evidence to support the allegation—"

"That we know of," says Todd.

"Right."

"So, maybe we can find something out today either for or against," I say. Both of them seem attracted to the idea. Personally, I don't much care what we do as long as I get to be with Todd. We could go pick peanuts out of turds together and I'd be happy.

"But let's go through the rest of this before we go out," says Todd.

Creed and I agree.

We seem to have hit the most pressing information first, however. The majority of that which remains, it seems, is irrelevant, boring information like class schedules, grades, and other academic stuff.

Another thick stack is a chronological history of Willa's incidents—interesting, to be sure, but not so much relevant, aside from the last month of her life, during which the only major recorded incident was the night she killed herself. Or whatever happened. This statement is written by the staff, however, so we read it with hopes that it will provide more clarity on the matter.

However, it is, if anything, less helpful than any of the others:

"Patient told staff that she needed to get something from her room for her costume. Staff told her that it was fine. Another patient asked the same thing and staff told her it was okay. The peer screamed and staff went to the room to investigate. Staff found Patient hanging from the ceiling with a length of bedsheet. She had removed the vent cover and tied the sheet around a pipe in the ceiling. Staff took the patient's peer out of the room while another staff stayed in the common area. Staff called for assistance, and when additional staff arrived, they took the peer to the time out room."

"I guess if I were trying to keep my ass out of jail, I would omit all of the relevant time frames, too," says Todd.

"Yeah," I say, "there's no way he just 'forgot' to write that down. He knew he should have been paying attention, and he knew that the way he worded it was misleading."

"Is there maybe one from the other staff?" asks Creed with more hopeful optimism than either Todd or I can muster.

In response, I pick up the next sheet of paper, which is indeed a statement from Kelly, but after a quick skim, I tell them that it yields even less than the first. Creed's optimism deflates at this, which, I feel, marks an excellent time to bring up the note from the lockbox. I started into the topic when I asked him about the key, but the subject changed. I'm surprised he hasn't pursued that more doggedly.

"Well, we do have one piece of evidence," I say. I pause dramatically for Creed's anticipation to mount. When his eyebrows are just shy of his hairline, I tell him, "The lockbox. Inside, there was a note. Written to 'Dubz,' from 'TE.'

"So, to Willa, from Thad?" Creed says.

"So far as I can figure, yes," I say. "It's a love note, too."

"Well shit," he says. "That is pretty decent evidence. I wonder how it never turned up? The lockbox, I mean."

"Well, it seems like a lot of the investigation was focused on the wrong places, largely investing in documents and witnesses and stuff. They were so happily reveling in the wealth of information available that they forgot to investigate it like a normal fucking case," I say.

"I guess that makes sense," Creed says, "but wouldn't someone have found it down the line? A peer or staff or the next person to use that bed?"

"It was tucked away pretty well, actually. And admission numbers did plummet pretty hard after she died. Maybe she was just the last one to use that bed. I doubt they could have convinced anyone to sleep in it after that night, anyway."

Creed nods along; my line of logic seems to pass his scrutiny.

Creed's phone rings, an earful of Crazy Train bursting into the hollow void of the cottage. He flashes us an apologetic look as he fishes it out of his pocket. He looks at the screen and his expression goes from confusion to enthusiasm before he picks up.

"Hello?"

I hear a female voice on the other end. I half expect it to be my mother (because apparently Creed is best friends with her), but the voice has none of the elegant grace my mother's has.

"Yes," says Creed. "No. I'm not representing anyone. I just want to talk. If you're open to it. Okay. Thank you. I'll see you then."

He hangs up the phone and, still wide-eyed, says, "You'll never guess who that was."

"You're probably right," I say.

"Madonna?" says Todd. Game on.

"Julie Andrews?" I say.

"Joe Pesci?"

"Former Kansas keyboardist and vocalist Steve Walsh?"

"The other Jackson Four?"

"*Supernatural* stars Jensen Ackles and Jared Padalecki?"

"A dog using a telecom service to infiltrate enemy lines?"

By now, Todd and I are laughing too hard to continue (Todd wins, as he got the last one in) and Creed's eyes are in imminent danger of rolling back into his head. Todd and I take a moment to collect ourselves before paying him our most devoted attention.

"That was Ginger Garrity. I called a while back to try to set up an interview, as I'm sure you remember. Left her a message. Figured she wouldn't call back after a couple of days, but there she is. She wants to do it this weekend."

"Fuck. You're right. I would never have guessed that," I say.

"Ah, babe, yeah you would've."

"Yeah, I probably would've."

"So, we have an interview with Ginger on the schedule," I say, "What do we do until then?"

"Dig up her therapy records?" says Creed. He retains his enthusiasm and reminds me of a dog, shaking in anticipation after its owner picks up its leash. I look the other way and Todd's face conveys the same message.

"All right, but we'll have to wait until dark," I say.

"So, yet again, we ask ourselves…what now?" says Todd.

"Well, I'm beat," says Creed, "so I'll probably sleep for a while. Maybe we could meet up back here around sundown?"

"Yeah, sounds good," I say. I almost ask where he's staying, but catch myself when I realize I'm on the verge of inviting a person I've only *really* known for a couple of hours into my apartment. I like Creed so far. But it'll be a while yet before I fully *trust* him, and all that may change in an instant. In reality, only Todd and Beth have ever earned a significant degree of trust from me, and both have shown over and over that they are worthy of it.

I'll admit that I'm fairly relieved that Creed wants to take a break; while I would be happy spending time with Todd in whatever capacity is available, a quiet afternoon in with him sounds divine. In the throes of constant chaos and resistance at every turn, to have things be…easy, even if only for a few hours, is a prospect that nearly brings me to happy tears.

FIFTEEN

Todd and I walk back to the apartment with the same casual ease as earlier. The noontime sun shines high and mighty, contrasting pleasantly with the nip in the air. The town's old buildings seem to be made of colors more vibrant and alive than they were yesterday, and the odor on the slight breeze is of the imminently shedding foliage of the mountain.

We pick up a few groceries before heading back, then spend some time cooking and eating together. I am an okay cook. I can whisk and poach and pare and mince. But Todd is a genius. Add to that that I haven't had the motivation to cook anything more extravagant than ramen over the past month, and Todd's homemade lasagna with from-scratch sauce makes for quite the delicious meal indeed.

We didn't plan the rest of the afternoon, but we never do. Never have to. The idea of doing anything right now is laughable, anyway.

So, as the Wyoming sun journeys across the sky, its rays shine upon the sleepiest town in the country, championed by Todd and me as the sleepiest inhabitants thereof.

The afternoon passes like a gasp, sucking in air and pausing for a moment, only to use its exhalation to blow all the blue out of the sky. Mountains rise and silhouette against the monochrome red canvas, like solemn guardians of the night.

Todd and I observe this from my western window. I feel a chill in my spine and don't know whether it's from a drop in temperature or the majesty of the moment. The romantic in me asserts the latter and I don't dispute it.

In my youth, I never knew a moment of pure tranquility, safety, peace. Even on the relieving nights my father spent out of town, when Mom, Trina, and I were able to have an innocent, quiet night and perhaps watch a movie, the threat of my father's return loomed in my mind. In retrospect, I think we all felt it—that the time we were enjoying was merely rented, time borrowed, and we were the more appreciative of it because of that. It wasn't so much celebratory as it was a last-ditch effort to convince ourselves that a normal life could one day be attainable.

A more aware version of me might have thought about the classically misquoted, "Eat, drink, and be merry, for tomorrow we die." But alas, six-year-old Remy hadn't had the biblical knowledge for that connection and was thus left to revel in the spirit and sentiment without the accompanying scripture.

Now, I reflect on that young Remy—naïve, sure, but with no remaining innocence to speak of—and wonder what he might think if I told him that one day he would experience serenity with such a simple completeness as this. In the drowsy evening of a quiet town, with Todd, undisturbed by car horns or sirens, listening to a silence whose only impurity is our own breathing.

My mother has invoked in me a sense of security I've never felt so solidly, and freedom is at the forefront of my mind. Logistically, I'm far less free than I was in Riverdell; I spend most of my time actively avoiding being seen, and thus I can't really do much during the day.

But what I have now is a freedom of the mind, a profound and underappreciated freedom in which one simply allows himself to think and feel, without the inhibitions and interruptions of fear, self-doubt, and distrust. As I learned almost a year ago (and as I continue to learn now), freedom of the mind and heart is more liberating than its literal counterpart will ever be.

As darkness hugs, envelops, and eventually extinguishes the last of the brilliant colors, Todd says, "Well, shall we go?"

I smile and nod. I'm excited to bring Todd and Creed along, and I figure that, to some extent, I'll become something of a tour guide. An amusing flash of thought occurs in which I am indeed a full-fledged tour guide, wearing an ugly blazer with a bronze nametag, exasperatedly answering Todd's many questions while also trying to keep Creed from touching everything.

As I lock the door behind us, I get just a small, nostalgic taste of the Good Ol' Days, in which Todd and I would go to Beth's house or to a movie. Maybe we'd go to the park, or sometimes we would set out with no particular destination in mind and go exactly there.

This excursion is different, sure, but I mentally strip those differences away and focus on the similarities.

We make our way through the darkness, and I take the lead when we get to the trail. The moon is bright enough, once again, to illuminate much of the path, but Todd feels more comfortable following behind me when it's dark.

"Man, this trail is a lot less romantic at night," he says, "and a lot creepier. You really did this alone?"

"What can I say? I'm an insatiable adventurer."

Todd laughs as we take teetering giant's steps through the tall grass surrounding the cottage, glowing in the moonlight's silvery sheen. The upper window on the west side is closed; Creed is here.

Todd and I climb through the window and head upstairs to find him sitting up against the wall with his phone out.

"Took you long enough," he says. It's hard to tell in the dark, but I'm pretty sure I see him wink.

We elect to leave all of our previously acquired documents there in the cottage. They may be useful in comparison to the others' notes, but we decide that we'll only use the trip for the *collection* of documents, and we can go through them when we get back here. That way, we won't get sucked into a vortex powered by the thirst for knowledge that's both present and strong in all of us. I'm definitely not fond of the prospect of spending another day at the school. Even so, I packed more food this time, just in case.

"We all ready, then?" I say. The others nod and we set off.

A sense of oddity lingers for a moment, but I think that's my brain struggling to make Creed fit into the distinctly Beth-shaped hole left in our trio. The feeling is gone in a minute, though— not because Creed fits into that space, but because I surrender to the idea that Creed is just Creed.

The three of us walk up the hill toward the falls, a steady *shrrr* growing louder by the minute. We don't talk much during the journey. Todd gets this way before exciting events: pensive, speculative, anticipatory.

Creed is just enjoying the ride. Perhaps his mind is as full as Todd's, but as it is, his eyes zip and zoom from place to place—even in the darkness—the whole way there. I pick the lock holding the chains together on the front gate, and we slip inside. So far, Creed has seen everything we've passed, but the alluring excitement of crossing previously uncrossed boundaries within these walls seems to hold him in a grip of trembling anticipation. He keeps looking around like we're in a building made of cheese, his fingers drumming audibly against his backpack straps.

"There's an unlocked door out by the cafeteria," he says. As far as I can perceive, the man nearly shits himself when I pull out my key and hold it up like a trophy.

"Where did you get that? I was wondering how you had been getting around so fast in there."

"From the program director's office. There's a whole drawer full of them."

"Also, Remy is a wiz at picking locks," says Todd. This evidently answers Creed's next question, as he remains silent after opening his mouth to speak. Instead he closes it and nods.

I open the door inside the lobby and we enter the small area with the office and restrooms, and I can practically feel Creed beside me, abuzz with excitement. I can't blame him; living here for as long as I have drove me to investigation, but I had the benefit of full access to the facility.

As we cross to the school hallway, Creed deflates slightly, but bounces back even more vibrant than before. I suspect that, from his perspective, it must have been a bit of a roller coaster: finally walking through a locked door only to find himself in the same hallway he's been in before, surrounded by the same old locked doors. But where there were previously barricades and obstacles, he must have realized, now there is a hallway rife with potential, brimming with things to be explored. And even better, being that it's been locked up, it hasn't been exposed to the same cast of vandals as the more accessible areas have been. Things will be all but undisturbed, ripe and ready to be juiced for the sweet nectar that is intel.

"First things first," I say. I beeline for the door marked 'Program Director' and open it. Todd and Creed follow me inside, but there's scarcely room for all three of us, so I make my business quick: I open the squeaky drawer and pull out one key each for Todd and Creed. Todd places his in his pants pocket, which looks almost offensively unceremonious compared to the respectful reverence with which Creed takes his and clutches it to his chest like a man who found his wedding ring after weeks of diligent searching. I expect him to kiss it, even, but he instead opts to hang onto it, keeping it clenched in his palm.

"Got a thing for tarnished old keys, do you?" says Todd. "Should Remy and I give you two some privacy?" Todd grins and Creed laughs, breaking his trance-like fixation.

"Right, then, all explorers ready? Let's get going on why we're here."

While I'm by no means averse to exploring more, I do find

relief in that I already know where I can find relevant documents. The thrill of every door and cabinet potentially holding important information was fun, but this errand can be completed quickly, which is the more prudent way to do it. Still, I suppose I can't very well deny Todd and especially Creed the chance to explore the school after giving them keys and seeing Creed light up like the Las Vegas skyline.

So, we pass through the school area, my two companions flitting from door to door together. I almost point them in the right direction, but the sentiment feels like I imagine a father might feel, watching his two voracious children hunt down Easter baskets. In a couple of minutes, they find their way to the courtyard door. Creed, in complete ecstasy, uses his key to unlock the door. The courtyard carries less mystery and enigma than my first time through; my not being alone has robbed the scene of its magic melancholy. In contrast, these two seem adequately enthralled despite that Creed has been to this area before.

Both of them look around for a minute, then gravitate toward the dorm building.

"Ah, yeah. It's all corroded. There's a broken window in the back where we can get in," says Creed before I think to. It's a strange sensation to be speaking so candidly about our shared experience, as it was so saturated in mystery and suspense last time the two of us were here—for me, at least. I wonder what that may have looked and felt like from his perspective. Probably he followed me from the cottage, certain he knew where I was heading.

We make our way around to the back, where I entered before, and the familiar disarray of the office comes into view. I take a moment to entertain myself with the thought that that was only a couple of nights ago. So much has happened in the past two days that it seems to have been much longer than that. But if any day is to feel so long, I'm glad it has been this one.

We clamber inside, Todd only slightly less gracefully than Creed and me. Creed uses his precious new key to unlock the door with a brand of childlike glee, and we step into the main area hallway.

Although there are three of us this time, the spacious hall seems more empty than last night. This time, I think, it's because my attention is largely devoted to my companions instead of filling up the floor and staircase with imaginary students and their loud chatter of varying emotions. No, indeed, the bare, hard surfaces echo our own noises rather than the parting of its former occupants.

"There's a classroom up there," I say, pointing toward the locked door on the other side of the hall.

"But wasn't the school area back there?" Creed asks.

"Yeah, but I think this one is more like study hall, a place to come and do homework more than to learn new material."

Todd and Creed both approach the door. Todd opens it this time, and the two walk in ahead of me, reaching the desk before I even get to the doorway. By the time I'm halfway into the room, Creed has already fished Ginger's folder out of the metal drawer.

"Shall we indulge here or later on, maybe at the cottage?"

"Later," I say. "That way, we can assemble all of the information we have and view it as a more complete picture."

Todd agrees and Creed, looking just the slightest bit put out, tucks the folder into his own bag and we move on. Recalling my first time through that room, I get goosebumps for a moment, wondering whether my stalker before is here with me again. But of course, that's only in the split second before I remember that he is, in fact, standing right next to us.

We make our way through the east doors, out to the vast main area containing the entrances to the dorm units. This time, I lead the way instead of indulging their curiosity, as there's nothing of interest between here and Willa's room. All the while, I watch Todd as we move; his razor-sharp memory is surely ablaze, taking mental images as we go.

I open the door to Willa's unit and show Todd and Creed to her bedroom.

"This is where I found the lockbox," I say, holding the mattress up. The three of us split up, looking through the rooms for anything else, but we come up empty-handed; my initial combing through seems to have been sufficiently thorough.

After declaring the unit useless, we head onward toward, in my opinion, the most likely place to contain further relevant information: the therapists' offices. If there were any telltale factors from Ginger's behavior leading up to the event, they will have been well reflected and well-documented over time, and well-preserved since then.

I open the door to reveal an office identical to that of Willa's therapist in terms of size and shape, but nothing else. The walls are covered in artwork that looks like it was done by the clients: psychedelic explosions of clashing colors, tastefully and artistically done roses, and festive pieces including hand turkeys, construction paper Christmas trees, Valentines, and what look like pumpkins, but may in fact be poorly painted sunsets.

"Interesting," I say, "I would think that someone with a sentimental attachment to this stuff would have taken it with her."

"Yeah, that does seem weird. Maybe she only put it up to please her clients, and never actually was all that attached to it," says Todd.

I shrug and open the closest drawer in the desk. This one, similar to the one in Batista's office, is filled with candy wrappers and decades-old snacks. My curiosity is not enough for me to keep that drawer open.

The next drawer is the one I'm after. I thumb through the names as Todd and Creed speculate imaginatively on the potential effects of consuming such ancient treats. Creed goes the food poisoning route. Todd goes the superpower route.

Looking through the names, I keep my eye out not only for Ginger, but for any of the names that have come up so far. Ellen, Josalyn, and Rhonda show up, and although I don't anticipate much of value, I take the folders and deposit them into my backpack just in case.

"On to the next one?" I say. The following office is Willa's therapist's office, and even though I looked through it last night, I'm now equipped with more names to watch out for. The fruits of that endeavor are files for Donna and Gina. As with the others', I stash them away and we continue.

"Onward and upward," I say, leading the others out the door

and into the tall hall. Indeed, we head up the next flight of stairs, an area I didn't cover last night due to sheer complacency (though the visit from that band of adventurous teens helped to usher me out). This floor is not part of the openness of the hall, and instead the staircase disappears up into the ceiling. And as we ascend into it, we find that there are no windows up here, rendering our flash-lights both necessary and safe to use.

Sixteen

This hallway is full of the kind of eerie silence that still just seems too loud. Our movements, rather than slicing a clean swath through the quiet, seem to be devoured by it *(eaten by it)*. The muffling quality is far deeper than we've encountered thus far, and a fearful, primitive side of me is grateful that I didn't explore this far when I was alone. Further introspection leads me to suspect that this comes from the same part of my brain that, in most people, generates a fear of the dark. I suppose a more complete assessment of a fear of the dark would be a fear of the aggressively unknown. An unsolvable puzzle flaunting its impossible curves and edges. Perhaps that's why I'm not afraid of the dark; I've been there, grappled with the monsters. I've seen worse in the light of day than darkness has ever delivered to me.

Beyond that, I've simply adapted to the darkness. I visited as a tourist at first, and decided I liked it so much that I turned in my flip flops and Hawaiian shirt in exchange for a mailbox. I'm not afraid of what goes bump in the night, because more often than not, it's me.

The probing beams of our flashlights set fire to masses of tangling webs, something I just now notice this investigation has had a supreme lack of.

The three of us stare at the geometrically perplexing series of webs both in the corners and spanning the width of the hallway.

"Well, then," says Todd, "let's go make friends with Shelob."

"I'll wear my mithril underwear," I say.

Despite that I'm not afraid of spiders, I get the unnerving sensation that webs are sticking to my face and neck, and the sensation grows more vivid and intense with every step. By the sounds of it, though, my discomfort is nothing compared to that of Creed, who would possibly have leapt straight into orbit were there not a ceiling above us.

Todd handles the situation as well as I do—no surprises there—and leads our small group with his signature poised calmness, progressing at a measured, steady pace.

Curiously, the walls are virtually barren—aside from the multitude of webs strewn all over the place, of course. No clever puns or silly nicknames grace this hall and no humorous attempts at being relatable and charismatic manifest. Instead, the sneaky webs are complemented only by various sizes of patches of missing paint, ranging from the size of a paperclip to that of a soccer ball.

In this side of the hallway, at least, there's only one door, but to my surprise, it has a window, the cross-hatched kind you always see in academic or administrative settings. The kind that says, "Mr. Important will see you shortly."

Todd presses his face up against the glass (a more paranoid bit of me objects, but I don't vocalize this), but he just shakes his head as he steps back.

"Can't see a thing," he says.

"Open away, my friend," I say. He inserts his key into the lock, but it won't turn.

"I believe your skills may be necessary here," he says. He steps away and gestures for me to step up.

With Todd's steady flashlight beam (and the less steady one from Creed), I insert my picks and set to work, all the while imagining what more could lie beyond these doors. As far as I can speculate, everything of relevance or importance is contained either in the school building or in the floors beneath us.

This lock, from what I can feel, takes a key cut from the same blank as the other locks' keys, but a couple of the pins are situated differently.

With a bit more effort, the door clicks and swings inward, revealing exactly what Todd relayed: nothing. However, the perceived 'nothing' opens up under the flashlights' beams, and we find ourselves in yet another hallway, lined on either side with still more doors, ending with one solemn-looking wooden one, facing us, at the end of the hall. None of them have labels, save for that last one, upon which hangs a plate reading "Copy." Upon closer examination, the doors without labels bear the odd, contrasting, faded marks of having *had* labels, but they must have been taken when the facility shut down.

"Oh boy," I say, "I really hope these doors take those generic keys." I count eight doors, excluding the copy room, for a total of nine. In desperation, I put my key into the lock of the nearest door and apply pressure, but it resists with the awkward uncertainty of the time-worn mechanism it is. I push a little harder in case one of the pins is stuck, but still no give.

"This is going to take a while," I say. "One of you want to check the other doors to see if they're all the same?"

Todd sets to work on the other doors, leaving me with the shaky assistance of Creed, but it's enough to complete the task.

Each time Todd tries a door, he reports his lack of success with a deflated, "Nope."

The shape of the keyhole is the same as we've been dealing with, but again, it requires a different key.

"Nope," says Todd.

I work the lock like always, and in time, it submits.

"Nope."

Inside, there's another office, but aside from the heavy wooden desk, it is completely empty. The walls have a few holes, and in a couple of places, there are patches where the paint has come up. This office was not always so barren, it seems; there must have been posters and photos on the wall in here, based on the tiny damaged areas.

"Nope."

I check the first of the remaining doors in hopes that Todd may have an oddly cut key or perhaps it simply didn't work for some reason, but that hope withers as the lock resists my key with an equally insistent "No."

"Nope."

I get my picks out and get them started. This lock must have been in better shape than the other, because it only takes a few seconds before it clicks open. The door swings open like the other.

"Aha!" says Todd from down the hall. His enthusiasm startles me, but Creed almost seems not to have heard it; his flashlight's beam shifts only slightly, and even then, little enough that it may just have been his natural unsteadiness.

I look down the hall to see Todd's silhouette framed in the doorway of the copy room. "Anything in there?" I ask.

Todd's flashlight beam flicks around the room, as though trying to find out for itself.

"The copy machine is still here. Man, it's like the second they heard they were being shut down, they all just up and sprinted from the building. There's so much stuff still around."

"Well, you're not far off," says Creed. He looks quite a lot more present than a few seconds ago; the mention of the school's history yanked his consciousness back from wherever it was. "When they closed down the school, their first order of operation was to close everything off as a crime scene. The presence of the tape and the lights, it was quite a lot to take in, especially for youth with histories of trauma. So they moved them, temporarily. By a convenient happenstance, the numbers were down on the boys' campus, so with some impressive finagling, they were able to consolidate the boys into two units, while the remaining girls took the other two. It ended up just *barely* working because the girls' numbers had gotten so low, too. From what I understand, there was a proper *line* of angry parents demanding to withdraw their daughters from the program.

"Understandably, of course. I would have been in that line, too, I think, had I been in their situation. Anyway, it was only temporary. But when they got back, of course, everything was different. Friendships that had been forged there disintegrated in the space of a week because of so many people having been moved and removed.

"So, when it happened again—they asked them to clear out, I mean—the administration, the therapists, everyone, they thought it was temporary again, that they'd get a nice little break and that they would just wait for the phone call to come back to work. They would have had to jump hoop after hoop in order to get in to retrieve anything, so it just wasn't worth the hassle to them."

"I wonder if the confusion was the product of deception or miscommunication?" I say.

"I've wondered the same thing," says Creed. By now, he's not only engaged in the present, but he's so much here that he resembles an ambitious conspiracy theorist vying to convince people that everything from the JFK assassination to 9/11 was an inside job.

"And what's this? I believe we may have our answer," says Todd. He holds out a single sheet of paper for us to read. "This was left in the copier."

I lean forward to take the paper, but I figure Creed will get more out of it (in terms both of divining information from it and of sheer indulgent pleasure), so I let him take it instead.

He reads aloud: "To whom it may concern, the facility will be closing for an unknown length of time, effective this Monday, November twenty-second. Please await our calls to return to work, and until then, enjoy your time off, and thank you for your patience."

"It's a memo," says Todd.

"They misspelled 'effective,'" says Creed. Todd and I laugh.

"So, either they themselves didn't think it would be permanent, or they did indeed deceive their staff. But even in the administrative offices—the directors, medical records, the likes—they also look like they flew out of here like bats out of hell," says Todd.

"Yeah. I think they really didn't know," I say. "Well, except for maybe that guy." I point toward the empty office.

"Yeah. But with their numbers dwindling, they may just have been letting people go," says Todd.

"Right. Maybe the other offices will offer something useful," I say.

With that, I get to work on opening the remaining doors. The one I opened before Todd found the memo turned out just to be a small break room, smaller than the one downstairs but nicer. It has a squashy couch whose original color I can't discern. The room looks like an upgraded version of its more accessible counterpart, in all aspects other than size; seven or eight people use this one, as opposed to the dozens who would have shared the one below.

The next office looks a lot more like the ones downstairs; posters and drawings litter the walls, and a neat stack of papers sits perfectly centered on the desk, the uppermost sheet bearing the company's logo in the upper left corner. That sheet, I find, is a letter penned by the therapist to be sent to the parents of one of her clients. Never to be sent after all, as it transpired.

Her files don't contain any names that ring bells, so we move on. Fascinating as it may be to rummage through therapists' notes about anonymous patients, looking through these offices may take some time.

"Why don't we split up?" says Todd. "We can cover them a lot faster that way, and if we all know what we're looking for, a single pair of eyes in these small offices is just as good as three." The man can read my mind, I swear it.

After I unlock the next door, Creed steps through its threshold, and Todd takes the next; my entry into the following room is hindered a bit by my having to pick the lock in deep darkness, but I get it open and step inside.

One word swims around the surface of my mind for the minute I spend taking in this office: *sweet*. It looks like a Valentine's Day advertisement cut out of a K-Mart newsletter. The office is adorned in all sorts of reds and pinks—streamers line the ceiling, little paper hearts pock the walls, and pink, white, and red doilies overhang just slightly from every surface, including the book-shelves and even the main desk. A modern-looking couch sits on one end of the desk, which is a surprising (but relieving) break from the trend of the rest of the room's obscene cuteness.

This is what happens to all of those girls who dot their 'I's with hearts, I think.

Even her client files are stored in red binders with hearts on the spines. Aside from the sofa, the eye's only reprieve from the ever-present reds and pinks is the hand-drawn art on the walls, given to her by clients, and even that isn't entirely free from it.

194

Surely in an attempt to appeal to the therapist, many of the pictures on the wall have hearts done in red crayon, or are themselves done on pink, heart-shaped construction paper.

Good lord, how did this lady not go crazy in this room?

Then again, perhaps she did. Or maybe she already was.

Once again, I find nothing important or relevant in the office. And, frustrating though that may be, I'd be lying if I claimed I wasn't at least a little relieved to be able to excuse myself from that office. I think I feel a cavity forming.

At the same time, Todd and creed exit their respective offices, shrugging: *nothing*.

A sort of full silence again washes over us for a moment, before we each select and enter one of the three remaining rooms. The one I enter is a janitorial closet—I opt to join Todd instead. Todd's is similar to the empty one, but lacks even a desk. There are no holes in the walls, and the paint remains perfectly intact. Neither of us can venture a guess as to this room's former function, but I note that there's an almost supernatural quality to its perfect square shape. Of course, my perception is subject to poor light and the inevitable fallibility of humans, but I don't need a tape measure to be sure, despite my humanity, that these walls are the exact same length and that the door through which we entered is exactly centered on its wall.

Todd and I exchange a glance that says, *Slightly more than nothing, but still nothing.* As we re-enter the hall, Creed steps out of the room he was in. Our hopes flutter slightly when we see past him and identify it as an office, but he shakes his head. No dice.

"Well that's confusing," he says. The same question rings in all of our minds, but none of us is willing to admit to our own groundlessness. *What now?* We've picked up some useful information, certainly, but our jackpot eludes us yet. That intrusive, full silence from before befalls us again, and while it's actually sort of pleasant, I'm eager for it to be broken as our next plan of action hatches.

"Let me think," I say. I wander through the hallway at a slow pace, peeking into the open doors as I go but searching more in my mind than in the inky halls and rooms.

It wouldn't just be that Ginger didn't have a therapist—they all did. It was part of the standard treatment program. So, either her therapist was one of the ones who up and left beforehand, leaving an empty office, or her therapist's office is one of these, just without her records for whatever reason.

I remind myself that this is indeed a possibility; with Ginger having been so close to the whole situation, the prosecutor may have requested medical records. Of course, most places would simply copy them, but perhaps they just never made it back to their original places?

As I think it, I look up to see the entrance to the copy room. Todd must sense my intrigue, because he comes to join me in my search.

SEVENTEEN

The copy machine is an ancient hunk of a thing, filmed over with dust and webs. There are a couple of marks wiped away where I assume Todd gripped the lid in order to look into the feeder tray. There's a small garbage can next to it, containing nothing but a plastic liner and maybe some spiders. On the wall to the left, a bulletin board sports an explosion of leaflets and flyers, in all sorts of colors.

Karaoke night, an autumn training, a reminder of the Thanksgiving potluck. The opposite wall holds a large cubby unit, with each slot labeled at the bottom. Most are empty, but two are not. One such slot belongs to Greg Ayers and offers a revision of a new policy that would never see implementation. The other belongs to Lyla Branville.

Lyla's box holds a thick manila envelope, marked in black ink as pertaining to Ginger Garrity. There's our jackpot after all. I guess that, if it had indeed been requested for use in the case, it was probably on its way back to Lyla when things went sour.

"Either of you come across a Lyla Branville's office?" I say.

Both Todd and Creed shake their heads no.

"I think this is our Houdini from the first office," I say. "Probably got canned or something right around the end of this whole thing."

"Lyla Branville," says Creed. The crude residual light from our flashlights is sufficient to display Creed in a state of deep concentration, trying with herculean effort to summon some memory from the vaults of his mind. Despite the effort, however, he can't quite seem to coax it into his consciousness. He shakes his head in disappointment. "I'm positive I've read that name in one of my articles somewhere," he says.

"We'll look her up when we get back," says Todd.

"In my opinion, we've found what we came for. You guys ready to call it a night?" I say.

My odd state of mind renders the return trip just the smallest bit disorienting, as though I'm continuing deeper into the facility rather than exiting it on a route I've already taken twice now. My perspective is just skewed enough to make the hard turns seem foreign until we reach the courtyard.

The courtyard, as before, whispers and gasps with the hints of a breeze just shy of a gust, the kind that twitches with life. I connect the sensation to standing in a patch of tall grass, the kind that reaches for the sky rather than bowing over upon becoming too long.

Minutes later, we exit the property entirely, shedding the mischievous mantle one wears when they're in a place they shouldn't be.

"So how did you find this case, specifically?" I ask Creed.

"Well, your mother told me where she was sending you, so to speak, and I followed immediately afterward. It was tough to get out of my undercover position with those idiots in LA, but I managed to slip away. Anyway, the group I'm with—Deliverance—we have a huge database. I'm sure we probably seem kind of eccentric, but we have all kinds of people working there, from accountants to security to IT.

"That said, some of the volunteers are there just to find the cases. They look through homicide, domestic violence, and missing persons files from across the nation. Of course, their local law enforcements have access to the same data, but when your trends only pull data from within the city or state, your scope is limited. So we have eyes all the way through this country, monitoring.

"Because of that, however, the cases we pull in are so many, and we are so few, that there's often fairly little we can actually do other than try to nudge the local police in the right direction. We had had our eyes on your father for quite some time. We were scratching our heads, trying to figure out what to do about him. When our system pinged a new homicide case in Riverdell, we feared for the worst. At first glance, we saw your father's photograph and thought maybe he had been caught, but when we saw that he was the *victim*, well, that was something of a relief.

"Anyway, to summarize, I followed you to Ghost Fork and got bored, so I asked the guys about anything active in this area. As it turns out, Deliverance was quite active in this area during the time this whole case was happening. In fact, the volunteers at the time had a very direct role in the case, calling for the extensive investigations and interviews. The local detectives were ready to call it pretty early on, passing it off as a cut and dry suicide. Eboncore's involvement wasn't brought into play until quite a bit of pressure finally cracked them.

"Of course, the legal case was closed, but in our own system, it was left open. Eventually, though, it got left behind, as the members who worked on it went instead to look into a series of missing young women along the Canadian border to the northwest. And there it sat until now."

"So, all of those articles and newspaper clippings," I begin.

"Yes, those came directly from our headquarters. Naturally, they're entirely public as far as the contents, but if you go and pull the records yourself, you raise red flags. Not to mention that it's already trimmed and organized this way."

"Wow. I didn't realize how big this all is. So, uh, who all knows about me?" I don't specify further; my intent is clear.

Creed hesitates before answering. "Well, a fair few," he says. "But you can trust them! They are the kind of people who fight for the same things as you...if a little differently in execution. I know it's not wise to trust so blindly, especially with information so heavy, but believe me, you're like a hero to them. To us."

I sigh. "I guess I don't have much of a choice but to believe you," I say. It's true: Whether or not I can concede to trusting them is irrelevant. Any way I look at it, I'm at their mercy. If they feel like it, they can expose me and turn me over to any number of people queueing up to spill my blood. I'm their bitch.

"In time, perhaps, we'll win you over," says Creed.

"I suppose we'll see."

By this point, we've put the crunchy gravel behind us, and now call forth a cacophony of the familiar *fshh-fshh* noise as we wade through the sea of long, wet grass in approaching the old cottage.

"So, into what treacherous territories does our newfound information lead us?" asks Todd as we sit on the floor of the conspiracy room (as he calls it) and unload our new documents on the ground in front of us. The scene is faintly reminiscent of children getting ready to barter their Halloween candy. Creed drums his fingers on the wooden floor, then interlaces his fingers, then goes back to drumming, finally coming to an abrupt halt when he notices that he's drawn both Todd's and my attention.

"Would you like to do the honors?" I say only half-ironically. I extend the thick stack of once-white paper in his direction and he snatches it from my hand with an urgent fervor I haven't seen in anyone for months. Maybe his thirst for action and resolution are mounting in much the same way mine did but manifesting more…intensely.

With our flashlights illuminating the pages from the back, Creed's eyes flit about busily and with a nimbleness equal to that of his overall grace. His brow does a dance of furrowing and relaxing over and over, interrupted occasionally by his left eyebrow jumping up without the companionship of its right counterpart.

"Huh," he says, after a few minutes and two dense-looking pages. He sets them down in front of himself and I see that he was reading from the therapists' notes. Creed then pulls a tiny notebook out of his back pocket.

"Look," he says, "every time there was an incident with Willa, there was also an incident with Ginger." He hands the small notebook to me, and points to a column on the left side of the notebook indicating a series of dates with corresponding notes. These are near-verbatim recounts of the notes from Willa's main file. Indeed, the lists of dates are nearly identical, save for a couple of smaller notes in between the more hefty ones.

"They don't seem all that related, though," says Creed.

At a glance, he's right. Willa self-harmed on a day when Ginger cussed out a teacher. Ginger had a meltdown on the same day Willa did, but Willa's was during breakfast and Ginger's was just before bedtime.

"They *look* unrelated, sure, but they rarely are," says Todd. "Everything that happens in those places is contained, but it happens around other volatile people. The first incident of the day sets off a chain reaction of different behaviors. Sometimes they wouldn't seem all that intertwined, but a lot of the time, you could predict how the rest of the day would go on your unit based on just the first hour. Not to mention, the two not only lived in the same unit, but they shared a room. It would surprise me if their emotions *weren't* tied at least a little bit."

"So, Willa has a freak-out in the morning, and then Ginger rides on the anxiety and tension from it until she's ready to have one of her own?" asks Creed.

"Basically, yeah."

"Okay, but in these two instances, the catalyst took place outside of the unit. I can see them being fairly connected on the unit and with the things that happened there, but how could that extend to their lives in the school? Didn't Ginger hate Willa?"

"Well yeah, exactly. In that hatred, that energy is focused on the other person, whether they like to admit it or not. So when the person they hate does anything at all, but particularly if they have certain behaviors or act out, it pisses both of them off. I'd be willing to bet that on those days that they had spaced-out behaviors, there was a lot of passive-aggressive back-and-forth between them throughout the day. Sometimes it's just a cycle of getting back at each other, sometimes it's a pissing contest of attention-seeking behavior. At times, they probably even got along, or at least appeared to. But the default, the way they woke up each morning, was in a sort of charged animosity toward each other."

"So these could, and probably do, indicate some sort of pattern, a correlation," I say.

It seems a bit iffy to me, but Todd nods with an authoritative confidence that gets me convinced. He knows the dynamics of a treatment facility far better than I do, after all.

"So where does that leave us?" Creed asks.

"I've been more and more on the Ginger-did-it wagon," I say.

"That she did it?" asks Creed.

"Well, yeah. Think about it. All they really have is Ginger's word to go on, which is perfect for her. She was her roommate, so she had the most access to her. There were a handful of matching testimonies that seemed to lend her credence, but one of them redacted her statement and refused to commit to a new one. Two of them were word-for-word identical, which screams *rehearsed*. Plus, the staff-submitted documentation of the incident was spotty at best. I don't know whether they counted that as evidence when this case was hot, but they sure as hell shouldn't have."

"Okay, so we have means and opportunity, but what was the motive? I know the two didn't get along, but this doesn't seem like a product of the heat of the moment." Todd's cop mind is taking charge now.

"I'm not quite sure on that one. But there is a little more involvement in the aftermath than I'm comfortable with."

"Even for a roommate?" asks Creed.

"*Especially* for a roommate."

"I don't follow."

"When there's foul play, people typically like to do one of two things: Get involved or get away. They want to cross to the greener grass."

"So wouldn't that mean that she would have wanted to distance herself, since she was in the thick of things?" asks Creed.

"Normally, yes," Todd confirms

"So, doesn't the fact that she wanted to get involved show that she was already a bit removed from it, rather than a killer?"

"That's the thing, though. She *was* in it, whether or not she did it. She was her roommate, so she was in it by default. So any other person would give out a few details, usually confirming what has already been discovered, then fade into the background to grieve and process things."

"What does it mean when they try to get involved like she has been?" asks Creed.

"Usually that they're trying to hide something. Often it's not necessarily part of the crime being investigated; one time I had a guy argue with me about showing me his apartment after his roommate offed himself. Of course, that put him at the top of our list of suspects, but as it turned out, he was just trying to keep us from his stacks and stacks of hentai."

Todd and Creed roar with laughter and let it peter out at a nice, slow pace.

"So, we like Ginger for it, then?" says Creed.

"I do," I say.

"I do, too," says Todd.

"Well, who am I to disagree with two detectives?" Creed says in resignation.

"So, let's figure out how this interview is going to go. If that's actually what happened, maybe we could get her to confess. Record it or something."

"Well, you're in the right ballpark, but she would need to be cautioned in order for it to be considered admissible evidence, at which point she would get suspicious and the ruse would be up," I say.

"Right, but we could at least submit it as new evidence to reopen the case, and maybe get a warrant to search her stuff or at least bring her in for formal questioning," says Todd.

"Hmm, I do like that," I say. "So how do we go about making it happen? We'll also have to have enough evidence set aside to make sure this can even get anywhere if the case *is* reopened."

"We could do with some conversation acrobatics, I think," says Todd.

"Yeah. I think I'll just have to familiarize myself with the details—both what she has given and what we've discovered—as intimately as possible. Then, if and when she slips up, I'll be poised to catch her on it and send her reeling."

"Seems solid. Plus, after all these years, I doubt she remembers everything she was supposed to have said and done regarding the case," I say.

"I don't know about that," says Todd, look up from a thick binder. "Ginger was not only one of their highest-functioning students, but they were going to have her tested, once they could find an expert. But they weren't able to find one in time."

"What were they going to test her for?"

"A couple of things. Antisocial personality disorder, for one. And savant syndrome."

"So she's a really smart introvert?" says Creed.

"Antisocial doesn't mean introverted. That's more along the lines of asocial. Someone who's antisocial is what most people would call a psychopath or a sociopath. Someone who has an interest in creating chaos in society."

"Oh. So she's really smart and really dangerous?"

"Yes, basically."

"...Oh."

"Yeah. So maybe going into her home alone isn't the greatest idea," I say.

"So, what do we do? Do you think she'd meet with me in public?"

206

"Maybe, but if she's as smart as that file suggests, she's most likely already on the defensive. She has to suspect that we know something, or else why would we be interested in some decades-old suicide and her involvement therein?"

"We could play it off like he's working a project—a report or something—on treatment facilities like that," says Todd.

"Hmm. Yeah. I think even then, though, she'll be hard to crack. Perhaps even more so, with the prospect of her words being published."

"What are you thinking?" asks Todd.

"We should try your way at first. The less intense it has to get, the better. But assuming that doesn't work, let's go on the offensive a bit harder. We can take the emotional route. 'Oh, how great your pain must be, I'm so sorry you have to carry that around all the time.' Tell her all about this massive, gnawing problem she didn't know she had, then offer her a solution. Give her a way she can stop hiding."

"But if she's antisocial, she may indeed be sociopathic," says Todd," in which case we'll have no real chance at getting at her emotionally."

"Correct. But if that is the case, she'll be subject to another weakness we can exploit: a profound certainty that she's untouchable. All we would have to do then would be to convince her, or get her to convince herself, that she's in the clear."

Todd thinks on it for a moment, then says, "I like it. Creed?"

It's escaped my full attention until now, but Creed has become increasingly unsettled—fidgety, even.

"That sounds like a bit much," he says. His eyes flit between me, Todd, and the floor, hardly pausing for more than a second.

Todd and I look at each other; he and I have always taken for granted our mutual experience as detectives. We walk into situations like this expecting to be one of two parts to a dream team. I've suspected that this might be an issue we'd need to tackle at some point, but I was hoping he'd be able to come through on this one. But I suppose interviews are best left, in their delicacy, to those with experience.

"Can one of you do it?" says Creed. He looks to be more pleading than asking.

"Remy can't," says Todd. "He could do it, I'm sure, but that would mean more visibility, more exposure. Especially if she's as smart as we're preparing for."

At this point, both Creed and I rest our eyes on Todd.

"Well, I guess I do sound enough like you. Enough to pass as you in person, at least," he says. He puts on his thinking face, a serious-looking but otherwise neutral phased-out glance at nothing in particular.

"I think I can do it."

"Perfect," says Creed. His efforts to conceal his relief aren't quite enough; he exhales sharply through a nervous smile, and leans back on his hands.

Eighteen

Esther

Esther Thorn washes her hands and dries them on a small, teal towel beside the sink. The sun has long since set, and the window above the sink shows not its normal charming view of a sage-studded foothill, but instead her own half-reflection, haggard and worn.

Esther glances at the pile of ingredients on the counter and mentally shrinks away from them; the energy she summoned to purchase them ran out while she wasn't looking, and now the prospect of turning the collection of parts into a meal is overwhelming.

Esther's depression has been held temporarily at bay by the prospective reunion with Jeremy (*No, it's Remy now, I have to remember that*), but now, after her attempts to connect with him in a manner other than geographical have been stifled, suppressed, postponed, and evaded for so long; the unstoppable energy with which she first sought him has drained away, devoured by the void she had worked so hard to replace.

But alas, such is a negative space hungry for the entirety of the spectrum of positive emotions, and specifically whichever of them may visit at night.

Or in the morning.

Or during the day.

Esther's shopping trip took place around three this after-noon, after waking up at nine in the morning and saturating in apathy for two hours before taking a shower (her first in three days), then sitting in the awkward timelessness of executive dys-function until the town's tolling bell finally roused her into ac-tion.

The trip took on a surreal quality, like she was watching some stranger pilot her body through the store, just observing through countless panes of glass. Before she knew it, the stranger had steered her back out toward the cashiers, paid, and taken her home.

And now it's coming up on nine o' clock, and Esther neither knows nor cares where the evening went.

She shoves everything into the refrigerator and orders a pizza online instead. She used to cry on nights like this, but these days, even the emotions necessary for crying are inaccessible. She can remember those sentiments, but now it just feels like her brain doesn't have the fuel left to fill the order.

Esther blinks and her slice of pizza is down to its crust, and she's lost her appetite more than she's become full or satisfied.

She checks her phone. For a time, she held onto a persistent hope that Remy would reach out to her. That hope suffered a brutal death some time ago, but she still checks her phone with a near desperate regularity. She chalks it up to habit at this point, but a small part of her she tries not to acknowledge scrambles at that old hope's ashes. For a while, he responded with religious attention. Until he found out who it was. Anonymity helped foster something of a dialogue between them, but it was forced and artificial, and she knew it. She knew that the anonymity was the life support of their relationship, and removing the mask doomed it to a floundering end.

An optimistic thought sometimes bangs on the door of the dungeon where her positivity has been locked, proposing that he's just busy, and that he'll get in touch when he has the time, but this thought is never permitted access to the upper levels.

She knew that putting Todd on his trail—however subtly—would eventually bring an end to her communication with Remy, but she also knew that it was right. Not just right, but the least she could do, only the beginning to her paying the emotional debt she had accrued in his name.

She had abandoned him at a critical time of his childhood. She doubted that she could ever make up to him the tides of hopelessness she must have inflicted upon him, but if she could send him any sort of happiness or reprieve from his own torment, she was obligated to do so, was she not? She knew that, but it was still hard to execute that decision knowing the inevitable side effects.

But no matter how she tries to look at it, she owes him that much.

She sets her pizza down and makes to stand up, when her phone vibrates at an incoming text message. The fullness of the following silence makes her think that perhaps she only imagined it, that her desperation has finally taken the plunge into delusion, but alas, the little LED light begins pulsing its friendly, enticing green: *New message!*

Still wary of the possibility that her mind is playing tricks on her, she rises slowly and crosses to her phone, a little black island on the white sea of Remy's countertop. Her heart does little flutters, alternating with fierce beats.

Just then, she hears a noise—a muffled bump. At first, she thinks maybe she knocked something over in her excitement, but she sits still for a moment and yet another bump sounds, this time accompanied by a clang and a crash.

The combined events of these thirty seconds—the text message and the subsequent events both—called forth the Esther who's been absent for almost a year. The one with focus and purpose; the one in control.

That Esther is the one she's been waiting for, whose return she has been praying for.

She pulls a drawer all the way out of its tracks and reaches deep into its space, grasping at a heavy handgun she duct-taped there the night Remy disappeared. She checks the magazine—full—and racks the firearm, holding it steadily as she makes her way to the back room.

Once there, she opens the window leading out into the desert *(slowly, careful now, don't make a sound)* and pushes the screen outward, resulting in a mercifully quiet *thunk* on the dirt outside. A warm breeze rolls in and caresses her face, and in spite of the imminent mortal danger she's likely to be in, she allows herself to enjoy it. She considers it to be an act of defiance, to enjoy herself in the face of such danger.

A loud *bang* sounds from the front of the house. Esther considers vaulting out the open window and escaping into the night, but she suspects that they—whoever "they" are this time—would have sent enough minions to keep one or two pairs of eyes outside, too; she considers it an act of providence that no one saw her open the window, but perhaps they were still focused on the front entrance at that time.

A flood of rushed footsteps works its way through the house. Esther hears one set in the living room and at least one more in the kitchen.

A deep voice speaks from the former, but the words are too muffled for her to comprehend. The tone, however, is audibly urgent—angry, even. Esther's heart threatens to beat faster, but she suppresses it, willing her body and mind into the calm state necessary to navigate the situation.

She listens, calculates; three (or more) of them together wouldn't take long to clear and secure the kitchen, living room, and hallway.

In her mind, she tracks them, listening for their footsteps, their voices, the sighing of the floor or creaking of doorframes. Cupboards open and close in the kitchen. One of them makes his way down the hallway, checks the bathroom, the storage closet. One, two, three steps down the hall, toward her. She breathes steadily, gripping the handgun with her signature calmness. She acknowledges that the first shot she fires will be akin to that of the starting gun at a track meet, setting the ball rolling but with the purpose of survival rather than achievement.

Of course, her reputation for steady consistency isn't

unwarranted. She's aware of this; the stories speak for themselves.

Maybe it's innate, but Esther is sure that her faux stability grew out of necessity as a result of holding herself together during Don's particularly bad rages. Putting on a face for the kids was a feat requiring more strength than any situation she's gotten herself into since. No number of guns or knives or threats has managed to instill in her the same intensity and volume of fear that she had when Don stormed around the house with a wrench, a belt, a spoon, whatever was arm's length away when his ever-tricky wire was tripped.

This has always raised obvious questions in her mind: would she have been able to contribute as much as she has to the well-being of other abuse victims had it not been for this on-call hard exterior to employ in the scenarios that drip with intensity? Would she have been able to navigate the tricky, delicate mazes in which she's found herself throughout her subsequent years?

She hates to admit it, but maybe some good did come from Don's life, if only by empowering her (and Remy, as she recently found out) to fight him and the filthy business in which he operated. Even if he had been the festering pile of shit he was, maybe his life had the silver lining of catalyzing the rise of those willing and able to fight it. To have inflicted such a wound upon the morality of humanity that the antibodies swarm to action, lending the whole their strength and immunity.

Esther waits in the closet, breathing.

In-two-three-four-five, *out*-two-three-four-five.

The bedroom door opens. They sneak as well as they can, but their weight on the floor causes that soft *fmm-fmm* on the

carpet. She feels their presence as much as hears it. One just outside the closet. If he slides the door open, she'll aim, fire. The
other waits by the door. She wishes she knew how tall he is; then
she could be just that much more prepared for the draw.

She becomes more aware of the gun in her hands, its weight,
its power—both familiar.

The closet door slides open. He's about an inch taller than
she.

Bang.

In the darkness, the man's blood and brains come out as an
inky black mess, painting a ghastly splatter on the wall above
Todd and Remy's headboard.

The second guy's voice comes from the door way: "Oh shi—
"

Bang.

This one's blood and being end up on the hallway wall; he
didn't have time to make it fully into the room before Esther put
a round into his face. Now the intense part: the life-or-death version of hide and seek. She knows that there are more, but she
doesn't know where, or how many. Beyond that, she doesn't
know whether or not they know where she is. Her best option is
to capitalize on her biggest asset: that she knows the lay of the
land, both inside and out.

She briefly considers escaping through the window she
opened in Remy and Todd's room, but she doesn't like the prospect of clambering through the open frame while holding a
loaded gun. The hall closet tempts her for the briefest moment,

but it would only be safe if they only had one more person. If there are multiple more, as she suspects, she could end up check-mating herself, pinning herself into a tight place with too many surrounding adversaries.

The kitchen has the opposite problem: too many entrances and exits. There are no hiding places out of sight from the windows and doorways, unless she hides in a cupboard—no better than the hall closet.

She then remembers the attic, with its two entrances. One entrance is in the kitchen—definitely not ideal—and the other is above the powder room just off the living room, at the end of the hall. If she can get up into it in time, without being noticed, she can creep around up there and make decisive moves without occupying herself with whether she's vulnerable to nearby doors and windows. If memory serves, the attic doesn't have any windows, so she won't have to worry about her flashlight being seen from outside, either.

This is enough for Esther. She slips into the powder room without being noticed and locks the door behind her. She climbs onto the counter and pulls the square door open before hoisting herself up and into it. As she replaces the door behind her, she hears more people, more footsteps, more voices. She's glad she didn't choose the closet.

The men file into the house, filling it like water flowing into an empty vessel. There are a *lot* more than Esther anticipated. Their footsteps sound less like their previous pitter patter and more like a thundering stampede.

Where did they all come from? Are there really that many

of…whoever they are? How on earth are they still organizing and mobilizing so effectively with both Keroth and Perkins out of the picture? Is their hierarchy really so deep and well structured that they can reform and regroup so quickly? And how in the hell is she supposed to handle this many of them? And if she does, will they just keep coming, in greater and greater numbers?

"Where the fuck did she go?" a voice yells. Again begins the process of cupboard and cabinet doors opening and closing, doors slamming, and the inevitable flurry of profanities.

Esther hears the door handle rattle in the powder room below her and hopes that she didn't accidentally leave any evidence of her escape into the attic; any fallen drywall dust could betray her.

As she expected, they immediately start slamming into the bathroom door; if it's locked, she must be in there, right? The first crash is loud and accompanied by the crackle of a splintering door frame. The second brings the door down, tumbling into the tiny washroom.

Good, she thinks, *if I left a mess behind, their own will disguise it.*

"She's not in here," says a voice. It's loud, powerful, like a lion roaring through a human's body. Esther knows right away that that's the guy in charge of this onslaught. She is drawn to the idea of hiding out in the attic until they leave, but she's too aware of the wake of destruction these people are prone to leaving. They won't just get bored and take off; they'll get bored, blow the place up, *then* take off. This leaves her with two options: take them all on or escape. Fight or flight. Their numbers are so great, though, that she has little confidence in either option. But she'll have to make a choice eventually. Before they make it for her. She listens to them flitting and swarming about, turning the house inside out in their fervent hunt.

Even if she turns into some action hero, dodging bullets while simultaneously landing her own rounds in people's heads, how many does she have left? Fourteen. Even if every shot lands and kills its target, she may well run out of ammunition before she manages to down them all. She could use their own weapons against them, but that's hard enough in theory and even more so in execution. By no means can she rely on that as an out.

But the more she thinks about it, the more she realizes that it's her only real option. She circles back through her options a couple more times (she considers calling the police, but more than likely they will have blazed through the house in its completeness before any help arrives anyway—not to mention that the sheer number of people here dwarfs the readily available police force in this tiny town), but her options allow for no wiggle room. Plus, she needs to commit to some sort of plan quickly; the seconds tick by with the insistent urgency of a flatlining cardiograph.

With that in mind, she listens closely, willing her mind's map to populate itself with these men's locations once again. The harder she concentrates, the more acutely she's able to pick out where the noises come from. In a moment, the sounds go from a frustrating onslaught of thumps and grunts to an intricate series of more identifiable noises—the cupboard next to the fridge slamming closed, the closet door squeaking open and closed, then again as someone else searches the same place.

By isolating these sounds in her mind, she's more readily able to pick out the pairs of shuffling feet. Three in the living room, four in the kitchen. Two wandering in the hallway. She only hears muffled sounds from the bedroom.

And none in the powder room.

Of course, she can only sense the ones who are moving or otherwise making noise, so she makes a mental note to allow for the possibility of more bodies than she counts now.

Esther uses a small pocket flashlight to illuminate the cramped attic. Webs hang like morbid streamers above and dust has piled up in a thick film, but the crossbeams are sturdy, and she manages to crawl across them without making the snapping and creaking noises she feared.

She stops to listen, still aware of time looming over her like a colossal tidal wave threatening to crash down and wash her away at any moment.

If she can shift the trapdoor—just an inch or so—without drawing their attention, she can start picking them off from above.

Esther once read that the human ears have great difficulty locating a noise that comes from above them. She hasn't yet had opportunity to test this out for herself, but she hopes it's true.

As soon as her gunfire draws return fire, she'll have to retreat to the deeper corner of the attic, and she can drop down into the restroom, around the corner from them; hopefully they won't have the deductive skills to infer that that's where the other entrance is. With timing, skill, a calm mind, and a shitload of luck, Esther Thorn may yet see another tomorrow.

Nineteen

As slowly as she can, she works her nails into the groove, digging deeper to get a good grip, pausing every couple of seconds to listen for changes in their movement or speech patterns, but senses none.

After a minute that seems like several, she has the cover pried loose enough that she can pull it away. She gives it a small tug, but quickly realizes that it'll take more than a small tug. A bead of sweat forms on her brow and slides down her nose, tickling her on its way down. She crouches and braces herself so as to maximize her leverage and control, a tricky act in itself while retaining her grip on the door and trying to make as little noise as possible.

She tightens her core and heaves the door. It moves this time, and faster than she anticipates. Panic grips her for a brief moment, but she regains control—of herself and of the door—quickly. No changes in their movements.

She takes a deep breath and kneels over the cover, awkwardly positioning herself to keep her weight on the crossbeams. The crack in the door allows her to hear them more clearly, assigning individual words to the various tones she's been hearing. As she further poises herself, she can see the men in the kitchen.

Two guys that look like they don't see much of the sun—or the shower—stand side by side, anxiously looking about in every direction but up. A burly man with short hair and a short beard leans against the table. He doesn't move his head, but his eyes are hardly as stationary; they make laps around the room quickly, but as with the others, they don't look up.

The pale ones would probably be safe to leave for after the burly guy; they seem the types to panic and freeze. The thick one seems like he would be most prepared to react. He'll be her first target.

A voice rises form the living room: "If we find her, do we get to have some fun with her before we kill her?"

The burly guy answers, "Oh, you know I'll make her my bit—"

Bang.

The cave-dwellers still have stupid smiles on their faces when the body hits the floor. As Esther expected, they both begin looking around with the intense paranoia of wounded cat, baffled that the windows are still intact, apparently certain that the shot must have come from outside, despite the volume of it.

One of them is moving, but the other seems too shocked.

Bang.

Thing One drops almost immediately; the shot hits him in the chest, and he has just enough time to spot Esther and widen his eyes in shock before the life fades from them. Luckily, he's out before he's able to call out or point to Esther's position.

This time, Thing Two freezes, and the others are beginning to gather in the kitchen, confusion spreading among them. Briefly, Esther wonders whether she herself would have the presence of mind to look up if she were in their shoes.

She assesses that she can still get a few more shots off before they notice her. Fortunately for her, the ones that are calmest, and thus the biggest threats to her hiding, are also the most still, making them the easiest targets.

Bang. Bang. Bang.

The three of them drop and the panic deepens. Esther's target practice surfaces in full force. The rapid fire, technical series of shots allowed by her semi-automatic feels like home.

Bang. Bang. Bang. Bang.

If the men in the kitchen are all who remain in the house, as Esther suspects, there are eight more. But Esther only has five more rounds in her weapon, so even though she may have the positioning to take them out, she doesn't have the ammunition. But maybe she could sneak out the back window in the midst of the chaos. In that case, should she use any more ammo here, or should she instead preserve it in case she encounters any of them on her way out?

She looks down through her thin crack. There are eight more men in the kitchen, all of them contributing to a cacophony of excited yelling that lands in Esther's ears as a muffled sort of roar.

In such loud circumstances, she's much less likely to be heard clambering over the crossbeams, so she hastens back toward the door through which she entered. That door is much lighter, and she lifts it out of its frame with ease.

Esther's arms strain as she lowers herself to the counter, a moment of uncomfortable vulnerability while she tries to make as little noise as possible. There's plenty of chaos to help disguise her, but with the door blasted off its hinges and lying among the bits of splintered wood on the bathroom floor, she still has to be careful about the amount of noise she makes; their own frenzied confusion will only mask so many decibels. The door leans against the counter at an awkward angle, forcing Esther to first drop onto the counter instead of aiming for the floor, then to make a little hop through the doorway.

She allows herself only the shortest second to look toward the kitchen area as she turns left to go toward the bedroom. Just as they were ten, fifteen seconds ago, they're looking out the window, their faces pressed up against it to block out the reflected glare of the kitchen light.

The words 'impressively stupid' streak through Esther's mind as she rushes through the hallway toward the back bedroom. Once inside, she waits for a few seconds to see whether anyone saw and followed her; she'd rather be aware and be able to stop and fight them than have her back turned to them as she tried to climb out of the window. But no one comes.

Do they have the numbers and presence of mind to maintain a perimeter around the house, or is the entirety of the onslaught contained in the kitchen, wondering where Esther disappeared to?

In either case, she doesn't have much of an option other than to flee. Sirens pierce the dry desert air; maybe the neighbors heard the gunshots and called it in. Esther is sure that she made the police's job quite a lot easier. At least, in terms of not getting mown down by fully automatics upon arriving on scene. The bloodbath will probably warrant quite a lot of paperwork, though. But better paperwork than the alternative. Esther has no doubts that these guys would have massacred the tiny Wometzia police force. She's seen it before.

She heaves herself up and through the window, hitting the dirt with a flat crunch. She wishes that she were wearing more appropriate shoes for running, but she didn't really get the notice necessary for such preparation; bloodthirsty perverts don't often RSVP.

Esther has yet another decision to make: run out into the desert or deeper into town? The prospect of the desert deters her quickly; too harsh, both at night and during the day. The drawback of running into town is that she may bring the chaos with her, but that's an inherent risk no matter where she chooses to go. If they expect her to go into town, she may as well *actually* go into town and be able to help if they make their way there.

So Esther sets off, squinting in the moonlight to try to step on the most tightly packed patches of dirt so as to minimize the noise she makes and to secure her footing.

Careful not to let herself be illuminated by passing cars' headlights, street lights, or the occasional pool of light spilling out from a back window or a security light, Esther eases her way into Wometzia's heart.

Dodging through the shadows, she thinks. *If I survive this, maybe Remy and I can bond over it.* The thought is facetious, but she holds onto it in a grim, austere way.

The sirens' scream fills the night air, fills it right up, like Wometzia has never seen before. Well, except for the night Remy left, about a month ago. Maybe tonight will be the end of it, and

Wometzia will return to its warm, sleepy tranquility after to-night—however it ends up resolving.

After she makes it farther into the city, she's lost for where, specifically, to go. She can't go to the police station (though that would have been her first instinct); they'll definitely hunt her there, if they have any bodies to spare. She doesn't know anyone, either. This is the result of not wanting to expose herself or en-danger anyone, reinforced solidly by the tidal wave of apathetic depression that swallowed her when Remy and Todd and Odin left. She could go get a room at the bed and breakfast, but she suspects that she may be found there, too.

She could hotwire a car and drive away, disappear just as her son did—just as she herself has done so many times, starting with abandoning Remy (he was Jeremy back then) and Trina all those years ago.

Not this time, no. Esther is so good at running away that she's confident she could make it up to the Canadian border with-out being caught. She knows she could, but…then what?

In that moment, difficult as it is, Esther decides to stay and fight—to assist in the eradication of these monsters. Her work has been important, no doubt, but never as anything more than an escape artist. The time to don her armor and stop playing from the shadows is now.

This moment, Esther stands in a mostly dirt lot, winded but not without the capacity to continue. Her resolution sharpens in her mind, strengthens. Permitting herself to feel such unfiltered emotion opens the way for one she didn't anticipate: retribution.

This time taking a lighted path, Esther sets off, back toward Remy and Todd's house.

TWENTY

REMY

I sit cross-legged on the floor of our apartment. The transition from 'my apartment' to 'our apartment' was fast, easy, and welcome, like a car pulling into its warm, sheltered space in the garage after being out in an unforgiving snow storm all day.

Even in an entirely new place (again), Odin settles quite quickly as well, evidently sharing in our sentiment that home is made by people, not geography. After polishing off a bowl of his favorite food (they didn't stock it in Wometzia, so its availability here may have played some role in his settling in so fast), he licks his muzzle, stretches out, and lies down with his head on my lap. He may appear intimidating to others, but this little softie is just here to melt hearts. Scratching Odin's head with my left hand and holding Todd's hand in my right, a sense of correctness settles in my mind like a nesting bird.

Until a small tinge of unrest prods at me from the unreachable void spaces of my mind, like that rogue tickle at the back of one's throat that they *swear* they've imagined until the full force of strep throat cripples them the next day.

These days, however, it's not uncommon for this kind of anxiety to show itself, and my brain seems to specialize in the kinds of obsessions with no immediate solutions—or, in this case, no immediate *problem*. Even so, I flick through the familiar checklist in my mind: Todd is here, safe, with me. Odin is slipping into a comfortable doze.

I consider calling Beth, but I'm still not familiar with how far this whole thing spreads. If it's far enough that they're watching Beth's phone, a call to her would invite throngs of these guys in a matter of hours, I'm sure.

But god I miss her.

Perhaps sensing that discomfort, Todd gives my hand a firm squeeze, scoots closer to me, and puts his arm around me. Todd has always been good at laying waste to my worries and insecurities, but even as I settle into him, I feel the persistent ember of doubt burrowing into my psyche, and even the rhythmic tranquility of Todd's breathing and heartbeat aren't enough to stamp it out entirely, each inhalation laced with the potential for some destruction yet unknown to me.

Even so, my position between Odin and Todd is a far sight more comfortable—physically and emotionally—than has been my standard over the past month, and even in the dull progression of the evening, I haven't felt so alive since the day I left. The events in the coming days—or weeks or months or years, even—remain unknown to me, and while I'm not exactly okay with that, I also don't have a solution to it; while Todd is skilled in speculation of the future and recollection of the past, he is not clairvoyant, and I am less so.

The lazy morning had blurred into a lazy afternoon with an anxious anticipation in the apartment—thrilling and with a sense of unrest, like cresting a tall roller coaster. Now, the day and evening have bled into night, where time always seems to hold still. Without the sun's rays moving, intensifying, and relenting, night's uniform inky darkness makes the world seem still and calm.

And then it's morning. Friday morning. The plan to have Todd pose as a journalist has the hidden benefit of not having to fit him with a concealed microphone. Instead, he can use his phone as a recorder and worry about it no further. Nothing to hide.

"What does a journalist even wear?" he calls from the bathroom, his speech obstructed by the toothbrush in his mouth. Odin sits in the corner, watching us both, picking up on the anticipatory static in the air. Todd rifles through a few of his clothes, tossing each aside as he deems it unfit for the task.

"I have a casual jacket on a hanger in the closet," I say. "Wear that with whatever shirt goes best with it. Maybe some slacks, but jeans will probably do. She'll be expecting more of a hipster look anyway, I'd imagine."

"Done and done." He finishes dressing quickly. "What do you think?"

Todd always manages to look better in my clothes than I do.

"Fabulous," I say with a wink.

Todd smiles and steps in front of the mirror to do his hair, then checks his watch. "I'd better be going. Wish me luck."

"Good luck," I say.

A knot I've been trying to ignore tightens in my stomach.

Last night, Todd asked me what I'm going to do with myself today. I told him I'd go with him, but he refused on account of the unknown number of people hunting me down. I hate it, but he's right; even if I committed to staying in the background, there's no guarantee that I'd be able to conceal myself to a satisfying degree. So, instead, I resolved to busy myself with tidying up the apartment. A part of me thinks into the future, of building a life with Todd here, but another, more hopeful, part dreams about being able to return to Riverdell, to the mild weather and to Beth. I long for this to be over, more than anything.

I kiss Todd goodbye and he heads out the door, and I amuse myself with how absurdly similar we would probably have looked to a normal couple—sure, this is me, just sending Todd off to work, getting ready to be the homemaker for the day.

Except Todd is going to interrogate a potentially dangerous suspect in a decades-old murder case and I'm going to spend the entire day itching for him to return.

Unlike me, Creed is free to be seen by anyone he pleases, so he is going to accompany Todd on this errand. Of course, he won't sit in on the interview, or even make it known that he and Todd know each other, but he'll stand by in a shop in the courtyard where Todd set up the meeting with Ginger.

The day, time, and place were all deliberate. Around noon on a beautiful Friday like this, that courtyard is sure to be bustling with hungry patrons eager to have their last lunch before the weekend. In that much noise, Ginger will have less to fear in terms of passersby overhearing what she says, and if she becomes agitated, there will be far too many witnesses around for her to do anything.

Many people find comfort and purpose in being busy; the tasks they assign their minds and hands are enough to pull them out of whatever else is on their mind, even if only for long enough to complete the task. For some, this is an effective catharsis. For me, it's a slow and frustrating torture, akin to the famous Chinese water torture. Busying my hands only creates a sort of background noise for my mind, allowing the rest of it to go wild with the possibilities of what's happening in Cheyenne. I'll keep checking my phone for updates throughout the morning.

But for now, nothing. I suppose I won't hear anything until this afternoon, if even then. Hell, the car ride alone will take up most of what remains of the morning.

Cleaning is a bust. I toss the rag into the laundry room and surrender, resolving instead to spend the rest of the morning with Odin. Surely, I could take him for a walk. We only need to slip into the woods, and if we go now, we'll have a nice, long time to be out before most people get off work. Todd must have forgotten his leash, but no matter—Odin is well trained and won't stray far, if at all, and he always comes when called. We head out the door.

Once outside, I look around to see if any passersby are around, but the lot is deserted and quiet. Upon setting off, I decide to go back to the cottage in the woods to see if I can figure anything else out from what's up there. Plus, it's a long enough distance away that it will give Odin some good exercise.

The sense of bated breath and anxious anticipation from last night persists into the day, even more palpable now that I'm not experiencing it through the soothing filter of Todd's presence.

Something big is going to happen today. I do my best to brush the thought aside; after all, of *course* something big is going to happen today, with Todd and Creed doing their business in Cheyenne.

Something bad *is going to happen today,* the voice persists.

Nonsense. This is just my well-practiced and well-lubricated anxiety roaring to life, flexing its muscles, baring its fangs. Even if something bad *does* happen today, I have no way of knowing that now. Plus, Odin seems happy, and if there is some sixth sense that picks up on impending doom, I'd sooner trust that of a canine than my own.

Odin makes more noise than I do trotting through the tall grass, what with having twice as many legs that aren't quite long enough to hold his chest and body over it. He wades almost as much as walks through this grass.

As we approach the cottage, Odin tenses and growls. At first, I think perhaps there's a squirrel, another dog, or even a bear or mountain lion nearby, but as it is, Odin is unmistakably glaring in the direction of the cottage, hackles raised. I kneel down next to him and scratch his neck to soothe him, but that doesn't work this time. His lean, strong body is rigid and focused. So much for my dog's happy demeanor.

Could it be Creed's scent? Maybe Creed's undercover work had, at one point, involved getting in close enough quarters with Odin that the pup picked up the scent. But then, wouldn't he have smelled it on me over the past couple of days? That can't be it.

Then maybe it's someone else. Maybe we're not as safe as

Todd and Creed thought.

I creep across the porch and press myself against the outer wall; if there is someone inside, I don't want them to be able to see me without coming outside themselves. I pull out my phone and see that I have no new messages or missed calls.

I tap out a quick message to Creed, asking about anyone coming by the cottage, then make sure my phone is on silent to ensure that, if someone is inside, they don't hear my phone buzz with the reply.

Fortunately, my phone lights up within the minute and displays Creed's reply: "Nobody's been by but you and Todd."

My phone then lights up with another text message: "My my, it looks like you've been busy."

It's from the number that was texting me before—not my mother, but the one telling me not to trust her. I decide to humor them this time—perhaps I'll be able to pull some clues out and figure out who it is.

"No more than usual. Probably less than usual, in fact." I hit 'Send.'

The reply is swift: "You didn't trust me before."

"Nor do I now."

"Shame."

I wait a minute for another text or further explanation, maybe an appeal for my trust now, but none comes. But I need to keep them engaged. If danger really is set to unfold, I need to milk any source I have for all the information I can.

"Should I have?" I finally type.

"Should have then, and should now." I can rule out anyone I ever formerly texted with regularity—none of them would have omitted subjects or even pronouns like that.

"Why is that?"

"Your lover, your friend, your mother—your whole world, really—they're about to meet an end."

"You told me not to trust my other stalker before, but that turned out to be someone helping me." My heart pumps fiercely, and for that reason, I'm glad that this conversation is taking place over text rather than in person. I can't lose Todd again. And while my relationship with my mom is tenuous, I've been warming up to her over time, and for once, I've been able to envision a happy future for it. I can't lose her, either.

I have difficulty reading the reply, as I'm shaky and a bit sweaty now.

"Yes, I learned about her identity shortly afterward. That's why I backed off—I knew you were in good hands."

"But I'm not anymore?"

"Those hands aren't available right now."

What the hell does that mean?

"So what now?" I know that I can't just trust them based on this conversation, but it can't hurt to hear them out. Even if their whole goal is to lead me into a trap, I'll have some insight into their resources and how they've allocated them.

"Are you armed?" My heartbeat doesn't relent. I don't know

whether to lie, but if I do, I don't even know which way to go. If this really is an ally and I tell them I'm armed, I may just be sent on my way into the crossfire of a crazy shootout. But if it's an enemy and I tell them that I'm *not* armed, they know I'm a sitting duck. I sigh and decide just to tell the truth.

"Just with my pistol." I guess that qualifies as a happy medium. Not armed to the teeth, but still able to defend myself if I must.

"That'll do, for now. One of Keroth's old cohorts is in Ghost Fork, and I suspect that more are on their way."

"How many?"

"I'm still working on that. Their numbers are dwindling, though, it seems."

Huh. I wonder if watching their leaders be put in prison or shot in the face might make them want out of that whole business.

"Why's that?"

"It looks like the result of your handiwork, in addition to your mother's."

"My mother's?"

"Get some firepower and find a place to lie low in town. They'll be coming from the west, but they won't be there for a couple of hours."

"And what am I supposed to do, just put a clip into the next car that rolls in from that direction?"

"Do what you need to, Remy."

Whoever it is knows that I don't go by Jeremy.

"Who are you?"

But I'm left with no answer, save for the calling birds and whispering winds.

Phasing back into reality, I draw my weapon and head around to the window. When entering a potentially hostile area, a window is a fair bit riskier than a door; you're left clambering through a hole without the cover of the door itself. However, I should have a reasonable vantage point from the window, and I can visually clear the room before I climb in.

Somebody else has definitely been here. There are Todd's and my footprints, and Creed's from when we forced him to enter downstairs rather than upstairs, but then there's a set of humongous prints that sweep more than step from one to the next, like he has a bad limp but in both legs. Beyond that, there's only one set, leading upstairs. My quarry (or perhaps my hunter) is still in the house, unless he took a different exit, and if so, I'll have no trouble finding where.

I remind myself that I could still turn around and walk away—there's a good chance that it's just another curious soul, shuffling along and exploring, just as I was not long ago. But then again, my *new* mystery texter alerted me that someone from that crew was in town, and I don't know how he would have known to look here, but this has been our meeting place of sorts for some time now, so it shouldn't surprise me that someone might come looking for us here.

Vanishing as one person is easy enough, but there are three people hiding here, and we all traveled separately, offering triple the opportunities to have been spotted or followed.

I climb in through the window and Odin jumps in after me, the light fur on his broad chest just grazing the pane as he does so. His landing is muffled, but the *sk-sk-sk* of his clawed feet still cuts through the quiet. The footsteps do an awkward sort of fox-trot in the living room, then patter off to the kitchen, where they circle back toward the stairs. The prints are harder to find on the stairs, with so much more concentrated traffic, but I am able to pick them out, even in the limited light.

I climb the stairs, and the upstairs hallway is too dark to see any more prints, but I don't bother anyway—I head straight for the Willa Frye room, its door closed. I stand outside of it, keeping myself as quiet as I can manage, and listen for any noise.

Silence.

I'm about to open the door when I hear movement from inside. I step back and crouch against the wall, my gun trained on the doorway, but it remains closed. Then I hear a voice from inside—a gruff, serious-sounding voice that rattles through the air like a marble in a blender.

"I don't like this. I don't like not knowin' why I do what I do."

A silence follows—he must be on the phone.

"Part of the job, sure—I don't ask questions, usually—but I've been hearing things, picking things up, and I don't think I can do it."

"I don't give a shit if your business depends on it, I don't give a shit if your *life* depends on it. I'm not doing it. Go fuck yourself."

He sighs and I hear a thump. Odin senses and catches on to my quiet and follows suit. Then I do what I've been trying to tell myself not to do the whole time: I knock on the door.

"What the fuck?" the guy mutters. "Who's there?" he calls.

"I think you and I might have some answers for each other," I say.

His conversation led me to think that this guy was hired on as some muscle for this mess. If that's the case, I just listened to him tell someone on the Keroth side of the field to go fuck himself, and that's the kind of guy I want on my side.

"Who are you?"

"Remy."

There's a silence for a moment—my name is significant to him. I back away from the door in case he comes charging, changes his mind and decides that he wants whatever money he was offered. Instead, there's the sound of shifting weight and the floorboards creaking. The door swings open, and a massive silhouette fills the doorway. His hands are at his side, without weapons in them.

"Remy, huh?" the man says. "So what makes you so fuckin' important someone was willing to pay two hundred thousand to blow your head off?"

"Probably that I put one pervert in jail and shot another one in the head."

"Perverts," he says, "like that Eboncore guy?" He gestures inward, toward the room and its obsessive décor.

"We're working on that one," I say.

"Working on it how?"

"Well, a lot of that case seemed fishy to us, so we're looking into it. But yes, perverts like that. I don't know who, specifically, hired you. Probably they didn't tell you anything valuable, either. But what we're up against is pretty big. It started in Oregon."

I pause for a moment, to give him opportunity to interject or stop me if he wishes, but he only nods and cocks his head a bit, so I tell him the entire story of Riverdell and Portland, Wometzia and Albuquerque, and how I ended up in Ghost Fork. When I've finished catching him up, he raises his eyebrows and exhales a gust through his nose. But still, he doesn't say anything more.

"So you're what, a hitman?" I ask.

He looks up and meets my eye. "Something like that. Hitman, mercenary. People with money come to me to do their dirty work. Some work is dirtier than others. But this...I can't be a part of this. My no-questions-asked policy is what brought in all of my business, but if that's what I'm a part of, I don't know that I can keep it up."

"You could always play for the good guys," I say.

He chuffs. "The good guys. Good guys and bad guys. Cops and robbers. Us versus them. When I was little, I thought it was easy. So black and white. They make it that way, you know, in books and TV shows. There's no question as to who the bad guy is. It's Wile E. Coyote, it's the dragon, it's the dog chasing the cat or the cat chasing the mouse. But life was quick to show me the extent of my naiveté. It all gets blurred when the people you love, the people who are close to you, are doing the same things as you see the bad guys doing on television. Then you start to think,

'Shit, maybe he's got a good reason for doing what he does.' And before you know it, you see it everywhere. You start to see the ulterior motives of the supposed good guys, and you start to give the benefit of the doubt to the supposed bad guys. I realized pretty fast that it's not so black and white, but we're all just muddled, splotchy gray."

I nod. "So what did you do with that insight?" I ask.

He shakes his head. "I just stopped caring. When you take the good and evil labels off of things, it becomes a lot easier to justify certain actions. I guess that's what started me on the path to where I am now. I figured if these people wanted to hire someone to do something, they would. Being the tool that they chose for that didn't bother me. Until now, I guess."

"I'm sure you're not a stranger to dark shit like this," I say, "but there's a difference between darkness and evil. Darkness is neutral. I don't mind darkness—I prefer it, even. But it doesn't have an agenda. It doesn't aim to kill or hurt, or to rob children of their innocence. It doesn't vie to proliferate or benefit from people's misfortune. It isn't greed or envy. It just is. Evil, on the other hand, is exactly those things. It wants only for itself, to gain and to grow and to spread, to create more evil."

The man doesn't say anything, but leans against the doorframe and nods, crossing his arms.

In a psychology class I once took, we were taught that crossing one's arms is a sign of a defensive state of mind. While I don't think this is inaccurate, I do think that this is often misinterpreted. When people appoint themselves as Body Language Experts, they'll see a person cross their arms and assume that the person is lying or trying to hide something, but that's seldom the case. In fact, as I've found, it's often a sign that they're confronting an uncomfortable truth. These uncomfortable truths make us feel vulnerable, and crossing our arms is a natural way to suppress those feelings of vulnerability. It's a way to feel safe.

"I suppose you probably won't tell me your name," I say.

"No way in hell," he says.

"Fair. So, what's next for you?"

"I have some thinking to do."

"I won't have to worry about running into you during this storm, will I?"

He laughs, a surprisingly pleasant chuckle, but not without the painful undertone of a wound reopened. "No. Y'know, it's a little strange. A week ago, I was pumped full of adrenaline, ready to find you and tear you apart. I would've enjoyed it, even, just thinking about the money I'd be earning. That's all it woulda been to me, you know?"

I know.

"Well, take care," I say, "and maybe stay off of Needle Point Boulevard. I think that's where your reinforcements are supposed to be coming in. Any idea how many there'll be?"

"Not many. From what it sounds like, something happened last night that really fucked them up."

"Last night?"

"Yeah. In New Mexico."

What the hell?

Apparently reading my look, he goes on: "Yeah. Some lady they were after shot 'em up big time. Took out like half of 'em. Not just half of those who showed up, either. Half of…whoever they are. That's why they hired me. They're skeleton crew right now."

"…Oh shit."

"I know, right? Crazy stuff you're mixed up in."

"I should go. Nice to meet you, and thank you for not killing me."

"Uhh, yeah, sure," he says. He grips his weapon one more time in what seems like an attempted comeback from the part of him that still wants to kill me, but he loosens his grip and drops the gun just as abruptly. He seems taken aback by my sudden urgency, but I have neither the time nor the capacity to explain what this could mean.

But just what all *is* involved here? My mother. I don't know what happened, but there was some kind of crazy shootout and she was involved. And by the sound of it, she handily decimated the mercenaries sent after her. How did they find her? Who did they send? And what the fuck happened?

I turn around and head back downstairs and out the window, back toward the heart of Ghost Fork, Odin trotting dutifully at my side.

TWENTY-ONE

ESTHER

LAST NIGHT

Esther watches the police zoom by, three squad cars screeching through the night, the red and blue lights just shy of painting the undersides of the clouds overhead. She jogs to catch up, hoping to warn them before they take any action that might get them killed.

She breathes quickly, but her body and mind are far from spent, and she ups her speed little by little until she's nearly sprinting. The wind playing at her hair and ears seems to be whispering encouragement to her, further filling her with the full-bodied strength of her essence—robust and strong, firm, unrelenting, and capable of love.

Powerful.

Thanks to Wometzia's small size, Esther manages to catch up to the squad cars before anything has happened. She makes sure to call attention to herself before she approaches, lest she accidentally take them by surprise and end up getting shot after all. She waves to attract the attention of Officer Kent, the cornerstone to Wometzia's police force.

Officer Kent looks to Esther wide-eyed and motions for her to duck behind one of the cars, where Kent herself comes to meet her.

"What the hell is happening? I thought you would've been inside, pumped full of lead by now!"

"That's definitely what they were hoping for," says Esther. The words come as easily and steadily as a canoe floating on a glassy lake. "I was inside, but I managed to escape. Not without a few...casualties, though."

"How many?" asks Kent, her eyebrows raised.

"...Eleven," says Esther.

"You and I are going to have a long talk after this is through. For now, just try to stay out of sight, okay?"

"You got it," says Esther. She means it, but she doesn't think Officer Kent would approve of how she intends to fulfill that promise.

Esther watches as Kent makes her way to Officer Simpson and begins talking with him in the hushed, serious tone with which Esther is all too familiar. She can't hear the words, but Kent delivers them in a calm but direct manner that seems to instill confidence even in Officer Simpson's nervous mind. After she finishes talking with him, she comes back to Esther, still in her crouch.

"How many more were there?" she asks Esther.

"A dozen or so. More, maybe."

"Christ. You people sure know how to piss other people off."

"It's in the name."

"Who are these guys, exactly?"

"Same as last time. The group that wants to find Remy and gut him for putting one of their leaders in jail and shooting the other one in the face."

"I guess they're not the forgiving type, then?"

"Doesn't seem like it. If you have reinforcements—or a SWAT team—it might be a good idea to call them in."

Officer Kent nods, then returns to Simpson to relay the plan. Reinforcements will have to come from Albuquerque, nearly an hour away—even ignoring speed limits. Esther doesn't know whether the rest of the men in the house will be able to sit still for that long, but she also doesn't intend to let the sand run out of that hourglass.

She kicks herself for not having armed herself better, but she reminds herself that she hadn't had the time to do so properly. She had hidden a few firearms around the house, like the one she has with her, but they're all inside, and accessing them would mean either approaching the house from the front, which would be the equivalent of red target waltzing up the length of the shooting range, or to sneak around to the back. The latter sounds like a decent option, but because that's where she escaped, it's probably being watched more intently now.

Adjusting to assist the flow of blood in her legs, Esther looks on toward the house from behind the squad car. They've turned off the kitchen light—smart. It almost looks like they've since taken off, but as Esther focuses, she picks up small bits of movement through the kitchen window—shiny objects glinting in the light for a split second, the quick wink of the oven's clock as someone moves in front of it and out of its way again. The whole property seems to be alive and festering, desperately longing to breathe again. *Save me, Esther. Heal me. Purge me of this evil.*

With only a few rounds left in her gun, however, there's little she can do. She briefly considers trying to steal a weapon from the officers, but is deterred by a vision of Officer Kent intending to draw her weapon and defend herself only to find her holster empty.

Maybe she can find a way to get one of the ones she's hidden in the house. There's one more in the kitchen—a tiny revolver perfect for a bad soap opera—tucked behind a sack of rice in the pantry. But the kitchen is definitely off-limits. There are two in the bedroom, one in the living room, and one in the bathroom. The living room is adjacent to the kitchen and is thus also a no-go. The one in the bathroom isn't very accessible, either.

In the bedroom, one is attached to the inside of a lip in the woodwork of the headboard. The other is underneath an armoire—right next to the open window. She reminds herself of the dangers of approaching the house from behind, but thinking about it now, she doubts that they would have very many people watching it anyway. And if she can find a way to divert their attention, even for a few seconds, she can get in, get her weapon, and get back out.

Before she knows it, she is backing away from the vehicle and circling around the side of the property, opting to close in on its east side—its only accessible window is in the bathroom, and it's both too high up and too opaque to be useful to anyone on the inside looking out. Still, she tries to keep her face hidden—a pale face is so often what gives people away in the dark.

She reaches the house quickly and listens for any sort of reaction from the inside. They're making a surprising amount of noise, but nothing rushed or panicked, as it would be if they'd spotted her.

She creeps toward the back and peeks around the corner. Nobody is there, as she expected. Before moving, she stops once more to listen for noise. She hears a couple of voices floating from inside the window. Once again, she can't pick out any individual words, but their voices sound fearful, almost reverent.

Good.

As Esther approaches the window, hugging the wall, the night goes still. The tiny, whimsical breeze that has been playing at her hair dies down and the clouds overhead, previously churning with the threat of a thunderstorm, seem to halt and freeze, as though they themselves don't want to miss this. Esther's footsteps crunch in the dirt and echo off the wall. She times them to the rhythm of the conversation inside in order to mask the noise.

She crouches even lower than before as she approaches the window. She can hear their conversation now, as clearly as if she were standing in between them.

"What if she comes back?" says one of them.

"I don't know, man."

"She took out *half of us*. They said this would be a quick job."

248

"With this many of us, it was supposed to be."

"How on earth did we fuck this one up?"

"She's good, man. We knew that coming in. JT said from the beginning we probably wouldn't all come back. And now look where we are."

"Where's JT anyway?"

"Went out to look for her, I think."

"I hope to god he finds her."

"Me, too. Before she finds him, at least. Or us."

Only two of them, it seems. Perfect. All Esther has to do is be consistent in her usual accuracy and hit rate (or even half of it), and she'll be able to grab the piece and run before anyone can get into the room. Still crouching against the window, she breathes slowly, steadily, hoping to invite in the sense of know-ingness she had earlier, when she could visualize exactly where the intruders were.

But it doesn't come. *I guess I'll just have to be quick on the draw,* she thinks.

Crouching beneath the center of the window, Esther stands up and sees them: a gangly-looking guy, maybe in his twenties or early thirties, with dark, curly hair and facial hair that makes him look like a used lollipop plucked from a barber's floor. The other guy is thick, slouched, and his eyebrows soar to his hairline just before Esther puts a bullet into him.

The curly-haired guy barely has time to look from his friend to Esther before he is delivered the same fate. Normally, Esther is much more discriminate with her shots. But she's happy to make an exception in the event of an invasion of child molesters.

As fast as she can, she hops through the window frame and reaches under the armoire to grab her fully loaded weapon. After vaulting back outside and stepping out of the room's line of sight, she checks the magazine, racks the weapon, flicks the safety off, and points the gun toward the window, right where she estimates a curious head might poke out to look for her. This doesn't happen, but she does hear much more commotion from the inside. Most of it is curse words, thrown out and strung together in creative ways.

Esther re-engages the safety and tucks the gun into the back of her jeans, its cold weight pressing against her lower back. Now keeping an extra careful eye out for anyone else who might be outside on the property, she works her way back toward the squad cars, where Officer Kent greets her with a wide-eyed rage.

"Where the hell did you go?" Kent asks.

"Sorry. I had to look around."

"I heard gunfire. You kill any more of them?"

Esther stays quiet but gives Kent her best guilty child look.

"You stay here now, I mean it," says Kent.

"Just so you know, I got a pretty solid confirmation on their numbers. I overheard two of them talking and one of them said that I killed half of them. He might have been estimating, but if it's true, that's thirteen down now, out of twenty-two. Oh, and one of them left the house to try to find me. So there should be eight inside. Give or take."

"Damn, girl. You're good. You're a pain in my ass, but you're good."

She knows. But she's always been good for herself, and now she can be good for Remy, too.

Finally.

She hates to be a pain in the ass (at least, to people who are doing good in the world), but Esther has things to do tonight, and she's already plotting her escape from Officer Kent's watch. However, her plan becomes moot in a few seconds, as the front door bursts open and the intruders start spilling out (*Thank you,* Esther hears the house say), sprinting in every direction—two even run directly toward the cop cars, and Esther imagines them all inside, drawing straws to see who got that duty.

Esther takes aim, but Simpson is too fast—he pelts one guy with a couple of rubber bullets, he topples, kicking up a barely visible cloud of dust. Esther watches for further movement, but he seems to be unconscious—she wonders if perhaps Simpson hit him in the head. Another runs just to the side of the squad cars.

He spots Esther crouching there and yells, "I found her! She's—" and Esther puts a round into his chest. She then looks toward Officer Kent to be chastised, but Kent is on the other side of the cars and doesn't even seem to have noticed the shot. Kent herself has a taser out and fires it at yet another man, who crumples less gracefully than the one Simpson brought down.

Eight men ran out of the house, as far as she could tell. Two are unconscious and one is dead. The other five simply ran off, into the desert or toward town. She doesn't suspect they'll return. They're all after saving their own skin at this point.

So what about the other one? JT, wasn't it? He's out looking for Esther, according to the burly guy lying dead in the bedroom. She is reluctant to let the other five get away, but she vows to herself now not to let this JT guy get away. Something about him—his implicit importance, his arrogant nature, the audacity of bringing two dozen guys to try to throw a wrench into Remy's and Todd's lives—it gnaws and burns at Esther's insides, and propels her toward vengeance. She can't let him escape.

But where would he be? Esther knows he's looking for her, and she considers giving herself up as bait, but she doesn't think that would work. This JT guy seems to be wary of the dangers of underestimating her, and he's shown that he's more than prepared to fight dirty. He won't offer himself up, even if Esther baits him out. She must seek him—hunt him.

Her first instinct is to call Deliverance; there's a good chance they'd be able to find him. But as she thinks it, she remembers that her phone is on the counter at the house. Unless one of the guys who fled has it. If that's the case, she can only hope that they don't have the resources (and brainpower) necessary to get into it and use it to manipulate Remy. Based on what she's seen so far, though, excessive brainpower isn't something she'll have to worry about, which allows her to focus more on finding this JT guy.

So where would he be? Probably looking for her, frankly. So where does he think *she* would be, if not at the house? She wonders what they know about her, and whether they know about her relatively limited familiarity with the area. She thinks about how the articles were written and what information was revealed in them, but there was nothing at all about her, thank god. Not that there is any reason there would be—this massacre will be her first time making news anywhere, at least as anything other than 'anonymous' or 'unknown.' She might have been able to get away with lying about her whereabouts tonight, but running into Officer Kent removed that option from the menu.

She runs through the town in her head, place by place, trying to determine where she'd be most likely to find JT. Not at the library, the gas station, or the bed and breakfast, certainly. Possibly the police station? It's the best she can think of. At least for now.

Once again sticking to the winding corridors of shadow—or rather, avoiding the blazing disks of light spilling onto the roads and sidewalks—Esther canters through the night. Every couple of minutes, she's forced to take refuge from sweeping headlights behind a bush or a parked car, but the journey is short nonetheless thanks to Wometzia's small size.

Instead of making a beeline across the street when the building comes into view, she works her way around the south, then to the west, behind the building. She crouches at the edge of the property line, just outside the hopeful reaches of the station's lights, and strains her eyes to pick out any movement in the darkness.

In the distance, a couple of dogs escalate a barking match. A beaten-up sedan rolls northward, playing some muffled hip hop that makes the ground rumble rhythmically. After a minute, however, the dogs have quieted and the car has left earshot, leaving the area to saturate in Wometzia's signature pregnant quiet. Ever since Esther came here, she's loved the specific brand of ambience produced in the town. The odd cricket chirping or passing vehicle seem like accents to the calm, rather than disruptions of it, like the whole town settles down to sleep at night.

She continues to watch for another minute, then creeps toward the building. The patches of light illuminating the ground are full and bright; Esther identifies the least luminous route to the building's south wall and takes it, stepping quickly but crouching to avoid being seen through the windows.

Aware that there's nowhere to conceal herself while she looks into the lobby, Esther resigns herself to pressing her body up against the wall and being as still as possible, hoping that, should there be any onlookers, the minimal movement is sufficient to evade their attention. She takes a deep breath and pushes her hair in front of her face—her pale complexion would stand out immediately in contrast to the dark, but her dark hair should aid as a shoddy camouflage, even if only for a few moments. Esther lifts her head to look through the window, slowly at first, then with a more confident swiftness. Her hair obscures her vision, but only slightly, like looking through a screen door.

There's soft light coming from floor lamps in the corners of the office as well as a desk lamp that somebody forgot to turn off—perhaps in responding to the massacre of the past hour. The surrounding flood lights burst in through the windows from behind Esther, their stark blue-white hue cut up into little rhombuses by the fortifying wire in the window. Seeing two such different lights compete for the same space is somehow dizzying.

Esther scans the lobby for any sign of…well, anything. But it's quiet. An older gentleman—the dispatcher on duty—sits at an archaic computer playing solitaire and doesn't notice the shadow Esther casts.

She spots movement near the door and is unable to quell the rush of adrenaline before realizing that it's just a frond of a tall, fake plant swaying in the breeze of a nearby vent.

Nothing to be found here, it seems.

Esther retreats back off of the property via the same route she used to approach the building, all the while wondering: *Where the hell did he go?* This started out as something of a 'Find him before he finds me' task, but the longer she searches for him, a furious conviction stirs and bubbles with rapidly increasing intensity, and she undergoes a transformation from prey to predator.

But, Esther knows that, as much as she would enjoy indulging these feelings, she also can't risk putting herself into a position of emotional engagement that might cloud her mind.

TWENTY-TWO

Still crouching in the shadows, Esther sifts through the contents of her mind, which shift like tenuous dunes in a windy desert—her memories of the articles written last month, mostly—to try to remember whether any of them had mentioned any locations outside of Albuquerque. Todd and Remy's house, obviously, but equally obvious is why JT definitely won't be there. The murder sites or dumping grounds, perhaps? No; those are in Albuquerque, and JT knows that Esther didn't take her car. He may have suspected that she would hotwire one, but even if that is the case, she won't have to worry about him being in town, because he'll be trying to head her off on the road that runs east out of Wometzia.

She considers making herself comfortable and keeping a closer eye on the police station, but instead the farmhouse charges into her conscious, like the Headless Horseman bursting into Sleepy Hollow.

Oh, she thinks. Without further thought, she knows that that's it. There are very few times that Esther can get herself to have confidence in such a concept as instinct, but in this case, it tugs at her like the master's call to a loyal canine.

She knows the location somewhat; her curiosity got the better of her one night and she explored the farmhouse herself.

Certainly, that's not enough of an edge to call home court advantage, but it's preferable to stumbling through the dark farmhouse to serve as target practice.

As Esther steels herself for the journey to the outskirts of town, her attention is called to her aching joints, her sore muscles, and the dull beginnings of a headache.

I'm getting too old for this shit, she thinks dryly, half-smirking in the darkness. But she sends those thoughts on their way; they have no place in her mind right now. Any thought that isn't directly involved in getting herself through the next couple of hours has a lesser priority.

A fresh wave of adrenaline surges into Esther and she draws her fresh, fully loaded weapon from her waistband, replacing it with the nearly empty one. She zips through the streets with a careful balance of speed and prudence, cutting across streets in the darkness and stopping at every corner to listen for movement. As she nears the western town limits, the quiet seems to embolden and encroach upon her. The heavy weight of her gun is comforting.

She turns northward and hears the first movement in what seems like hours—a sort of raspy chuffing, like an extremely old machine chugging to life. She turns around to see a (wolf?) dog running straight for her. It seems to morph and sway in strangely alien ways, until she's able to focus more fully and realize that it is, in fact, *two* dogs, chasing after each other playfully in the dark.

This realization comes a second too late, however; Esther steps back and loses her footing on a large rock near the side of the road and stumbles onto her backside. In the process, her handgun slips from her hand, clattering to the ground and off toward the curb. Esther's worst fears are confirmed when she hears a faint but distinct *splish* as her weapon makes its dive into Wometzia's limited sewage system.

Dread threatens to well up inside her, but with tremendous effort, she keeps it at bay. With luck, the next person she encounters will be JT, and with a little more, he'll be the *last* hostile person she encounters tonight. She closes her eyes, takes a deep breath, and pulls the first gun back out, reminding herself that it's only a few rounds away from becoming a paperweight.

She continues north—not long to go now.

As she looks upon the old, creaky house, she wonders about what angle would be best to approach from. Her one and only visit here was also during the night, so she didn't get much of an idea of the surrounding terrain. She expects that JT is already here, waiting. He would have gotten a head start, and there's a good chance he came straight here, rather than having made the detour at the police station (and being frightened by a couple of loose canines), like Esther did.

She looks up at the barn and the house, silhouetted against the night sky with a graceful subtlety. It would be a beautiful night, if it weren't so full of death and blood. As she observes the house, she thinks there may be a blind spot in the back, and if she's careful, she can make her way around to the other end of the property without being seen. Assuming, of course, that JT is in fact here at all.

Oddly, she has no doubt that he is.

Esther steps carefully through the umbral cover of the night, hoping that her footfalls on the dead grass aren't audible from a distance. In time, she looks at the house from the northwest. From this angle, it seems to lose some of its charm, its innocence, but perhaps it's also because she is aware of its past and present—and maybe a bit of its future.

Well, she thinks, *it's now or never.*

Keeping in as much of a crouch as reasonable, she trots in a straight line toward the house's back wall, then flattens herself against it. She steps along the perimeter toward the screen door at the corner, eases it open, and steps inside, holding her firearm at the ready all the while. The screen door closes behind her and she holds her breath, listening for movement. For a brief moment, she wonders whether this was how Remy felt when he came through here only a matter of weeks ago.

She wonders whether the blood is still upstairs—one thing that television shows don't cover is the macabre aftermath of a crime scene. Typically, if the scene is on private property, the local police will give them the number of a professional cleaner and send them on their way. But, being that this house is abandoned, that probably hasn't been the case. Not that there was a murder here, but there was some gruesome violence upstairs, and Esther suspects that that hasn't quite been taken care of.

She crouches against the wall near the door and holds her breath, listening. A surreal kind of quiet holds the room with an austere firmness. It would strike Esther as unsettling, but she takes comfort in knowing that if JT so much as scratches his ass anywhere in the house, she'll be able to hear it.

She considers going into the pantry and the basement, but

knows that it's not necessary. He's upstairs. In the room where Remy and Todd found Stan Romero, sliced open and left to bleed to death. JT may even have been involved back then. Who knows?

Sure enough, she hears an abrupt *thunk* from upstairs, followed by the creaking of floorboards.

Her first option is to sneak upstairs and pray that she's quicker on the draw than he is. She's confident in her own skills, but without having any knowledge of *his*, it's a hard gamble to make.

Her second option is to hunker down and wait for him to give up and come downstairs, but she doesn't know how long that could take. Minutes, maybe, but the possibility also extends to hours or even days. And, even through her famous disciplined resolve, she's not so arrogant to think that she would never let her guard down during a vigil so long and constant. On top of that, the couple of guys who managed to slip away from Remy's house may be headed this way (or even already here), and that's a variable far too unpredictable to calculate for.

Her third option is to notify the police, but she would have to make a phone call to do so, which would mean either having an audible conversation in the house or making her way back outside to do it, far enough from the house so as not to risk being heard—a task that would be a feat in and of itself. In retrospect, perhaps she could have contacted the police sometime in the past half hour, but they're also chasing the others all over town, no doubt.

The silence is broken by the gradual rising of distant sirens, likely the reinforcements called in from Albuquerque finally arriving. Esther hears the house's other occupant shift once more—possibly moving to a window to see if he could spot any of the flashing blue and red lights.

That he's moving about strikes Esther as a good sign for two reasons: First, because it means he's fidgety. He's on edge and spiraling. Of course, this can lead a person to be more dangerous, but Esther is prepared for that, anyway. Second, because it means he's most likely unaware of Esther's presence. If he had any idea that she was in the house, he wouldn't dare make a sound.

Option one it is.

She takes a deep (but quiet) breath, flicks her weapon's safety off, and begins up the stairs, praying that they aren't creaky enough to alert JT to her approach. She takes each step at a glacial pace, her practiced patience in a fretful duel with her desire to put a bullet into JT.

At last, she's outside the bedroom where Remy found Stan. She presses herself against the wall by the door frame, listening with all her might. The sirens still blare in the background, but at this distance, they're not full enough to drown out even JT's breathing. Esther steels herself, feels the weight of the gun in her hands, and tries to visualize how the following few seconds will occur.

But as she places her weight on her back foot, the tired old floorboards betray her and let loose a brief but audible *creak*. There's an immediate shuffle from within the room, and Esther knows that the time has come. JT heard her, knows that she's here, and is coming for her.

261

In slow motion, she can almost see him rising to his feet and barreling across the room, even through the closed door.

Thud—one step—*thud*—two steps—the door swings open and there stands a man, smaller and more fearful than Esther had imagined. He's holding a gun, but the look in his eyes isn't so much murderous as it is flooded with panic—despair, even. He lets out a yelp.

"It's you," he says. His face pales, visible even in the tiny slivers of moonlight filtering in through the grimy window. He begins to raise his weapon, but Esther is far faster on the draw. She sends a shot into his left shoulder, the force of which carries him stumbling backward to the center of the room, his dropped gun clattering toward the open closet. Esther's ears fill with a ringing, punctuated by JT's anguished grunts.

The pallid light glints in the pooling blood. Esther steps toward him and he attempts to push himself away, but with his good arm wounded, he only makes it a few inches before gasping and collapsing into a heaving, bloody heap. She kneels down and looks at his face, and suddenly she understands: These aren't the fearsome monsters she's made them out to be. Monsters, yes, but not fearsome.

They aren't the domineering type, out to flex their muscles and intimidate the world into submission. They're the quiet cowards. More than likely, these guys are *patrons* to the filthy business, blackmailed or otherwise coerced into helping clean up the mess that Keroth and Perkins left for them. JT's eyes buzz with a disoriented, pained terror.

Even as she thinks it, however, the fear in his eyes is, for a brief moment, abated by a desperate surge of boldness, which allows JT to strike at Esther. A nasty left hook, his fist collides cleanly with Esther's face, throwing the room's tricky lighting into a dizzying pot of streaks and flashes. The room's ambience and the far-off sirens are once again subdued by a prominent ringing in Esther's ears, and she feels herself hit the ground, stunned and disoriented.

Through the commotion, she focuses with everything she has on lassoing the world back into focus. She hears JT struggling toward his gun. She wills the walls to stop spinning around her, and slowly, they do. To her relief, she finds that she managed to maintain her grip on her own weapon this time. She holds her gun out toward him, trying to steady herself enough that she can line up and squeeze off an accurate shot, but conceding that she may have to take a less clean shot if she can't get herself steady in time. As the two images of JT in her vision blur and settle into one, Esther lines up her sight over his shoulder, predicting where his head will bob as soon as he manages to retrieve his firearm.

From outside, Esther hears a series of four *thumps*: car doors closing. She looks around the room for flashing red and blue lights but finds none; these reinforcements aren't hers. Seconds later, the clattering of an old door being slammed shut fills the air.

JT perks up. "Guys!" he yells. "I'm up—" *Bang.*

Three rounds left. Judging by the four car doors closing, there will be at least as many guys—but perhaps not all at once. This time, instead of waiting and watching from the shadows, Esther must act quickly and decisively. She considers grabbing the gun from JT's corpse, but the thundering steps on the staircase indicate that there's not enough time for that. Her only immediate option is to pray that they split up so that she can deal with them in a less concentrated manner.

She moves quickly and quietly toward the closet just in time to avoid being visible from the hallway. If she manages to deal with the first one or two quickly, perhaps she can buy herself enough time to pull the gun off of JT. A huge, dark figure steps into the room and Esther puts a round through his head.

A second, slightly smaller figure follows. He's more alert, but not quite enough; Esther's next round plunges into his chest, and the light in his eyes dims and dies before he slumps to the ground. She can hear the other two (or three?) in the hallway, afraid to enter.

This is my chance, Esther thinks. She steps over JT's cooling body and lifts he gun from underneath his left hand. A wedding ring clinks against the metal of the gun as she does so. She feels the weight of the revolver in her hand, but the balance feels off— quickly, she ejects the chamber to inspect it.

It's empty. Big Bad JT was carrying a gun without any ammunition. He bluffed himself to death. The other two also had guns on them, but she can't retrieve them without entering the hallway's field of vision.

One round left, she thinks, *What I wouldn't do for a blade. Or another few rounds.*

While she knows that her next move is crucial, she also knows that she doesn't have much time to calculate it. She holds her own gun, with its one remaining round, in her left hand and

JT's impotent piece in her right. She looks up and takes aim…and hurls JT's gun at the window with all of her strength.

The glass shatters dramatically and she can still hear shards tinkling to the ground outside when she hears one of the guys say, "Did she just jump?"

Two men run in, but only one has the presence of mind to look in her direction—the other makes a beeline for the window. The former takes a bullet to the chest: her final target. She crosses the room toward the bullheaded one, who turns around in time to see her charging at him, aiming him through the window frame with all her might.

Her shoulder connects with his chest, but with more force than she thought she'd need; the minion sails through the window frame and Esther teeters at its edge for a second, but is unable to reclaim her balance so she, too, goes toppling through.

The sensation of falling felt unusually slow-motion. In that second, Esther sees a driverless four-door sedan with its headlights on; a smattering of glistening glass shards on the ground below; the (hopefully) lifeless body of the man she pushed out the window; and the rapidly approaching ground.

TWENTY-THREE

REMY

My mind zips all over the Midwest, trying to piece together what happened with my mother while simultaneously fretting about Todd's and Creed's safety. I don't like that we're apart, but I also can't see a realistic method of fixing that. This leaves me with nothing to do but either evade or confront the incoming hunting party.

Evading them sounds ideal, but there's a part of me—call it exhaustion—that just wants it all to be over. The part of me that has, for the past month, been sapping me of purpose and drive and emotion, of the will to be anything other than alive and breathing. It protests my escape plan before it's even hatched, insisting that in this opportunity I have to drive the final nail into the coffin of this whole ordeal; flight is not an option.

Beyond that, how many more people—how many more kids—would I then allow to fall into harm's way in my endeavor for self-preservation? I imagine my own childhood, my own desperate longing for some powerful, authoritative adult to swoop into my life and pluck my father from that household.

Indirectly or otherwise, I could be that person for scores of children.

I notice that my walk has escalated to a hurried canter, Odin padding along at my side. At this point, I feel I no longer need to conceal myself; my pursuers are already en route. I've been found. On that happy note, I spend the remainder of the morning frequenting the local businesses. I introduce myself to the small-town shopkeepers, in full awareness that it's not likely I'll be seeing them again.

First, a bakery—Dunn's Buns—which turns out to be the source of the delicious cinnamon smell that wafts through town in the mornings. I buy a cinnamon roll and proceed to an antique shop, a tailor, a coffee shop, and a twenty-four-hour diner themed for the town's ghostly reputation. After a quick bite (pancakes topped with vanilla geistcream), I visit a butcher, where I buy an entire steak for Odin—if either of us deserves it, it's him.

As I watch Odin wolf down his meal, a breeze sweeps into the quiet street and I take in the scenery, for once not concerned with being invisible. The gust carries with it a wash of melancholy; what a shame I won't get to know this town more intimately. Simultaneously, my resolve is strengthened with the task of providing protection to the small city and its inhabitants.

Having spent the precious hour that I could afford on visiting and enjoying myself, I must now focus on the incoming figurative storm, thunderheads flexing menacingly in a sea of ozone and danger. The clock at town hall clangs out eleven o' clock.

Whatever time I have left must be spent carefully, and I reason that my best use of time, right now, is to acquire a more intimate familiarity with the lay of the town. My time here so far has yielded an adequate knowledge of the surrounding geography, but if there are any obscure alleys or useful climb paths, having prior knowledge of them may determine on which side the coin of fate lands.

In the ambiguous, ethereal moments before big events, there are things I think about often; a sort of slow-motion, intensifying drumroll. I think about Todd and his impact on my life. I think about Beth. I think about Odin. Lately, I've been thinking about my mother. I feel a strange connection to my body, like my brain exists throughout the whole thing rather than just in my head. I become hyper-aware of my movements and their minute details and angles. I assign importance to otherwise unimportant things, like a baseball cap left abandoned in the road or a neon sign with a couple of letters burnt out. I soak in the quiet and visualize the rotation of the planet, blindingly fast and unbelievably slow all at once, big and awesome and important, but at the same time, quiet and subdued, like a heavy, windless snowfall.

I've always thought of this as a curious phenomenon, but one without much use to me. But as it happens now, in the rural streets of Ghost Fork, I understand why I do it.

It's to remind myself of the things—little and big—that often escape my notice. It's the important things in my life chiming in before my big moment to say, "Hey. I matter." Perhaps this serves as a bookmark, so that if the big moment alters my way of thinking or my view of the world, these last memories and musings can draw me back in and tell me, "This is how things were."

I continue through the streets, trying to balance these meta thoughts with the micro ones. In the latter field, I focus on committing to memory every alley, including the locations of dumpsters, exposed pipes, window ledges, or anything else that I could climb. My inaction during my time spent here has done a disservice to my muscles and lungs, but I figure I still stand a fighting chance, should it come to that. After all, it's barely been over a month.

Twenty-Four

Creed

Todd and Creed roll into Cheyenne, the windows down and the radio off. They had it turned on, but the mountainous Wyoming roads offered little more than static, and the endeavor of hunting down a clear station proved to be more work than it was worth.

This came at both of their dismay, as the drive itself has been long and dull, and contained awkwardly little conversation. As it turns out, their mutual experiences produce a cocktail that's hard to talk around. They quickly reminisced through all of their shared memories, and subsequent conversation or small talk seemed even smaller and less relevant; when most of your experience together is quantified by the exploration of an abandoned treatment facility, it saps what little interest is left in small talk.

Creed agreed to meet Ginger at a café in a strip mall downtown, with plenty of outdoor seating. Todd will be taking his place to conduct the interview, but Creed will take post in a Mexican fast food restaurant, which has windows looking out into the plaza. Fortunately, since they've never met face-to-face, neither will have to conceal or disguise himself.

Todd parks the car about a block away from their meeting place and gives Creed a minute's head start; they don't want to be seen walking in together.

Creed enters the restaurant and makes his order, self-conscious about mispronouncing his entrée. Even though he told himself he wouldn't, he finds himself looking over his shoulder—toward the windows—while he waits for his food. Afterward, he takes a seat at the window and scans the crowd for Todd. Fortunately, the plaza isn't as densely populated as they had anticipated, being midday on a workday, and he finds him with ease, striding with a bold confidence into the heart of the court.

Having picked him out, Creed feels more at ease, and pulls out the paperback Todd gave him to help him appear subtler and less aware, a well-loved copy of *To Kill a Mockingbird*. He opens the volume to a random page and fixes his eyes on a spot near the corner, paying attention only to Todd, whom he can see just out of the corner of his eye.

Within the minute, she appears. Ginger Garrity, the star of the show and, with luck, the key to revealing the truth about just what happened to Willa Frye. She enters the plaza from the far end, looks around for a moment, and spots Todd waving her down.

Creed's heart rate threatens to pick up, but he wills it back down.

Ginger approaches Todd, who stands to shake her hand. They appear to exchange pleasantries, small talk. If she suspects anything, she masks it well. The two of them walk into the café's interior.

Twenty-Five

Todd

Ginger has a peculiar air about her, and Todd hasn't yet figured out whether it's due to what he already knows about her or something he doesn't. Her voice is confident and bold one moment, but the next shrinks into a Disney princess. Her eyes flicker with mystery, and every time he thinks he can get a good read on her, she slips into a different dimension and becomes another creature entirely, and the puzzle begins anew.

"I love this place," says Ginger. "I come here all the time with my friends." She flashes Todd a quick grin (Is that mischief? Innocence?) before striding to the counter to make her order without a glance at the menu. She has exact change ready before the barista reports her total.

Todd follows, makes his own order, and pays the barista. An unsettling quiet befalls them while they wait for their drinks. He leans against a wall near the counter, doing aloof. Ginger paws absentmindedly at a pendant around her neck, a tarnished brass piece engraved with an intricate design that he can't quite see while she toys with it.

Though she appears absentminded, her eyes zip all over the place, resting at each stop for only a moment before speeding off to their next destination. He can feel an odd, insubstantial tension intensifying, but before it mounts, their orders are ready.

Ginger grabs a chair and makes to sit down, but Todd interrupts her.

"Actually, do you mind if we sit outside? It's a bit cramped in here. I don't do well with tight spaces." This serves a double purpose, one of which being Todd's plan to remain in Creed's line of sight and the other being a trick that Remy taught Todd. When questioning a victim or a witness who might be reluctant to reveal information, it helps to make yourself seem weak. *Look, look how vulnerable and broken and relatable and human I am. Now tell me...*

He has his doubts about whether this will work with Ginger, but it's certainly worth a try.

"Oh, sure, no problem." She flashes him that pixie smile again, pushes the chair back in, and leads the way to the door. She moves with the nuanced fluidity of a snake, sleek and purposeful and graceful, with undertones of power and menace.

Todd shudders.

They return to the table where he sat before. As he's trying to figure out how to start the interview, Ginger saves him the trouble.

"So," she says. She takes a sip of coffee and continues, "You wanna know about Willa?"

"Yes, I do," says Todd. He pulls out his phone. "You don't mind if I record this, do you?"

"Not at all." Her eyes sharpen and flick from Todd's face to his phone and back again.

Todd taps the red button to begin recording and tries to steer himself away from sounding more like a cop than a reporter.

"First off, the details haven't been very clear with what the living situation was like. Did you have your own bedrooms at the facility?"

"No, we shared. There were two to a bedroom, at the time. I was Willa's roommate."

Ginger's poker face is almost perfect, but she keeps looking up over his shoulder when he tries to meet her gaze. Contrary to what many seem to think, eye contact is not a surefire way to get the truth out of someone, nor does it necessarily mean that they're lying if they don't make very much of it. But, to Todd, there *is* something fishy about the way she won't meet his gaze at all, especially when five minutes ago she was shooting him all sorts of mischievous smiles.

"Okay. That much was true, then. Can you tell me, in your own words, what happened? I'm sure you've told the police several times, but I couldn't find much that was publicly available."

Ginger exhales and looks down, gripping her coffee in both hands like her whole being will freeze over without its warmth.

"I'm sorry, it's just…give me a moment. I try not to think about that day."

"It's okay, I understand. Take all the time you need."

She doesn't need much time. "Well, we were having a little party on the unit. The staff were helping us do our makeup and costumes. For Halloween, ya know? Willa asked if she could go to her room to get something. After a couple of minutes, I started to worry; she never dawdled. Ever.

"So I asked the staff if I could go to the room, too. I told them I needed to get something, too, but I just wanted to check on her. She had been having a rough time for a while, and I needed to know she wasn't doing something drastic. But I guess I was too late."

Ginger doesn't look up. She sips her coffee and sniffles, and her lip starts to quiver.

Bullshit.

Instead of calling her out right away, Todd decides it's his turn to play games. He puts on his pensive, perplexed face and waits for her to look up and notice him. Eventually, she does.

"What?" she asks.

"I guess some of my research must be wrong," Todd says.

Ginger's right hand flies from her cup to her pendant, which Todd can now see is engraved with a depiction of Kali, the Hindu goddess of destruction and power. She has four arms. Two of her hands hold a sword and a severed head, and even in the tiny engraving, the head looks anguished.

"What research? What did they tell you?"

"My sources told me that you weren't all that close to Willa. That you hated her, in fact."

"Well sometimes we didn't get along, but—"

"They also told me that you were jealous of her." This one is a lie, of course, but he sees that her labored coolness is coming unraveled, and determines that this is the best way to capitalize on his momentum.

Ginger laughs and it comes out more like a bark or a yelp than anything joyous or mirthful.

"Me? Jealous of her? For what? Her connect-the-dots acne or her rotten pear body shape?"

"Because of Thad." Todd intended this to reign her back in, but it has the opposite effect.

"Thad? *Thad?* Please, he never wanted anything to do with that bitch."

Careful not to reveal his surprise, Todd only tilts his head toward her, inviting her to continue. As he does, he sees the twisted and mangled remnants of humanity leave her; she's now pure monster.

She grips the sides of the table, as though to keep herself from rocketing into the sky out of pure fury. "Thad was *mine*, you imbecile. I don't know how anyone ever believed he'd be into *her*, but it ended up being a convenient cover. Even *she* believed it! All because she found a note he gave me. She thought it was meant for her."

"Dubz," says Todd.

"*I'm* Dubz! He called me Double G, for my initials! When he got lazy, he shortened it to Dubz. But like everyone else in the goddamn world, Willa thought it was about her, and she went over the moon about it. I told her over and over that things weren't the way they seemed, but if I told her *how* I knew, she would have told on me.

276

"So I just let her believe it for a while, but good god, she got so *smug* about it! She carried that *stupid* lockbox around with her everywhere. I swear to god, I kept wishing she *would* kill herself, would've saved me the trouble—"

She stops and looks at Todd wide-eyed, locking eyes with him for the first time, and now he knows why she avoided it before. There's nothing human left in them. She knew that if she let him look into her eyes, he would see the void, the blank darkness, and figure it out.

"I—I mean," she stammers, hands shaking.

After a moment, her hands relax. "Fine. Fuck it. I did it. I choked that bitch out. She knew she had it coming, and she's lucky I let it go on for as long as it did." As she regains her composure, she twists back into the snake, but rather than small and defensive, she looks coiled and hungry. Maintaining eye contact as much as possible, Todd slowly reaches out, stops the recording, and sends the file to Remy.

"I have to go to the bathroom," says Todd. He leaves his phone behind to show that he's not simply going to call the cops. When he walks away, she still looks like some foul, predatory creature from the pits of hell.

Todd walks into the café from which they just got their coffee and flags down the barista.

"Hey, how many times have you seen that girl I came in with?" he asks.

"Never, in all the time I've been here," he says.

"How long is that?" Todd asks.

"Six years this December."

The other lies he could understand, but why lie about being a regular?

Because this is exactly where she wants me, he realizes.

He should have brought his phone with him.

TWENTY-SIX

CREED

Creed fiddles with the corner of the page but pays it no attention. His nerves tighten as he watches Todd stand up and walk back into the café. Even from afar, he has noticed that Ginger is much more a wild card than he could have anticipated, and he thus worries about the number of directions this whole ordeal might take.

But, as he promised Todd he would, he sits tight and tries not to focus on the tenuous fragility of the forthcoming events, instead prodding his mind in the direction of potential escape routes, should he need one. Doorways, alleys, fences, and climbable exterior walls congeal into a messy sort of road map in Creed's mind as he scans the courtyard through the window.

Even with his distraction, however, Ginger's slightest movements seize and lock his gaze back on her, almost against his will. He watches as she pulls a small object out of her purse, removes the lid of Todd's cup, pours something into it, replaces the lid, and stows the item away, all within the space of about eight seconds.

He sets his book down—subtlety be damned if it means Todd is in danger—and unlocks his phone, desperately pulling up Todd's number. Even as he does so, however, he sees Ginger pick up Todd's phone—he must have forgotten it when he left for the bathroom—and, presumably, shut it off. Indeed, as Creed watches his frantic text message on his own screen, the delivery report remains unconfirmed.

Creed's heart thuds more violently in his chest as he feels the heat, the life, draining from his skin, as though his core has morphed into a tiny black hole, sucking the vitality from him with ruthless fervor. The 'what-if' machine in his brain kicks into overdrive, but promptly sputters to a hissing stop as he tries to visualize a feasible solution.

As if he has turned into a beacon of fear, Ginger turns slowly and looks straight at him, smiling a wicked smile. If possible, Creed's veins turn even more frigid, as he realizes: This has been her plan all along. She's confident, careful, and precise. And she's not alone. Just as Creed is here, hidden in plain sight (or so he thought) as Todd's backup, any number of the passersby could be just that for Ginger.

But how many? Who are they, and where? And more importantly, would they be susceptible to diversion, if Creed were to manage to cook one up?

Before any conclusively beneficial plan comes to mind, he spots Todd walking back toward his table from the café's front entrance. He sits down and picks up his drink. Creed stands up, making for the exit, but the most enormous person he's ever seen obstructs his path. He stands at least six-foot six, and is built solidly, like a tree trunk. He glowers at Creed and spreads out his arms, which are as big as small logs themselves. He's wearing a nasty sneer, barely visible underneath a poorly kempt mustache.

He sports a too-small black tee shirt and jean shorts that expose his legs, thick and pallid and sturdy. Creed is quick and agile, but the combination of surprise and the man's sheer size prevent him from routing an effective path to and out the door.

Creed glances—for as long as he dares—back out toward the courtyard and sees Todd holding his paper cup, sloshing it about as he talks animatedly. So, Creed does the only thing he can think to do: he kicks the giant in the groin and pushes him backward with all his might.

The man looses a howl, but it morphs into a wail as he tumbles backward through the glass door. The glass doesn't break, at first. Instead, the door absorbs the colossal weight of the man and flings open with mighty force, then the glass shatters upon colliding with a bike rack. The tinkling of broken glass is just barely audible over a passerby's scream and the huge man's howling (which has dulled to a raspy roar and now transitions gracelessly into a growl).

Creed looks up from the sprawling mass of human in front of him to Todd, whose coffee cup sits safely on the table. He watches as Todd assesses the moment and stands, staring Ginger down in an intimidating manner that Creed would never have expected Todd capable of.

A few seconds pass—or possibly minutes; it's hard to tell—before the pivotal moment takes any sort of direction. But just as abruptly as time halted, it lurches into motion once again, with all the vicious potency it had a minute ago.

He stumbles over the mound of a man in the doorway and approaches Todd and Ginger. Just before he reaches their table,

Ginger lets loose a shrill screech and, in an instant, she morphs from a perilous she-devil into a whimpering child. Her eyes swim with tears, her lip quivers, and she draws her arms in toward her midsection defensively. The familiar hush washes once again over the courtyard, this time with the people's attention directed hostilely at Todd and Creed. It dawns on Creed, now, exactly how the scene looks to passersby: Two grown men, looking angry or at least frustrated, standing square, fists clenched, with a small, pretty woman who's cowering and shrieking in fear.

Todd eases up on his intimidating scowl, softening up again. Creed unclenches his fists and folds his arms, placing his weight on one leg in a desperate effort to seem casual and unbothered. The eyes of maybe thirty bystanders still rest upon them, during which Creed swears he can hear Todd's and Ginger's minds whirring at equal paces, both trying to route into a checkmate without surrendering his or her own king. Ginger capitalizes on Creed's and Todd's inability to do anything (without incurring the wrath of the odd courageous onlooker, at least) by simply retreating. She gets to her feet, flashes them one more devilish smile (or does Creed imagine that?) and flees to the east, down an alley between a dry cleaner and a jewelry store, her steps punctuated by the odd sob.

Todd puts his hands in the air and looks down in a surrendering manner, and Creed follows his lead. Some of the surrounding people shake their heads in disgust or whisper to one another, but after a minute, the commotion dies down and one might never know anything happened.

"What now?" asks Creed.

However, Todd needn't answer, as the next step manifests in the form of perhaps half a dozen men entering the plaza from various directions. Some are armed with guns, but a few only have a baseball bat or a crowbar. Creed knows well that he could easily maneuver past the ones without firearms, but doesn't know how well Todd would be able to do so.

"This way," Todd says before beginning to weave through tables and patrons, moving southward.

Whether due to luck or a profound lack of planning on the part of the adversary, they've consolidated their armed stooges at the north end, which means that the men approaching from the south side can only be as effective as they are fast, and judging by their physiques, Creed suspects Todd isn't encumbered by an excess of worry in that regard.

Creed follows Todd out through the crowd, both of them keeping attentive eyes on the men running (or hastily waddling) toward them, weapons in hand. In any other circumstance, Creed might trust the bystanders to intervene somehow, but as they were just painted as the bad guys a minute ago, he figures they probably won't receive much aid this time around.

Todd and Creed reach the threshold of the food court, thus escaping the forest of tables and chairs. As the two emerge, though, two of the three men in that direction have also reached the same place. Creed ducks the swing of a bat and rolls through, then looks back in time to see the other guy move in with an overhead strike aimed at Todd.

Creed's heart sinks for a second—he's not close enough to intervene—but Todd makes it apparent that he doesn't need his

283

help, as Todd himself lunges in toward the man, blocks the strike at his wrist, and plunges his fist into the assailant's midsection. The man lets out a strained *Mmph!* before doubling over and falling to his knees. The man with the crowbar winds up for another strike, looking much like a baseball player, and Todd gives him much the same treatment as the first attacker, stepping in close to nullify the power of the strike, but this time aiming his punch at the face rather than the midsection. The crowbar clangs to the ground as its former wielder yelps in pain and reels backward, blood streaming down his face and over his chins.

Without missing a beat, Todd sidesteps the guy and follows Creed. The would-be third attacker from that side of the plaza is nowhere to be seen; perhaps he realized he has no chance against Todd and fled to safety.

A wide opening gapes at the south end, glowing with a bright contrast to the shady food court, welcoming them out of the arms of danger and into those of potential freedom. They zip through and around the corner, heading east; they daren't return to the car before being sure that they're safe.

The two hurry onward, but their momentum is jolted when the sound of gunfire cracks the air, two quick shots followed by a mess of chaotic yelling. Creed looks back at Todd, who reveals no intention of stopping or turning back, and they race onward, seeking whatever form of asylum they can take advantage of.

After a minute, they spot the shady refuge of an alley cutting into the exterior perimeter of the plaza. They duck inside it to catch their breath and regroup.

His heightened adrenaline makes it seem to Creed like one

might be able to listen closely from anywhere within a mile and hear their heavy breathing and pounding hearts.

"Do you think anyone got hurt?" Creed says between breaths.

"No," says Todd. "No sirens. There are probably cops on the way, but no sirens."

Creed nods. He and Todd stand crouched, taking turns puncturing the relative quiet with their breaths until they gain more control over their respiration. It feels like several minutes, but Creed reminds himself that it's probably only two, three tops.

"What now?" says Creed for the second time in a five-minute span. He has a vague awareness of the logical facets of his mind, buzzing around like a mosquito, telling him that the correct course of action is to stay put until the threat dissipates. However, his body is pulsing, vibrating with the need to *do* something. To fight or flee, as it is.

Todd pulls out his phone—apparently, he had the presence of mind to snatch it up during all of the commotion before, when the giant man tumbled through the glass.

"Remy hasn't opened the message I sent him, but he has received it," says Todd.

"What did you send him?"

"The audio recording I took with Ginger. I figured she'd probably try to delete it as soon as she got the chance, and I had every reason to let her fall into that sense of security. So I removed the lock on my phone for a minute and told her I was going to the bathroom."

Creed is impressed with Todd's quick and smooth thinking, but any praise or commendation for it will have to wait; a casual set of footsteps approaches and a figure halts at the end of the alley, at first silhouetted against the early afternoon sunlight beyond their shadowy sanctum.

"Call it fate, chance, whatever," says a sultry female voice, "that we should have been pushed together after all this time."

Creed's eyes are still adjusting to the sudden dimness, but the voice is unmistakable: Ginger Garrity.

"What do you mean?" asks Todd.

"Oh come now, don't pretend you don't see it. Feel it. *Know* it."

Creed suspects that the message is directed at Todd.

"Dear old Dad gets put in jail by the *oh-so-heroic* good guys, and they don't even have the decency to acknowledge his daughter?"

"Dad? Who, Keroth?" says Todd. His eyes widen and his brow furrows in a simultaneous flash, like someone who just found out that the cook spat in his food.

Ginger doesn't answer, instead raising a single eyebrow and lifting the crook of her mouth just the slightest bit. Clearly, this is a satisfying moment for her.

"When you first called me," she says, shifting her gaze to Creed, "I was panicked. I thought maybe I had been found out, that I was going to jail. But I talked to some of Daddy's old friends, and they were *very* interested that people would be asking about that mess all these years later. After all, they worked so hard to cover it up back then. They didn't want all of their toiling to have been in vain, now, did they?"

"What? You, too? How are you people so goddamn *every-where?*" says Todd.

"I wouldn't say *every*where, no. But *you* people certainly have a way of sniffing us out, don't you?"

Creed thinks he detects just a note of irritation, possibly even anger, in her voice. This is good; If they can push her over the edge, thus separating her cognitive facilities from their usual stoic pilots, Ginger will become less of a threat—less predictable, but also less potent.

"We go where the wind blows us," says Todd. "I guess it's a habit of ours to get tangled up in shit along the way."

Ginger's breathing intensifies and her hand flees to her hip. Creed becomes abruptly aware that she may be armed now, a calculated step in her careful plan to deliver her idea of justice to Todd and Creed. For now, though, her hand remains stationary, hovering a few inches above her hip, ready to reach for her weapon and draw it like a nervous cowboy.

"You guys just have to ruin *everything!*" she shouts.

They've succeeded in ushering her out of the realm of rational thinking and into that of delirium, but with the knowledge that she's armed, Creed finds himself second-guessing the plan to incite an emotional reaction. Their current situation is a delicate one indeed, a rough-around-the-edges stallion edging on the thin border that separates its wild, unruly side with its newly developed domesticated one, and Creed knows that Todd will handle the reins to this beast much more masterfully than Creed could ever hope to.

"Keroth is your *father*?" says Todd. His voice is an intriguing combination of sweet and smooth and bold and confident, like a seasoned pastry chef's famous caramel topping enveloping her latest work. "I thought all of his family lived with him."

Ginger scoffs. Her hand twitches, but goes right back to where it began. "All of the family he wanted people to know about," she says. "I was the bastard child. When he was in his thirties, he had quite a wild sex streak—no surprise to you two, I'm sure—and he ended up sleeping with a prostitute during a weekend of partying. He thought nothing of it, of course. Neither did she. Until she found out she was pregnant with me."

"Did this happen often?" asks Todd. Creed picks up on his strategy: stall until either some help shows up or a visible crack in her defenses is available for exploitation.

"Plenty," says Ginger. Her rage seems to have been replaced with a sort of petty spite toward Keroth, which is much more malleable than the former. "Thing is, most of them bugged him until he paid them off and told them to shut up. Most of them got enough money for an abortion and a few years' worth of vacation."

"But not your mother?" says Todd.

"No. She wanted more. She wanted love. She spent her life trying to reunite me with him, trying to force a relationship, but it wasn't happening. I didn't really care about him at first, but in the end, he came through. Probably it was just because my mom had gotten sick and he knew he wouldn't *really* have to commit, but he started visiting. And he paid all of her medical bills. *All of them.* She didn't have insurance, and I didn't have a dime. But he took care of us."

"So now what, you have a dutiful obligation to avenge him now that he's in jail?" Todd's words border dangerously on antagonistic, but his calm, controlled tone keeps them carefully in line.

Ginger laughs, a shrill needle of a sound puncturing the air. "Sure, he doesn't *want* to be in jail. I mean, it's not ideal. But do you think he would be there if it weren't by his choice? Attorneys, judges, jurors, they can be contacted, bribed, coerced. You can't. Remy can't. He knew he had to cut his losses and be safe for a while before doing anything more.

"He underestimated you. You and your people did a good job at cornering him, and he knew it was only a matter of time before he was caught. He also knew it was more likely he'd be caught by Remy than by the police, and Remy almost certainly would've killed him. It was a means to an end. Not ideal, certainly, but don't fool yourself into thinking he slipped up and got caught by accident. Surely, you can't be that naïve."

Creed hears more yelling from the courtyard, followed by the echo of a clanking, clattering commotion. Both noises cease before Ginger seems to notice them.

"It was a matter of resources. When it was Daddy versus Remy, he had all of his guys at his disposal. But Remy cut him off from his resources, isolated him. Daddy tried to do the same to Remy, but there were two problems. The first was that Remy was so used to being alone already. He never operated with an army under his command, so there was no army to strip him of. The second problem was you and Beth. See, even later on, after he identified you two as Remy's supporting cast, he couldn't find a way to separate you three. He had Beth kidnapped and you two found and rescued her. He tried sending someone for you in the hospital, but you were watched constantly."

"You might call that loyalty," says Todd.

"Oh, you don't have to lecture me about loyalty," says Ginger. Just then, a fire seems to ignite somewhere inside her, in that barren, desolate plane deep in the distant reaches of her emotional landscape, the dark and shadowy terrain ruled by id. Her eyes gloss over with that mischief again, her eclipse goggles intended to shield her from the light of external feelings and truth. She smiles a nasty grin and pulls a handgun from behind her at last.

For now, at least, the firearm remains pointed at the ground, dangerous and wary like a rattlesnake, but still subdued.

"Like I said, my father and his people helped me out of my pickle all those years ago. It wouldn't be right of me to let you walk away." Though her voice drips with a malevolent venom, Creed can't help but wonder if he detects a trace of doubt on it.

A sinister quiet befalls them, complemented rather than interrupted by a car's poorly aligned serpentine belt, a calling bird, and an odd rhythmic thudding. Ginger's gun is still pointed at the ground, but her finger is on the trigger and the hand which holds the piece twitches now and then.

Creed looks from Todd, breathing his slow, calm breaths, to Ginger, whose respiration has become labored and intense. Ginger is having to work harder and harder to maintain her façade of untouchability, while Todd's calm is cool and consistent. But, while he's winning this psychological battle, she's still holding a presumably loaded gun, and entirely unpredictable.

Their circumstance has become something of an Icarus situation. If Todd steers her back to her more stable mental state, she has access to a much cleaner stream of thought, which may afford her opportunity to gain an upper hand (even beyond where she is now). On the other hand, the less stable she becomes, the more likely she is to lose control entirely and smash through any remaining inhibitions keeping her from shooting them where they stand.

A car with the squealing belt seems to be idling nearby and that odd thudding grows and diminishes in volume, grows and diminishes, but with each cycle seems to net an increase, like a tide coming in, pushing and pulling but with just a little more push than pull.

Creed looks back to Todd, whose gaze remains fixed on Ginger. He seems to be focusing on her eyes, but Creed knows that Todd is watching the armed hand intently, as well. Now, Ginger's breaths have become more regular, but are no less intense. Indeed, they seem to be getting deeper, heavier.

The squealing car finally peels away, leaving the thudding ever louder in its wake.

"Why can't you all—" shouts Ginger, her eyes filling with tears of the most reluctant kind,

Thud-thud-thud-thud

"—just fucking—"

THUD-THUD-THUD-THUD

"*die?!*"

Ginger aims her weapon at Todd, hands shaking.

TWENTY-SEVEN

REMY

As the morning yawns and stretches into day, I begin to worry; is this a red herring? Have I been stationed here to wait for a threat that's not coming? And if so, what possible reason might my enemies have for that?

I pace the streets for a while, without a destination but still adhering to some obscure guideline that I can't fish out of my subconscious. Before long, I'm back at the apartment's parking lot, still waiting for the sounds of roaring engines or yelling or the thundering cracks of gunfire.

But they don't come.

It's then that the horrible thought occurs to me: I'm not the target.

Not *now*, at least. They know about Todd. They know he's here.

He's the target, and he's two hours away.

Before I realize I'm doing so, I'm pulling desperately at car doors in the parking lot, hoping to find one unlocked, which I can then enter and borrow. Fortune smiles upon me when I try the second-to-last car on the lot, a sedan with peeling paint; not only does the door open, but its poor owner has accidentally left the keys in the ignition. I make haste, lest the car's rightful driver return, perhaps only taking a load of groceries inside. The car revs to life, and before I know it, I'm crossing the city's boundary en route to Cheyenne.

Even after the past few days, my extended time spent without contact has rendered my phone's buzzing an unfamiliar phenomenon, and it thus startles me when I receive a message from Todd. First is a text message that urges me more than perhaps anything else could have, composed of only two words: *Get here.*

The second is an audio file. I download it and press play, nervously glancing back and forth between the road and my phone (I normally refuse to use my phone while driving, but such dire circumstances cannot be ignored), and my phone begins to regurgitate what I assume is Todd's interview with Ginger.

I don't know how, but things must have gone awry. Without much time or mental bandwidth with which to plan, I forward the message to Beth's E-mail, with a quick message:

"I'm alive, but here's in case I'm not for much longer."

Within the minute, my phone buzzes itself into a frenzy, reporting the reception of what seems to be a flurry of E-mails, texts, and phone calls from a furiously concerned Beth. I force myself to compose one more message to Beth, still anxious for any time spent distracted by the device.

"I don't have time to explain now, but I might in a few hours. Hang tight and I'll give you any updates I can. If you don't hear back from me, send that file to the police force in Cheyenne."

I have no time to read the messages she's sent me, but I'm confident they're littered with profanities and threats of various methods of castration. My phone continues to buzz for the remainder of the journey, and I appear to have made great time; today's graciously clear weather has made visibility a non-issue and the roads are clear, not only of precipitation, but of traffic and construction as well.

Now, I'm in Cheyenne. I only hope I've arrived in time to be of any aid at all. Todd's message came only a few minutes ago, so, with luck, whatever crisis was in progress at the time either is still in the air or has resolved favorably. Of course, Todd isn't helpless, and Creed has demonstrated a fair amount of competence himself, but my unrest isn't one that can be settled by my confidence in Todd's and Creed's merit. Not with the threat they're up against.

I park the car (poorly) as close as I can get it to the northern entrance to the plaza where Todd was supposed to meet Ginger, only pausing to lock the vehicle out of a sort of apologetic courtesy to the owner. I approach the plaza at a sprint, keeping my eyes trained for anything suspicious-looking, anything hurried or hunched or armed, but for now, I see nothing.

I crouch low, hurrying between the rows of cars, which laze on the lot like a lounge of lizards sunning in the afternoon shine. The air around me seems to be abuzz, like the anticipatory chatter before a headlining band takes the stage, or like the way the atmosphere crackles and simmers with ozone before a violent thunderstorm. Each step I take seems to contribute to this pent-up chaos twisting through what would otherwise be a pleasant warmth.

Still at the height of my sensory awareness, I close the distance to the curb. Well-groomed trees sway gently in a barely palpable breeze, and a bird's shadow zips across the concrete, startling me for a split second. I reach the plaza's outer perimeter and press myself against the brick exterior of what smells like a seafood joint.

I peer around the corner, into the central plaza, where Todd should be. I don't see him, but I do see two men—one on his hands and knees, the other on his back, evidently out cold, blood streaming down his face. If that doesn't speak for Todd and Creed's trail, I don't know what does. I start making my way toward them, ditching my crouch in favor of a casual, inconspicuous trot.

I notice more signs of commotion—an overturned bistro table, a smashed-out glass doorway and its glass guts being swept up by a panic-stricken worker wearing an apron and an expression of exasperated disbelief.

The tension in the air, building up like a river into a small reservoir, seems to be approaching a tipping point; the first ominous cracks have broken their way into the base of the dam, and the water will burst forth at any moment.

Then, it does.

"There he is!" yells a voice from underneath a nearby awning. I look toward it in time to see two guys jump to their feet and break into a run in my direction, reaching to their hips as they do so and drawing guns.

I have to think fast. I have no doubt that I'm faster and can out-maneuver them—even if they're firing at me. The problem is that there are bystanders. I can't risk them getting hit by a missed shot. In an effort to minimize the risk, I move westward, putting myself between my attackers and a brick wall. They run toward me, but one trips on the leg of a cast-iron bistro chair and stumbles into the other—and here's my best chance to resolve this encounter.

I've walked too deep into the plaza to make a retreat before they recover, but they've made the mistake of coming too close to me. In that second, adrenaline primes my neural pathways to make the moment quick, calculated, and decisive.

One of the guys stumbles just ahead of the other, and a step to my right lines them both up in front of me, so that the attacker in front obstructs the line of sight between his partner and me. As the one in front tries to adjust his aim while simultaneously finding his footing, I lunge in toward him, grip the barrel of the gun, point the firearm upward, and throw my body weight into him, hoping that it's enough to toss him into the other.

Alas, it is not. However, the shock of the body hurtling toward him sends him teetering backward anyway, and the general mess of the food court comes to my aid once again as he loses his balance and falls into an empty chair over its armrest with enough force to send the chair dangerously over toward its other side. The man flails his arms to try to retain his balance, in the process losing his grip on his gun and tossing it away. It lands on the ground and discharges, cracking the air like lightning and embedding a small round in the concrete planter beside it.

I realize that I'm still holding the first guy's gun. Part of me wants to make use of it, but with the commotion that's erupting around me, I figure it's best not to be running around with a loaded gun. To that end, I eject the magazine and toss it to the ground, then leap to the other gun and do the same.

By now, both guys are recovering and angry, like wasps that have been swatted at by a flustered gardener. The one closer to me charges like a bull. I take a step back at a slight angle and plant my hand on his shoulder blade as he approaches, dropping my weight onto him as I do so. He collapses to the ground with a pitiful *mmf* and stops moving. I look up in time to see his partner charging me in a similar manner and lift my knee to meet his face. I feel a sharp pain, just above my kneecap, where I assume I've just knocked several of his teeth out. He makes a sort of gargling howl and collapses with his hands over his face, blood trickling through his fingers like the first spring runoff after a snow-heavy winter.

I almost make the mistake of feeling proud of myself, but I remember that these guys were only an *obstacle* on my path to a different goal. I know Todd and Creed are around here somewhere, and my best bet of finding them is from the rooftops, rather than on the ground where my line of sight is apt to be obstructed by people, buildings, cars, and small trees.

I slip into the nearest alley and climb up a length of pipe on the side of the building (my shoulder aches from its month-old wound, but the pain serves to fuel me rather than to hinder me). Upon finishing the climb and vaulting over the lip of the building, I begin to run southward, toward the opposite gate of the plaza, checking the perimeter of each building as I go, and making leaps between the close-quarters rooftops. I don't worry about security spotting me; if I find what I'm looking for, it can only be helpful to have some badges around to assist in that mess.

Building after building, my panic bolsters, threatening to take charge of my psyche. In most of these small alleys, there's nothing but day-old garbage or boxes that need to be broken down. One alley is the setting for what looks like a drug deal, and one has been deemed fit for an impromptu (I hope) make-out session.

I reach the south end of the plaza having found nothing of interest. There's an archway over the southern gate, made up of a series of thick iron bars welded together, and I use this as a bridge to the east half of the plaza, where I'll head back north. The buildings on this side aren't quite as even as they were on the west side, requiring more climbing and rolling as I ascend or descend to their varying heights. The biggest drop is maybe ten feet or so, and threatens to obliterate my ankles, but as I drop down onto the lower rooftop, I'm able to roll out of the fall and minimize the impact of it.

Suddenly, I hear voices. It takes a moment of concentration to isolate these calmer voices from the still-frantic ones from the plaza, but I hear a controlled, measured, unmistakable voice speaking from the east, off to my right somewhere. I run to the north end of the building I'm on now and don't see anything in its northern alley, but the voices have become louder, clearer, and more recognizable—indeed, I'm able to pick out Todd's easy tone. The voice that answers him is a female's—Ginger's, presumably—but she has none of the careful, practiced undertone that I heard just a second ago.

I continue to work my way toward the source of the noise (this next alley, surely) and when I slow to a halt and peek my head over the lip of this structure, there's a woman with fiery red hair (what is it with redheads and trying to kill the people in my life?) pointing a gun at Creed and Todd, both backed into the corner of the alley. A delicate situation to be sure, but Todd has been talking smoothly and calmly so as not to throw any unexpected wrenches into the mix. Ginger yells something, but the only word I can pick out is 'fucking'. She has Beth's mouth, apparently.

In what little time I have, I try to assess my safest plan of action. I can't very well hurl myself down there, as she might (accidentally or otherwise) pull the trigger as I land. If I alert her to my presence too early, she may well decide that her best option is to do away with Todd and Creed before turning the weapon on me. I need to disarm her quickly and safely, without drawing any attention to myself.

But at that moment, the last grains of sand in the hourglass slip into its lower chamber as I hear Ginger scream, "DIE!"

I take a step to the east—parallel to the alley and toward the parking lot—then grab onto the lip of the building, letting my weight swing me back westward, toward the three. Ginger still hasn't noticed me, and the commotion of her screaming still hasn't quite finished bouncing around the alley. In my descent, which seems to take place in slow motion, Todd and Creed flatten themselves to the north and south walls, respectively. Ginger fires and a chunk of brick cracks out of the wall where Todd had been half a second earlier. My feet hit the ground perhaps five feet behind Ginger while she's still reeling from the recoil. I roll toward her left side and come up just in front of her, gripping the barrel of the pistol and aiming it skyward.

Ginger's eyes widen (whether out of fear or anger, I can't tell) and she pulls the trigger again. My ears ring and I feel the heat left behind by the round as it exits the barrel. Ginger's eyes zip from the now-raised firearm to my own eyes and I see recognition, anger, and fear wash over her. She tries to thrash and rip the gun out of my hands, but she only succeeds in forfeiting what grip she does have, and within a couple of seconds, it's completely in my control, her fingers trying desperately to cling and claw at my hand to get it back.

I use my hip to push her backward, which I'm sure will throw her into a frenzy, but now that she's disarmed, I have little fear of such a frenzy. She can scratch, kick, claw, and punch at me all she wants—without the gun, there's very little chance that it will be fatal, and with Creed and Todd here, I'm confident that she can be subdued until authorities arrive.

"Welcome to the party," says Todd, smiling a welcome (if facetious) smile.

I smile back, half at him but half at Ginger, as she starts swinging wildly at me, like a three-year-old who just declared war on a piñata. Blocking and dodging these strikes isn't so much difficult as it is exasperating, and it only takes a moment for Todd to jump in from behind and seize her arms. He drags her backward to the corner, only a foot or so from where her bullet punched a hole in the wall.

She grunts and thrashes for a few seconds, but then puts her forehead against the wall and begins sobbing. Every few seconds, it turns into an angry yell, but she doesn't thrash anymore. As an added bonus, her sobbing will help lead the cops to our location.

I take a moment to absorb the scene. Creed is standing well out of our way and looks like he's waiting for someone to tell him what to do. Todd continues his restraint on Ginger and holds her in the corner looking like he's removed himself mentally. For the second time in the past few minutes, I realize that I'm holding a gun, and for the third time, I eject the magazine and toss the piece aside—I'm unwilling to risk her (or anyone) gaining control of the weapon and re-escalating the situation.

Sure enough, some cops show up within minutes. Part of me wants to be critical of them for taking so long to arrive, but then I remind myself that, though it felt like hours, the time that has passed since I arrived has been perhaps five minutes, and this area isn't exactly the type of urban density that would have ten available units within a minute's notice.

TWENTY-EIGHT

The rest of that afternoon is a blur. Later on, as I reflect on it, I remember only a distinct handful of things. I remember the more significant events, of course—watching Ginger as she's detained (on multiple charges and warrants), e-mailing the audio file to the police, sitting with Todd and Creed in the police station. I remember the sirens and the crowd's excited commotion (things are *happening*, get the camera!). I remember the ambulance carting the unconscious pedophiles off to local hospitals.

I remember getting a call from a hospital in Albuquerque— incidentally, the same one where I left Todd to heal up after his own gunshot wound—and hearing, from the other line, "Is this Esther's son?"

I don't remember the details of the conversation—those memories have been replaced by the details of the emotions I felt. Mostly of overwhelming *wrongness*. Unfairness and ugliness. I don't remember what look I had on my face, but when Todd saw it, he copped it immediately and squeezed my hand. It was meant to make things easier, but it tugged me that much farther into the zone of vulnerability, allowing a few tears to escape and roll down my cheek.

What the hitman said to me about my mother had been on the back burner of my mind the entire afternoon, but for a few reasons, that was the extent of attention I was able to give it at the time. This phone call succeeded in calling it forth from its neglected place and setting it at the forefront of my mind. Apparently, my mother was involved in an epic gunfight last night.

Her (Todd's and my) house, in New Mexico, was swarmed by a ragtag team of mercenaries in Keroth's group. By some miracle, she managed to kill quite a few of them and escape the house unscathed, but got seriously injured when she hunted down the leader of the pack, some guy named JT. JT is dead, and my mother is in the hospital, in critical condition. She hasn't been conscious, but according to what evidence they've been able to pick up, she confronted him in the same room where Todd and I found and rescued Stan Romero.

She conquered him and two reinforcements who ran in—one with a bullet, but the other by ramming him through a window and toppling outward with him, falling from the second story onto the hard gravel driveway below. Nobody knows for certain how long she lay there before ambulance arrived, but the estimate is around half an hour. Fortunately, additional ambulances had been called down from Albuquerque a while beforehand, in order to treat any who may have been wounded during the night, but as they found, everyone (with the exception of my mom) was either unscathed or dead.

I remember stumbling over words to communicate to Todd what happened, but trying to recall exactly what I said or how he reacted is like trying to snatch a fish out of murky water using my bare hands. Then we left.

The road rumbles timidly beneath us as we speed toward

New Mexico. Some time ago, I acknowledged the possibility that I may never be returning there. To be doing so now isn't shocking, but the circumstances are. I'm not sure who accessed my mom's phone in order to retrieve my contact information, but whoever it was must have sent those digits to Trina, as well—she called me some stretch of time ago and let me know that she was boarding the next flight out of New York.

Hearing her voice was strange, especially when observed through the distorting lens of my exhausted desperation. She was emotional, borderline distraught, but underneath those layers of hysteria, I detected the truth of her character: She had grown into quite a strong woman indeed. Uprooting and moving to the opposite coast must have been a daunting venture in itself, and she faced it with the fearless determination that echoes in her voice now.

She ended the call with a quick, "Bye, Remy, love you." I suppose this should have caught me by surprise, but instead, it pulled at some deep-seated and long-dormant strings of my soul, the ones whose sounds reminisce of the toasty interior of the house on chilly winter nights and Mom's cooking and the dull but insistent pull of sleep while curled up in blankets, as the rain taps out a lullaby on the window. It shouted, didn't whisper, *home*, in a way I didn't think could make me feel good. During the time since that phone call, the pleasant memories, long forgotten, have been oozing forth steadily.

At some point, my stream of thought, barreling down the accessible conscious lane of my mind, flicks on its signal and drifts over to the subconscious lane as I fall into a shallow doze, my tenuous stability eased only by Todd's presence and his calm command of the vehicle.

I don't remember much of my dreams—only that, for the most part, they were stressful and anxiety-inducing. I do recall, however, that they ended on a positive note. Or, at least, a neutral one, which is still a net improvement from the general tone of my slumber. There was some kind of resolution, some sort of relieving finality.

As the tired car comes to a halt at the Albuquerque hospital, the luminous clock in the dash reads eleven o' clock on the dot. Night has fallen and I rise from my sleep with a pulsing spot on my forehead—the spot where I rested it upon the window, evidently. Todd rolls the windows down a crack, kills the engine, looks at me, smiles in his *I don't have the experience to empathize properly, but you have my full support* way, squeezes my hand, and opens his door. He gets out and over to my door faster than I can even undo my seatbelt, and he helps me out, strong and secure and solid.

"What if this is a trap?" I say sleepily. The thought only just crossed my mind, but I don't stop or even slow my path toward the hospital doors. At this point, I only want the whole ordeal to be over. If the hospital is my end, so be it.

"This isn't a movie," says Todd.

I agree, but I still shoot him a look I know he'll understand to mean, *What about the past year managed to convince you that our lives are grounded in any sort of normal reality?*

"Right, but still. I think it might actually be over."

If it were anyone else offering such speculation, I would dismiss it as wishful thinking or unfounded optimism, but there's something about Todd that makes me believe him. Perhaps what I need right now is to believe that, even if I'm incorrect. There's only so much paranoia a mind can handle.

I try to steel myself for the emotional ride I'm about to go on, but the combination of Trina and my mother in the same place, without the tremendous weight of my father's presence, is a prospect I'm drastically underprepared for—if someone handed me a shield and a sword and informed me that I was next in line at the colosseum, I would still be more prepared than for facing reuniting with Trina and Mom.

So instead of spending my mental faculties laying a foundation for a building whose shape and material I don't know, I instead try to clear my mind of the day's (and decade's) events, which, in my worn-down state, proves to be much easier than expected.

Todd and I must look like a designated driver assisting his extremely inebriated friend as we enter the hospital. He does the talking, thankfully, and guides me with his anchoring presence toward the elevators.

A minute later, we walk into my mother's room.

The hospital bed, accommodatingly wide and long, dwarfs my mother and, for the first time since she re-entered my life, I see her as *small*. Her skin is scored with cuts and bruises—some minor and shallow, but others marked by stitches—and her unconscious head is supported by a C-collar, and is covered with purple-blue-black bruises and a series of tight gauze bandaging.

The hospital-issue blanket is pulled up above her chest, and on top of that lies a blanket I recognize as one that she herself knitted for Trina when we were kids. I have a matching one in a box, somewhere. Trina's is periwinkle blue, with intricate stitches and interesting geometric designs knit into it, like a fuzzy mandala design. My mom used the same pattern for mine, but with red yarn. She gave them to us on Christmas Eve in 1999, and that night, Trina and I stayed up, wrapped in our blankets, coloring in old coloring books until neither of us had the strength to keep our eyes open any longer.

And speaking (thinking?) of Trina, there she sits, in a chair in the corner, fiddling with her nails and waiting for me to notice and acknowledge her. As soon as she sees my eyes travel from our mom to her, Trina stands up, crosses the room in two big strides, and throws her arms around me.

I feel—or perhaps 'sense' is a better word—Trina trying to navigate her own emotional storm, and in the space of a moment, we become each other's anchors, each of us too flimsy to deal with the storm on our own, but together solid enough to have become immovable by the tempest. Todd is helpful to me, but in regard to this particular type of storm, he's in another dimension, and the storm thus pays him no notice.

She continues to squeeze me close, wordless for a time, before finally releasing me and stepping back to her chair. Her eyes swim with tears, but so far, none have made the grand escape onto her plump cheeks.

She looks, more or less, exactly how I thought she would. Her thick, dark hair falls down over her shoulders and spills over her white blouse. She has an average figure—which by today's media standards, would be considered full- or plus-sized—and has always known how to dress it. Even in her distress, she looks beautiful, like a melancholy music video. I'm stricken by memories of her experimenting with makeup, at first a well-guarded secret from both parents, until Mom not only embraced it, but began to share her makeup with Trina and give her tips and instructions. The two of them would sit in front of the vanity in Mom's bathroom for hours, me sitting on the end of the counter, watching with innocent and absent-minded fascination.

"Who's this?" she asks, ripping me back to reality.

Such rudeness is uncharacteristic of me, but I'm sure she'll understand, given the circumstances. "Oh, this is Todd. My boyfriend," I say.

Trina stands up again and gives him as tight a hug as she gave me, and I step back to take in a moment that five-, ten-, or twenty-year-old me would never have believed: My family, sans daddy, together and welcoming my partner into the otherwise oh-so-exclusive circle. It's my turn to tear up a little.

Trina sits back down and I ask her the question I've been afraid to ask since my arrival. "How is she?"

TWENTY-NINE

Trina shakes her head; apparently, the question moved her to a darker part of her mind. "Not good. The doctors aren't sure what to expect. She's in a coma, and there's really no telling when—or if—she'll come out of it. Aside from that, her physical wounds are hard to read, as well. Her spine is all fucked up from the fall, so even if she does come out of the coma, they're not sure she'll be able to walk. And depending on the brain damage, she may not be able to do much of anything—even speak—for the rest of her life."

I exhale and feel the stinging of my eyes tearing up again, the room blurring into an ugly stew of synthetic whites and blues and chromes.

"Remy...what's been happening? I just heard about Dad less than a year ago, and well, that was whatever, but now Mom?"

I look to Todd—I need someone to tell me what to do—but his returning gaze says, *You know perfectly well what to do.*

So, I tell her everything. I start with two years ago, when the case for Ellen Dodge appeared on my desk and I discovered that our father was the murderer. With reluctance, I move on to disposing of him—if there's anyone who will understand this, it's her—and the subsequent shitstorm that forced Todd and me to move to New Mexico. I tell her about Andre and Stan Romero, and the ever-present and perpetually flailing tendrils of this evil organization. I tell her about how I left Todd—in this very hospital, in fact—to flee, in order to keep him safe. I tell her what happened to Mom and why. I tell her about Mom's own heroics and her work with Deliverance, about the reputation she acquired and how that led to the eventuality of a bright red target appearing on her back. At certain parts of my recount, such as my getting shot or my mother showing up at my doorstep, I think I hear her stir, but with no more certainty than if I imagined it.

As I tell my (and Todd's and Mom's and Creed's) story, Trina sits in solemn patience, nodding along. Sometimes, her face shifts into shock or even horror, but it always defaults back to a concerned attentiveness. When I finish, she nods but doesn't speak; she seems to understand what few do: that there's nothing she can say right now that will make it any better. Her support is implicit and thus needs no spoken message.

Then, it's Trina's turn to tell me her story. I know that she moved to New York to sing, but that information is about as informative as the title of a novel alone.

To my great relief, she hasn't been bothered by Keroth's army of goons. Admittedly, I didn't give that much thought, particularly when Todd, Beth, and my mother occupied my thoughts so commandingly.

When she ran off to New York, she had every intention of cutting us—all of us—off completely. To cross the rickety bridge to an adventurous new land and slash the ropes upon reaching the other side. Of course, she knew it was in her nature to be dramatic, and she figured she'd probably override that decision before too long, but it felt good to revel in the drastic finality of her action. She had been awarded a scholarship with a generous living stipend, so she didn't have to find work—at least, not right away.

Her arrival in the Big Apple (which she learned not to call it within two days of landing in it), while well-timed for her, seemed to come at a pivotal and detrimental time for those around her. Her charm has always been good at getting her friends, and college was no different. She fell into a circle of classic New York artsy hipsters, just a couple of trust funds in excess of a perfect *Rent* cast, with the immersive bohemian lifestyle on display, but secretly (and not disappointingly) better funded. Exposed brick walls, independent coffee joints with live local talent once a week, and organic, grass-fed, gluten-free, and vegan options on every other menu. And on top of all of that, she had finally created a substantial distance between herself and her past. Geographically, at least.

Of course, she was aware that creating physical distance from an emotional issue would do no more to subdue it than closing the closet door would make the monster vanish, but it made it quite a lot easier to focus on the present knowing that her former life, full of fear and struggles and strife, was a sharp four thousand miles away, ticking on in her absence.

Then the present struck.

New York, which she trusted as a fertile new land into which to put down roots, lost its glamour of novelty in time, and reality dawned on her: She was alone. Her support system, she realized, was only as strong as the relationships she was able to build with those in the vicinity, and while she enjoyed them, she'd have been kidding herself to think that they were any better than tenuous. This thought didn't occur to her often, but when it did, it swept a chilly gloom into her heart like the first biting gale of winter.

Indeed, although she had a knack for building relationships quickly, she had an equally prevalent knack for setting them ablaze and inadvertently pouring gasoline on the flames with any efforts she made to remedy the issues. She hadn't received many great gifts from her parents over the years, but among them, her emotional intelligence and ability to maintain relationships were by far the worst.

Chief among these catastrophic attempts at human connection was by far the worst and, at the time, the most puzzling: Gunther, Trina's Ex—with a capital E.

The circumstances under which she met Gunther were innocent—playful, even. She entertained the idea of a romance with him even more eagerly when she thought of telling her peers the story of how she'd watched him walk headfirst into a tree due to his nose being buried in a paperback. He heard her giggle—not a malicious laugh, but one infused with an innocence that, in her, had died long ago—and chuckled himself before introducing himself.

They hit it off immediately. As it turned out, the book he had been reading was Roald Dahl's *Matilda*, and a well-loved copy at that. This was Trina's favorite book growing up—I have distinct memories of her pointing her fingers at objects in the house in hopes that they would submit to her commands and zip around the house like drunk flies. At times, when she was angry at Dad, I'm sure I even caught her jabbing her finger in his direction (behind his back, of course). I'm not certain what she was visualizing in these moments, but probably something satisfyingly punitive.

As every hopeless romantic and rom-com aficionado knows, a mutually loved children's book is one of the most powerful means of establishing an instant love connection with a total stranger. This case was no different, and as one might expect of *Matilda*, talking candidly about the book—what they love about it and how they relate to it, specifically—paved the path for the disclosure of their pasts which, it turned out, they also had in common. She seems to have had a romance not terribly unlike Todd's and mine—from the start, at least. Perhaps humans are just drawn to humans with similar degrees of brokenness.

In terms of compatibility, it sounds like the two had a connection to rival ours, even down to the subtle, less celebrated things that I find to be the most endearing, like sharing a space without the implicit obligation of doing anything together, or the way we pick up on each other's moods and act accordingly without verbal communication.

However, like me, Trina gets panicky upon getting close to people—but this is where our parallels end. My panic manifested by way of convincing myself that I'm not good enough for Todd, and that he could be happier with someone else, or even alone. I braced myself for the day that he would realize this and abandon me, but that day didn't come, and over time, through his own means of communication, he told me that he wasn't going anywhere.

Trina's panic tore through her mind like a mighty tornado of paranoia, shredding any rational thoughts and reasoning that dared enter its path. I suppose Gunther just wasn't as successful in communicating his commitment to her as Todd was with me.

I reflect for a moment on whether Todd and I would still be together if his methods of addressing my insecurities was similarly unsuccessful, but dismiss that thought and shift my attention back to Trina.

This was the beginning of how things went sour. From the start, it was salvageable—a boat with leaks, but patchable ones. However, neither Gunther nor Trina were equipped with the emotional tools necessary to mend the vessel and stay afloat. Water came aboard faster than they could bale it out, and that was that.

"Are you still in contact with him?" I ask.

Trina shakes her head.

A nurse walks into the room, a tiny thing who, at first, reminds me of Gale Quispitt, the little nurse with a big personality, who worked at the only hospital in Riverdell. However, a moment's observance reveals that this nurse's demeanor and way of carrying herself differ vastly; she moves almost without making a sound, and only acknowledges our presence in order to excuse herself as she squeezes around the side of the bed. She checks Mom's vitals—no notable changes—and slips back out the door, her brief presence having felt no more substantial than that of a spirit.

"No," Trina says, "I got clingy and he ran for it. I wish I knew then what I know now. I'm a lot better at these things now.

Maybe still not as good as…most people—" Translation: non-abused people "—but I'm getting a lot better at setting boundaries, both for myself and for others."

"Well, maybe you'll cross paths again some day," says Todd. Despite his bookshelf full of horror and thriller books, Todd is a romantic at heart. I'm more of a realist, but I quite enjoy when Todd gets on his romantic kicks.

"Or maybe you'll find someone who will leave no room in your mind for those doubts and insecurities," I say.

Trina seems to be somewhat removed; she just shrugs.

The ambitious morning light begins to brighten the window, sapping its inky blackness and leaving a dull, unremarkable gray in its place. I guess some part of me knew how much time was passing, but during the fact, it seemed more like we were on a dimensional plane removed from time itself. Now, presented with direct evidence of time's relentless march, I'm plucked unceremoniously from that realm and deposited back into this one, the one where my mother is in a coma with no end in sight.

Trina stands up, straining her body into a long stretch, then goes to look for a doctor, perhaps hopeful for an updated, more optimistic prognosis.

"This has definitely been interesting," says Todd.

"It has," I say.

"Seems like she's been put through a hell of a gauntlet on her own."

"Yeah, no kidding. Thorn family trait, I guess."

"Must be."

Todd and I sit in silence until Trina returns, by which time golden bars of sunlight slice through the blinds and lay across my mother, as if to impress upon us the prison her mind is in.

"No news," Trina reports from the doorway, "I guess she's relatively stable for now, so all we can do is wait until she either gets better or gets worse." I hear her voice catch on the latter.

She crosses the small room to her chair.

"Knock knock," says a voice I know all too well.

THIRTY

"*Beth!*" I say. I nearly knock Todd out of his seat as I fly out of my own—he breaks into a laugh as he regains his balance.

I hug her close and hear her say, "You didn't tell him I was coming?"

"I figured he could use a surprise of the fun type for once," says Todd.

Beth hugs me tightly and I feel her figure relax. I make a quick mental note: *Beth Connors is being vulnerable and affectionate.*

"I've missed you, friend," she says.

"I've missed you, too," I say.

I pull away and Beth looks at me, her always laser-focused eyes simply observing instead of boring a hole into my mind like they used to. I introduce her and Trina and the two shake hands and smile.

"Man, all that shit in Riverdell seems so long ago," I say.

Beth nods and looks away, her mind clearly taking a detour through those intense few days last November.

"So fill me in. What's been going on?" she says, snapping back to the present like a compressed spring jumping out to its relaxed shape.

Fortunately, catching Beth up requires far less re-telling and context. Additionally, Beth sits and listens with the same earnest patience that Trina had.

When I finish, she sighs wearily and shakes her head. "Christ. What are the odds that some random-ass case from twenty years ago ends up in a showdown with Jeremy Keroth's *daughter?*"

Todd and I just shrug and shake our heads, and Beth changes her emphasis:

"*Jeremy Keroth's* daughter. Fuck, Rem. What happens now?"

In response, my phone speaks up before I have the chance to do so. It buzzes aggressively as I take it out of my pocket, as if aware of its message's urgency. It's Creed.

He begins speaking as soon as I pick up. "Remy, big news, I'll shoot you a text with a link. All's well here. Gotta go. Odin says hi." Indeed, I hear my German shepherd whine before Creed cuts the line, and a second later, my device *ding*s as it receives the promised text message.

The link directs me to a blog *(Happman's Happenin's, Musings of a Woke Bloke)*. The first post on the blog is explained in its title: *Suspects in Massive Child Porn Operation Exposed, Charged.*

"Holy shit!" I say. Todd, Beth, and Trina look up and six eyebrows rocket up into their respective hairlines (well, five and seven eighths—Todd singed off a small chunk of his left eyebrow when he was learning flambé).

Rather than read the entire article out loud, I skim it and recite the highlights. The text is occasionally interrupted by a photograph, and indeed, every single mugshot goes into a sinister corridor of my mind with associations and memories of my ordeals over the past year. My memories of it mingle and collide, though, and I can't match the mugshots to where, specifically, I saw them.

Near the end of the article, the author (Charlie Happman, perhaps sired by a Chaplin fan) mentions the massacre in Wometzia. Of course, that story has been all over the news (local, state, and even a couple of national and international news stations did stories) since yesterday, but in today's media climate—that is to say, one where any kind of violence gets a free ticket to the front page and a featured piece on the nine o'clock news—it was overtaken shortly by a Florida man who made a bomb threat using a metallic suitcase full of what seemed to be discarded phone chargers and various other retired USB cables.

I finish reading the article and we stand in awed silence for a time.

"Holy shit," says Beth. "So...does that mean it's over?"

"It's hard to say. But I think so," I say.

There are many superstitions that deal with "tempting the devil," and while I'm not a superstitious man, it's hard for me to believe that the text I receive from Creed now is a coincidence.

It says, "Uh-oh." It's accompanied by yet another link.

The link leads to yet another news site, this one telling of a complex jailbreak led by (and for the benefit of) none other than Jeremy Keroth.

"But this could be good, right?" says Todd. "Most of his guys are either dead or in jail now."

"Yes…but I don't think he was planning to use them, anyway," I say.

No, indeed, when I visit the image of Keroth in my mind (or, rather, when his devilish grin erupts into my nightmares), he is no longer a creature of reason. Millennia of evolution and established civility melt away from the core of his mind, like breaking the mold away from a freshly cooled piece of metal, leaving nothing but the sharp and the dangerous—the vengeful.

The times I've had thoughts (conscious or otherwise) about him have been relatively few, but each of them leaves me with a sort of insidious residue, a stain on my mind and soul. No temperature of water nor any intensity of scrubbing has yet been sufficient to wash that feeling away, and it often leaves me feeling weak.

"What is happening?" asks Trina.

At this moment, surely Todd's and Beth's minds are going at the same rate mine is, if in slightly different directions—if our thoughts were represented visually, they might look like a forking lightning bolt. But although Trina is bright, she doesn't have the experience or the mindset that we've had to adopt for our professions.

"Do you remember Dad's friend, Jeremy Keroth?" I ask.

But I'm asking Trina. When I told her about the events in Riverdell, I refrained from using his name, but now, I see that it's the most effective tool for her to see exactly the depth of depravity we're dealing with.

Todd and Beth were ones I had to tell about Keroth. I had

to explain to them the horrors that he and my father committed while I was growing up.

But I don't have to explain that to Trina; she was there. She experienced it alongside me. She and I would endure the same thing, often back to back, then go our separate ways to cry it out and try to process what had happened, only to meet up again later in the day or evening to pretend that nothing had ever happened.

We were good at that. No matter what had happened, no matter how bad things had gotten, we were always able to support each other in the endeavor of burying it all.

But now I'm asking her to do the unthinkable: I'm asking her to fish out the rusty key from her mental keyring and plunge it into the lock that she undoubtedly hoped, all these years, she'd never have to touch again.

Through her face and eyes, I can almost watch her as she performs that mental task—a hurt expression at first, which then morphs into sadness and, finally, anger. She remembers and, now, she understands.

"He got out of jail?" she asks. Her voice is flooded with emotions now, each fighting for dominance in her words; it's hard to tell which is winning. "What do we do?"

"Hope that the police find him before he finds us. Or me, more specifically."

"You think he'll come after you? I'd think he'd just go into hiding somewhere, lie low for a while," says Beth.

"There was something in Ginger's voice that reminded me of him," I say. "I couldn't put my finger on it at first, but then I got it: revenge. He's careful and methodical, sure, but even as coolheaded as he usually is, that all takes a back seat to retribution in his mind. And not only does he want me punished, he wants to be the one to deliver it."

"Do you think he knows how to find you?" asks Todd.

"I think he thinks he does."

He looks at me, his eyes pleading. "You're not thinking of running off again, are you?"

A pang of guilt stabs through me, quick and merciless. I was indeed considering doing just that, but the thought passed quickly.

"No. It wouldn't do you guys any good. When we were in Riverdell, his most powerful asset was his army of minions, right? Guys he coerced, threatened, or blackmailed, or the odd nutjob pervert who genuinely wanted to help him. Using them, he could, in effect, be all over the place, all at once, without ever leaving his fake white-picket-fence lifestyle.

"But he no longer has that. Without his and Perkins's leadership, the whole operation has been flailing for weeks. Even if he wanted to, he no longer has the influence he used to. If he so much as sends a carrier pigeon to one of his old contacts, there's always the chance that they turn him in. He can't manipulate people into obedience anymore.

"So, where does that leave us? What do we do now?" asks Beth.

"We go to Riverdell," I say.

THIRTY-ONE

Beth looks surprised.

Todd nods his head.

Trina looks mortified.

"Will you come?" I ask.

Just like her memories of Keroth, Riverdell itself beats with a sinister rhythm, building with an ominous ebb and flow like the *Jaws* theme.

For the most part, I've been desensitized to the memories of Riverdell due to my presence there for most of my life. But Trina ran out amid constant fighting, abuse—trauma. In this small moment (which is no doubt a huge moment for her), I wonder whether she's given much thought to what it might be like if she ever did return to Riverdell.

"I can't," she says. The emotions that were previously struggling for her voice have settled—and anguish won.

"I'll stay here with you," Todd says to Trina. "We can hang tight while they go sort out what they need to."

An uninformed onlooker might see Todd's offer as a copout, an act of cowardice, but it's quite contrary. Todd is offering to let me leave him behind so that my sister, whom he's only known for a matter of hours, can feel safe and comfortable in her first trip west of the Mississippi in a decade. He spent a month in a state of constant worry about me, finally set out to find me, and within a week of finding me, offers his own mental well-being in exchange for Trina's.

This is the farthest thing from a selfish or cowardly act.

Considering all of this, I tear up a little before having to turn away—I don't want my own emotions coming into play with Trina's decision-making.

"I'll go," she says. Her anguished look has transformed into one of determination.

"Trina, you don't have to. I know what memories that place has for you."

"I know, I know. The place has haunted my nightmares for years now. I never wanted to go back. Ever. But maybe it will bring some kind of closure. Maybe confronting the memories—acknowledging that they're memories, and not just my imagination tormenting me—will allow me to be at peace with them.

"Or, you know, maybe I'll spend the entire trip in a fit of panic and flashbacks. Either way, it's something I have to confront. If I do it, then I'll know, from then on, that it will never have the same power over me."

Two hours later, we're boarding a plane to Portland, Oregon. In terms of secrecy, it's a relief to be moving about in a public, crowded place without worrying about who might see me—without running the face of every single bystander through my mental database to see if maybe I recognize someone as a threat from my past. I guess I didn't notice how much of a toll my secret life has been taking on me.

I feel a little bad for leaving my mother alone in her hospital room, but she is unconscious, and I'm sure she would understand if she knew the circumstances. I make a mental promise to return to her as soon as I'm finished with my business in town.

We're on a larger plane, with four seats in the middle section—perfect. Beth sits on the left, then Trina, me, and Todd. Trina has been talkative since we left the hospital—more so than I've seen her so far—but now, as the plane prepares for takeoff, she quiets down. She puts her head back and closes her eyes. I don't think she has any intention of sleeping, but I leave her alone anyway. If she wants to feign sleep, she has every right to do so without intrusion.

The flight is only a couple of hours long and goes smoothly with no turbulence. The second we touch down in Portland, Trina's eyes shoot open and she takes several deep breaths. I squeeze her right hand and she nods, steeling herself.

We step off the plane into the cool, humid Oregon air. A shiver runs through me, but not from the cold.

One hidden advantage of flying is that, if Keroth has any of his old resources available, he'll most likely have some way to have seen that I flew to Oregon, and he'll thus receive my message: *No more hide and seek. No more bullshit.*

We shudder to think of the state Todd's house might be in, after this time of neglect. We didn't sell it, as we figured perhaps we could return to it some day, after all of this ended. Maybe that day is today. When we left, we were under constant siege by the less intelligent of Keroth's clutch, ranging from the mailbox being smashed to a brick being hurled in through our front window. We repaired the window before we left, but both of us brushed Riverdell into the darker, less attended areas of our minds, acknowledging that it may continue to be a target for vandalism.

We're pleasantly surprised to find that the house has remained, more or less, exactly how we found it. In its abundance of Oregon moisture, the grass needs to be cut and weeds have overtaken the small garden, but regarding the structure itself, it stands strong and proud, like a guard dog hailing its returning masters. The windows remain intact and even have a hint of their glossy newness underneath the residue left by months of Oregon rain.

I'm certain Keroth is waiting for me at my childhood home, but even so, I do a lap around Todd's (and my) old dwelling just to be sure it's safe. As much as we can with what little we packed, we get settled. I note the distinct hollowness in it since we moved out but, probably by association, I still take a unique and powerful comfort in being here.

We're spared the awkwardness that should be settling over us by yet another text from Creed: "You're not doing what I think you're doing, are you?"

I reply with a smiley face.

"Oregon? Right after Keroth escapes jail? You've lost your damn mind."

"Gotta end things somehow. I'll let you know if I survive tonight."

He doesn't reply.

"How are you planning on tonight going?" asks Beth. Following her question, Todd and Trina, too, beseech me with their gazes.

"I'm going to the old house. Alone. He only has so much sleeve left to shove tricks up into. But if he manages one, I'd rather it be me who goes down than any of you. I'll give you a time limit. If I'm not back before then, get out of here as fast as you can. Out of Riverdell, out of Oregon. Just get gone. If I'm right about his intentions, he'll leave you alone. He wants me."

"You're not going alone," says Beth. Her protest is breathy and intense.

"There's no reason to endanger more than one of us. If I go, he stops and it's over. If one of you goes, he'll keep going until he gets to me."

"We're not as helpless as you think," says Beth.

She's getting heated now—she can't see it. Even though she's been a part of it, she can't see the wake of damage, of pain and trauma and of death, that I've left in my path.

In the beginning, I thought of myself as a vigilante of sorts. I wanted to do good for the world, and that goal coincided with one that would bring me a measure of closure regarding my past. But that one action—big and decisive as it was—set into motion a series of events I couldn't have foreseen at the time. To think of the events that have come as a result of those actions gives me a sense of despair, but when lain parallel to the thoughts of all of the kids who would have suffered at their hands otherwise, I can't bear either timeline.

Have my actions been worth it? Has there been a net increase of comfort and safety and happiness in the world due to my vigilantism, or have I spent almost a year poking at a wasp's nest with no real promise of eradicating the swarm?

No, indeed, to invite them to accompany me on this last dangerous endeavor strikes me as selfish and outright ludicrous. Beth and Todd have had my six throughout this entire ordeal. Sometimes I have asked them for help, and other times it has been at their insistence, but now, as with my departure from Albuquerque, I can't ask them to accompany me. And beyond that, I can't *allow* them to accompany me.

My adventure's collateral destruction ends tonight.

To my relief, Todd seems to understand.

"Do what you need to do, Remy," he says. An uncharacteristic unrest befalls him, manifesting in his clenched jaw and tepid movements. Once again, his universe is demanding that he let me go without the guarantee of my return, and once again, he surrenders to it.

On the same mental notepad on which I promised to return to my mother as soon as possible, I vow never to ask Todd to make a decision like this again.

"What?" Beth's protest begins to escalate. I've seen this woman on the tail end of a kidnapping and hostage situation, but this moment is the most unraveled I've ever seen her.

In the borderline telepathic communication that's become Todd's signature, he looks at Beth and tells her, *Even if we come out victorious, Remy won't be able to live comfortably knowing he asked us to risk our lives for him any more than he already has.*

Beth takes a moment to receive the message, then looks back and forth between Todd and me, wrestling with her hysteria even as her eyes well up.

"Fine," she says. She folds her arms, sniffles sharply, and looks away—first at the floor, then to the ceiling, then around at the walls, as though watching a ghost zip through the house's rooms, unseen by the rest of us.

At last, my gaze shifts to Trina, whose being has been tugging quietly at my attention for the past minute.

"It's all so real now," she says. "No more pretending that it never happened, or that this—"she gestures in a vast circular motion—"is a made-up town, or that what happened here all those years ago isn't a part of me today. I guess in order to acknowledge that it's all coming to an end is to acknowledge that it happened in the first place. All of this, on top of what's going on with Mom… It's a lot to process. I keep thinking I'll walk through a doorway into the next part of some psychedelic dream, then I'll wake up in my apartment and go back to my old life."

"I don't think so, sis," I say. I put a hand on her shoulder. "I think that whatever happens tonight will mark the start of a new era for both of us."

THIRTY-TWO

Big events have a way of splicing one's life with the same efficacy as a new act in a play. Things are notedly different, and the context and mood we associate with act two are markedly different than those we associate with act three. And now, this play is entering its final act, the one that swoops back to the beginning to finish the journey like a roller coaster settling back in to its station. *Thank you for riding, please wait for your lap bar to release, and enjoy the rest of your day in Riverdell.*

A couple of unceremonious minutes later, I step out the door and into the inky night. My joints feel stiff and inflexible, but I know that sensation will melt away after I've been moving for a minute. It's only a few minutes' run from Todd's house to my childhood abode; the ideal distance to get myself warmed up without expending too much energy.

There's very little light pollution that emanates from Riverdell, which on many nights allows for a breathtaking view of the stars, but thick clouds coat the sky tonight, heavy and pregnant and full to bursting. Indeed, before I've cleared two streets, I feel the beginnings of rainfall. By the feel of it, this isn't our normal, coalescing-in-midair rain, either. These are fat, substantial drops—the kind you'd be more likely to encounter in Hawaii than in the mainland northwest.

331

Riverdell's geography unfolds in my head as much as, if not more than, under my feet. One of my goals in moving to Wometzia with Todd was to take an axe to my roots in this town. From what, specifically, I couldn't be sure, nor do I think I could have chosen individual things from which to separate myself. My childhood, certainly. But as I traverse these familiar streets underfoot, my wellspring of memories erupts, and on every corner, I see myself or Beth or Todd. I see us eating sandwiches on park benches and dripping ice cream from cones outside of the café.

An unfamiliar emotion streams steadily into me. Resentment? No, not quite. Longing? Partially. Perhaps this emotion is my soul reacting to me trying so hard to cut off a part of the town where it was cultivated. I've spent much time telling (and re-telling) myself that it's only a matter of geography, but the painful truth is that it's far more significant than anything that can be represented by maps or GPS.

And after identifying this emotion, I feel an unexpected one bubble up: a quiet but deep appreciation for this place: Riverdell, its town, its people, and even my history here.

I don't want to lose my focus, but curiosity and a wan sense of insecurity prod me to look upward to better perceive the clouds.

They move with an uncanny gusto, eager to rain their rain and perhaps strike their lightning. As I think it, I smell the telltale odor of ozone—the olfactory version of what it tastes and feels like when you put your tongue to a nine-volt battery.

As I cross north through the park, the rain picks up with uproarious swiftness, like a higher power had dumped a jug of

Drano down through the clouds to clear out the plumbing. Maybe this is to be a reminder of the dark deed I committed in this very park. The raindrops plink into the pond's surface and, reflecting the few lights cast from lampposts and storefronts on main street, they look like a school of tiny golden fish, eager and frenzied at feeding time.

I'm only two streets away from the house now. Home sweet home. Back where it all began. Not nine months or a year or two years ago, but decades ago. As a whole, my life has been colored with the blacks and blues of despair, but the recent chapters in my life have taken on the brighter, furious hues of retribution.

As if the strength of the storm pulses from my childhood dwelling, each step I take *(squish squish plit plit)* seems to crank up the intensity of the deluge. When I round the next corner, I see the first dazzling flash of light, from a bolt that touched down who knows how far behind me. It illuminates the suburbs before me like a low-budget horror film, and even amid the battering rain, my soaked clothes, and my fired-up muscles, I feel a current run through my spine, as though some of the lightning's charge splashed away from its striking point and found the next target over.

Thunder follows the lightning rapidly, amplifying the sensation.

During my college days, I found an app that came in quite handy in helping me sleep. Its function was simple, but effective: It simulated ambient noise, such as rain, a ticking clock, a whirring fan, a crackling fireplace, thunder, whippoorwills, a babbling creek, or white noise. The volume for each individual effect could be adjusted, as well as the frequency of the occasional effects like thunder or the call of the whippoorwill.

However, one day, as I finally drifted off toward the relief of unconsciousness, I picked up on a sound within the ambient noise, one I had never noticed before. It was a rhythmic *plit, plat, plit, plat* that made it sound like an anxious person was pacing back and forth in the puddle, up and down, up and down, toward me and away again. While I was pretty sure it was all in my head, it still made me uneasy enough that I had to turn the app off and begin my journey toward repose anew.

Now, I delight in a sense of beautiful irony that my own rhythmic *plit-plat-plit-plat,* splashing away through the rainy streets, may well be the sound of my adversary's impending demise.

Will be, I remind myself. I have no room for self-doubt here.

And there she is. Two stories, stacked thick and deep with unsavory memories.

With no logical alternative, I make a beeline for the house.

I normally operate according to the more prudent faculties of my mind (which scream at me to *take it slow it's a trap what are you thinking you're going to get shot as soon as you open the door*), but the more emotionally inclined portion of my brain (though only recently reawakened, admittedly) knows that Jeremy Keroth is one for spectacle and drama.

He won't kill me right away. He'll want to point a gun to my head and monologue for ten or fifteen minutes first. Even if he's booby-trapped the entire house, I'll be debilitated at the worst upon entering. As I cross Ripple Drive, lightning strikes again, once more framing my old home in ghostly white against its oily black surroundings. (Was that a person in my old bedroom window? Was that Keroth?) Thunder follows the lightning strike almost immediately—that could have been as close as the park.

I pull out the spare set of lock picks that I had left at Todd's house when we moved—though it's not so much a set as it is a tension lever and two flimsy picks. But, before I even draw the aluminum pieces from their leather pouch, I find that the door is unlocked. *Come, then, and meet your demise!*

The storm door swings and thumps against my back as I swing the proper door inward. I step inside.

Before the last echoes of the door's closing have faded away, a voice speaks from the darkness. I expected as much, but it still does a lot to accentuate the chill already coursing through my veins.

"Old friend," says Jeremy Keroth. I panic at first, unable to locate him, but lightning strikes again and the left half of his figure is illuminated, rocking in my dad's old recliner—Keroth knows this. Spectacle and drama, I say.

His hands rest neatly on his lap, his legs crossed daintily underneath. Certainly not the hardened version I expected to see on this side of his (albeit shortened) prison time.

"Sure, let's go with that," I say. "Old friend. Dad's old friend, I guess. Mine? No." Uh-oh. I feel myself getting heated.

I cross the small dining room in three strides (Was it always so small? When did it get so small?) to where it borders the adjacent living room, where Keroth sits. He continues rocking in the worn chair, right at home in the old bastard's favorite spot.

Keroth cuts me off. Good—I need a second to cool off. "What, after all we've been through? Oh, and I heard you met my offspring."

"Offspring, huh? Sounds like you two are close."

"Some of these whores just don't believe in Plan B anymore. Most of them will fuck off after a while, but not that one."

"Such a tragic, beautiful romance. Better copyright the idea before Nicholas Sparks gets ahold of it."

"I see you're still as elegant and respectful as ever," says Keroth. He folds his arms and I wonder if he has a gun tucked at one of his sides, now inches away from his fingers.

"I'm sorry, what exactly have you done to earn my respect? Was it when you and my pops bonded over pedophilia? Was it the lifetime of trauma and nightmares? Was it the sense of being *repulsed* by the very thought of intimacy? Was it the emotional roadblocks? Was it the bright and shining gift of never being enough? *The guilt? The abandonment?*" Without realizing it, I lifted my voice right out of the 'hushed but firm' range, and now I'm bordering on a yell.

Keroth maintains a cool façade, but I can almost watch my mighty waves of rage wash over him, each one bathing him in a fresh coat of fear. Most likely, he expected me to float through this encounter emotionless, calculating, methodical, and level-headed, per my reputation. He's never seen me tap into emotions—and boy are there a lot of them.

I draw breath to begin again, but he's been waiting for this moment. He grins and I watch as, in slow motion, he pulls a revolver out from his side—he had been concealing it between his hip and the armrest, as I suspected.

Fortunately, I've been waiting for *this* moment. He thought he could take advantage of my emotional state by catching me off guard, but I was ready. He rolled a Trojan horse on in through my open gates, but little did he know I had an army ready to slaughter the invaders the second they emerged from the mighty wooden steed.

I step forward at an angle as Keroth aims, fires, misses. I hear the round *pock* as it burrows into the ceiling and the subsequent hiss of plaster showering down. The fear in his eyes is more prevalent now. He tries to adjust his aim, but I cover the distance too quickly. In his seated position, he's quite easy to overpower and I wrestle the firearm out of his hand with ease. I slide the cylinder out of the frame and rap the piece against the nearby end table to shake loose the remaining ammunition.

As the rounds *tink* onto the table and fall to the floor, Keroth pushes at my torso which, combined with the unsteady rocking of the recliner and his bucking hips, is enough to unseat me and send me careening backward. I roll onto my back and Keroth lunges at me with his fists clenched and a bloodlust in his eyes, visible even in the minimal light.

I draw my legs to my chest and kick at him with full force, but he steps aside and swats my legs away. I'm unable to retract them before he lands on top of me in full mount, his face twisted into a monstrous horror and his fists cocked and ready. He

337

pummels at me, but without accuracy or power. Using my legs, I push my hip upward—Keroth teeters at being unweighted—and turn, tossing him aside as I go.

Capitalizing on that momentum, I roll up on top of him and prepare to unleash the same flurry of blows he tried to deal—only with power and technique. Instinctively, Keroth covers his face, which at this angle is a frightened, ghostly white. That's fine—a right hook doesn't give a shit about your stupid nose.

I connect with his temple, knocking his head to the side, out from underneath his protective forearms. I follow this blow up with a left hook, which lands just above his cheekbone. I pummel him for a few seconds before becoming aware that I'm speaking (growling? yelling?) again.

"This is from Trina." Right hook. "This is from Mom." Left. "This is for dad." Three jabs in succession. "This is from *me!*" I seize his lapels in my clenched fists, stand up, take a big step backward and, turning, I hurl him right over the top of the chair he occupied only a minute ago.

He collides with the wall in a mighty crash. Some thrift store paintings drop to the floor and join him in his pathetic heap. Even in the dark, I see blood pooling around him. I'm not sure whether he acquired more wounds from the throw or the blood is just from my beating him, but I don't care—the more the better.

In a sense of calm that strikes me as eerie (but necessary), I step back toward the revolver and the discarded ammunition. I pick up the gun and a single round, then marry the two properly.

Keroth is losing more and more blood from his head wounds; the point where his head hit the wall is marked by an immodest amount of it. He's still crumpled on the ground, making a sound that can't quite decide whether it wants to be a whimper or a growl.

Now it's my turn for a dramatic spectacle.

"I can't change what you did in the past. I can't change the effects it had on me, my sister, or my mom. I can't change what you've done to countless innocent children since then, nor can I change what you doubtlessly did to myriad kids prior to that. But what I can do is make damn sure you never do so again."

Still face-down, Keroth lifts a shaky arm and flips me the bird.

I pull the trigger.

Ten months ago, when Keroth went to jail, I felt a sense of closure. Doors were closing on chapters and sub-chapters of my life, each with a satisfying finality marked by the echoing *thock* of a deadbolt shooting home.

But those chapters were shorter. Those were the chapters I started only a year prior. They would be titled *Plotting Dad's Death* and *Executing Dad* and *Discovering Sexuality* and *Emotions are Things I Have*.

The doorways marked *Childhood Trauma* and *Abandonment Issues* still stood wide open, equally uninviting, and with no signs of moving anytime soon. Cobwebs formed around their handles, and if you poked your head into either of them, you would see only darkness and hear the isolated cries of a child in tremendous turmoil.

But now, with Keroth gone—permanently—those doors

creak shut, their decades-long yawns finally ending as they slam into their respective jambs.

Tension I didn't know I had eases up and down my spine. I take a deep breath. Scores of blocked-up emotions pour forth, pinging all over the spectrum.

It's over.

Lightning illuminates the room again, followed by the growling rumble of rolling thunder.

I drop the gun without pause or ceremony; it thuds on the floor, impotent and powerless.

Outside, the rain has maintained its heavy and steady fall. I inhale deeply. *Ah, yes. My first breaths of air drawn from a world without Keroth.* It smells sweeter than it did before. More alive.

Lightning rips through the clouds, forking and forking and forking until it's a brilliant, dazzling web weaving through the thunderheads. The subsequent thunder cracks and booms and shakes. I take this as an applause for a job well done.

The journey back to Todd's place is more leisurely, but I hurry anyway, so as not to keep my family waiting too long.

Rather than burst in, I knock at the door, to avoid startling Beth and taking a bullet to the face. Such a victorious night would be marred by dying at the end of it.

Within three seconds, Todd flings the door open and pulls me into a rib-bruising hug. Beth and Trina join us shortly afterward, the four of us bunched in an awkward clump like Antarctic penguins huddling against the cold.

As I relate the story to the others, I notice, with fascination,

340

that the parts at which they individually grow tense varies from person to person. Beth borders on losing her shit when I tell her about Keroth lunging after me. Todd's height of suspense came when Keroth fired his first shot at me.

For Trina, the tension built and built throughout the entire story, ebbing slightly here and there, but mostly building, finally releasing when I tell her that I put a bullet through the sick fuck's skull. Her hands, clenched into fists throughout the whole tale, become celebratory rather than tense at that moment, her arms pumping at her sides like an enthusiastic spectator at a sporting event.

Our business in Riverdell complete, we prepare to spend the night. Even with my shouting, I don't suspect we caused enough commotion to have roused the neighbors, and with that house being abandoned, there's no reason anyone should stumble across Keroth's body before we're able to make a clean escape.

Keroth's body.

The phrase feels good, empowering. I've been witness to (and deliverer of) a lot of death lately. For most, even including that of my father, the transition of their being from present to past tense is uneasy, tenuous, like trying to assemble one's own parachute while plummeting toward the earth.

But not Keroth. His was a life that stuck around in the present for far longer than warranted. Time after time, he demonstrated that his life was a plague, and even given the chance to stop—not necessarily to cure the world of his deeds, but at least to stop inflicting them—he discarded that opportunity in favor of further treachery, greed, and—there's no other word for it—

evil.

I rest easy, like my soul just took its first shower in decades.

EPILOGUE

Our initial plan was for Mom's funeral to be quiet. Small, intimate, subdued. Of course, Deliverance was not unaware of her passing, so instead of the single-digit number of attendees we gave the funeral home as an estimate, the staff worked themselves into a frenzy fetching more chairs as more guests arrived: dozens upon dozens.

Now, the total count is just over one hundred mourners. Most of these people I don't recognize—former colleagues and contacts through Deliverance, I suppose. There are a few I do recognize, such as our neighbor from across the street, Nancy. Her house always smelled like freshly baked goods.

When the staff are satisfied with the new seating arrangements (we had to move to a different room than anticipated, and chairs fill virtually every possible space, leaving very little walking room), the ceremony commences.

Trina reads Mom's obituary as an introduction; most of the mourners wear deep smiles—partly from knowing that the good things written about her are true, but mostly from the secret knowledge that that truth is far from complete.

Next, Todd speaks. Those who know my mother's true history (which is to say an overwhelming majority of the mourners) know who Todd is. As such, they also know for how little time he has known her, but how much they meant to each other any-way. He delivers a striking metaphor about their relationship be-ing akin to the blooming of Japanese cherry blossoms—breath-taking and beautiful, if short-lived.

Now it's my turn.

I don't have as much of a case of nerves as I anticipated. I haven't done any sort of public speaking since giving presenta-tions in college, but thinking upon it now, this event is decidedly distinct from public speaking. This is intimate, even in its large number. This group has much more in common than a class schedule and I find peace in that common ground.

"For a long time, I resented my mother's actions," I say. I have only a dull awareness of the direction I'm taking this, but matters of the heart seldom come with a compass.

I continue. "The emotions I harbored toward her ranged from disappointment to sadness to flat-out anger. But at the root of all of those was something that I had difficulty acknowledging: a deep love for her. I missed the things she did for Trina and me, sure. She gave us two hundred percent. Of course, as kids and teenagers, we took that for granted. But beyond what she did for us, I missed who she *was*. I missed hearing her sing while she was cooking. I missed the way her voice could take you right out of this world and into one with no violence or anger—only that sweet, melodic serenity."

Todd, Trina, and Beth sit on the front row, an empty seat between Trina and Todd where I was sitting. Each of them, even Beth, is tearing up. I feel my own throat catch, followed by that newly familiar sensation of salty tears welling up in my own eyes.

"A lot of the time, we see people on TV or in magazines with a lot of strength. We see someone with one leg run a marathon. We see someone beat cancer, then start a successful charity to help others do the same. But the type of strength I want to acknowledge in my mother was a quiet one. It didn't have magazine articles written about it because, to all but the most observant, it flew undetected under the radar.

"It was the kind of strength that would offer you the last bite of its only meal of the day. It would pick up on the harshness of *your* reality while saying nothing of its own. It bore the pain of ten lives to lessen the pain of yours. Hers was a strength that uplifted, protected, and inspired. It bled into those she met—"I need a moment to clear my eyes, my mind"—and instilled them with that very same strength.

"Even if all the strength you needed was enough to say, 'I'll try again tomorrow,' Mom was there to give it to you. Often in the form of soup or cookies or hot chocolate. And while I spent so long resenting her absence from my life, the only regret that remains is that, after she returned, I didn't spend more of my time with her.

"Her absence will leave a hollowness in the world. As demonstrated by the number of you who showed up, she influenced the lives of many. Her hand has been one of comfort to her loved ones, and one of protection against the rest of the world."

I swallow hard. "And if there's a chance that you're somehow here, listening beyond the grave, I want to tell you that I love you, I miss you, and I forgive you."

Trina stands and hugs me as I return from the podium, then

she steps up to it herself, still teary-eyed.

To the staff's horror, I'm sure, Trina then opens the floor to anyone who wishes to say anything about my mother.

A surprising (though simultaneously unsurprising) number of the volunteers are children. After a couple of them, I begin to sense that they've been instructed not to divulge the details of how they know my mother, but the word 'hero' comes up a lot, and each time, Trina gives my hand a light squeeze.

The adults who speak are much more eloquent in their disguises of how they knew my mother. The most striking thing, to me, is how confident and self-assured they seem to be. Knowing about my mother's history, and thus Deliverance's dealings, I suspected maybe those she helped may be timid or uncomfortable, but again and again, the floor is taken by confident, radiant women who seem to ring with one word: *Free.*

Though it first seemed like a never-ending supply, eventually the line of those waiting to speak about my mom dies down, and the ceremony can draw to its reluctant close.

Funerals are supposed to be a time for mourning and reflection, but in reality, they're more a way for survivors to come together and grieve openly. The true reflection occurs in the hours, days, months after the funeral. After a mourner arrives home and removes his tie, then lies on the couch to "rest his eyes." That's when the reflection happens.

In my case, my reflection has been ongoing for the better part of my life. The frames and lenses through which I viewed my mother have not changed often, but when they do change, they do so spectacularly. From protector to traitor, then back to protector. Now, to martyr.

The few of Riverdell's attendees to her funeral all ask me the same thing: "Why here? Why not back at home?"

Like much of the day, the specific way I answer these questions escapes my memory, but the sentiment was raw and powerful and present: Her journey was a noble one. It was fierce and powerful. And one of the most poignant aspects of her journey is that, as much as it was a voyage toward a redemptive ending, it was an escape from an oppressive and traumatic past.

Riverdell was not home to her. Hell, Wometzia wasn't, either. I'd wager that Washington wasn't. Her home wasn't geographical; it was social and familial. Her home was always Trina and me. As for my own home, I'm not sure where that might end up. And while I don't know nearly as much about my mother as I would like, I have no doubt that nothing would have pleased her more than to know that she is at rest in a place close to me now. Her home.

The details for the burial itself aren't shared with most of the mourners, and they understand. Although I've never met most of them, they aren't shy about approaching me, offering condolences, and wishing me luck in the future.

I suspect that many of them will be checking up on me whether I like it or not.

I do.

Graveside, I stand in solemn fortitude with Beth, Trina, and Todd. Away from the mass of mourners, a sensation of surreal removal has stolen into my mind, and I can't quite shake it. Todd or Trina or Beth crack jokes here and there, but the humor lands with the uncertain shakiness of a feather on a gusty day, and it's all I can do to offer a half-smile in acknowledgement before getting swept away into the unreality of it all once again.

Later that evening, the spell is finally broken as I sit down to dinner with the three of them. Maybe their unrelenting support simply overwhelmed the thick, murky film that had settled over my mind.

Wometzia's setting sun casts a brilliant yelloworangeredpurple blanket across the sky. To the west, I almost can't tell where the restless earth ends and the drowsy sky begins, but the four of us sit in pensive silence until the horizon becomes a seamless black silhouette. I look over my left shoulder and nod toward Orion, making one of his first journeys across the southern night sky.

And I breathe.

ACKNOWLEDGMENTS

Many people have contributed to Remy's journey, and I would be remiss not to show them gratitude. First, to my parents, JP and Lisa. Not a day goes by in which I'm not grateful for their influences in my life—for raising me, yes, but even more so in my adulthood, in which they continue to teach me about life and the world. Their belief in me has always surpassed my own, and in times of doubt, I know I can draw on their encouragement to steel my resolve and prime my motivation.

In a similar vein, I want to thank many of my friends for their encouragement. Often, I feel like my rants about writing, editing, etc. border on esoteric nonsense, but they're happy to listen, commiserate, and empathize as much as they are capable. There are far too many of them to list, but I want to give a special and specific thank-you to Rachel and Bethany—you're rock stars and I love you both!

Lastly, to the folks at Vulpine Press and to my editor, Sarah. Many people fear that they'll surrender control over their work by publishing traditionally, but my experience in this journey has been one of excellent communication and cooperation. From the editing itself to the promotion and cover art, working with Vulpine Press and with Sarah has been a dream, and I look forward to further opportunities with them.

ABOUT THE AUTHOR

Michael Lilly was born in Provo, Utah. He has lived in that area his whole life, and splits his time between reading and writing books, cooking, hiking, martial arts, and being around his family. He has six siblings who, along with his parents, fostered and encouraged his interest in writing, and he is grateful for his closeness with them. Mike loves to travel and see new places, and carries a passion for other languages and cultures.

Follow the author:

Twitter: @AuthorMLilly

Facebook: @MikeLillyAuthor

Instagram: @mjlilly92